PRAISE FOR STINA LINDENBLATT

"A feel good, sensual, intoxicating and sexy love story; if you love contemporary romance you do not want to miss *Decidedly Off Limits*." —Slick, Guilty Pleasures

"Sweet, sexy and invigorating, *Decidedly off Limits* is a friends to lovers story that is truly a breath of fresh air!"—Read & Share Book Reviews

"Oh my goodness this book was so much fun!!!"—For the Love of Books (*Decidedly With Baby*)

"There are steamy moments but you are just left with feel good melty moments more"—Books Are Love (*Decidedly With Baby*)

"Be warned dear reader, this book will have you giggling and blushing as you devour it"—The Subclub Books (*Decidedly With Love*)

"...a truly unique and utterly swoon-worthy romance." – Mary Dubé at Frolic/USA Today's HEA (*Decidedly by Chance*)

"Stina Lindenblatt writes an emotional, heartfelt story about single parenthood, friendship, and love. Add to that great chemistry and tons of feels and this is a great book for anyone who enjoys this trope." – Ari at Red Hatter Book Blog (*Decidedly by Chance*)

"I can't wait for more Daniels brothers."—Mary at USA Today HEA (*Cowboy Most Wanted*)

"Are you in the mood for a fun, hot, sweet, romantic read that will have you blushing, laughing and glued to the pages then look no further than *Cowboy Most Wanted*."—The Subclub Books

"HOLY HOTNESS!! Not only this book was a fun read, but it was so sexy as well!"—Blog on the Run (*Cowboy Most Wanted*)

"I'm loving this series!"—Red Hot Blue Reads (*Once Upon a Cowboy*)

"Holy words, batman!...Stina NAILED this book."—Garden Of REden (*Fix Me Up, Cowboy*)

"...it's an opposites-attract romance that will evoke all the feels." —Mary at USA Today HEA/Frolic (*Fix Me Up, Cowboy*)

ALSO BY STINA LINDENBLATT

CONTEMPORARY ROMANCES

Carson Brothers Series

One More Chance

One More Secret

One More Betrayal

One More Truth

SPICY ROMANTIC COMEDY NOVELS

By The Bay Series

Decidedly Off Limits

Decidedly with Baby

Decidedly with Love

Decidedly with Mistletoe

Decidedly by Chance

Decidedly with Luck

Decidedly with Wishes

Copper Creek Series

Cowboy Most Wanted

Once Upon a Cowboy

Fix Me Up Cowboy

Visit stinalindenblattauthor.com for more books

WHILE YOU WERE SPYING

STINA LINDENBLATT

*To the women and men who have fought (or still fight)
to protect the freedoms we hold dear.*

WHILE YOU WERE SPYING

1

ISABELLE

I nod at the jogger heading toward me. Six foot. Maybe six foot one. Marathoner. Early thirties.

Good-looking.

Single.

It's also possible he has a girlfriend or wife, but she doesn't like to run with him. Every day, rain or shine. Or as is so often the case during our regular morning runs overlooking the bay and marina...the fog.

He nods back like he does every time he sees me, his long stride effortlessly eating up the distance—the opposite of how the run is for me. My legs and lungs burn, beg me to slow down. Possibly even take a *siesta*.

Not much farther, I remind them. *You can do this*. I mentally break out the pom-poms and cheer my legs on while I keep an eye on my surroundings, noting anything unusual for this time of day.

That's not to say I live in a bad neighborhood and have to watch for thugs and whatnots. But the number one rule of being an operative with Quade Security and Investigations is to be aware of your surroundings. The people, the location, the vehicles. Nothing is ignored. Nothing is considered insignificant.

Truth? I'm not an operative.

I'm the office manager—the person those five hot alpha men couldn't survive without.

But although I enjoy my job, I have a different career aspiration. I want to be more than just an office manager.

I push myself a little harder and a little further, then slow my pace for the cool down. Even though the temperature isn't exactly warm, sweat soaks through my T-shirt and running shorts. I can thank the last round of *fartlek* training—sprints that left my legs burning with resentment and resignation—for that.

I can also thank, with a healthy dose of cursing, Jayden Price.

My best friend. My colleague. And in his mind, my personal trainer.

Who is currently away on a mission, being all dark and dangerous and hot, helping to take down a Russian mafia crime boss.

I power walk across the street to the familiar Victorian-style bungalow, sandwiched between two taller houses. Their exteriors are light blue. Mine is rose pink—the color my grandmother on my mother's side painted it many moons ago.

When she died five years ago, the house became mine, and I decided to keep the colors as they were: warm and eclectic.

I approach the stairs to the porch. Mojo, the big goofball of Bernese mountain dog, lumbers to his feet. His face shifts into his friendly doggy grin.

"Hey, boy. Anything exciting happen while I was running?" Despite his size, Mojo sucks as a running companion. He doesn't like to run. At. All. Relaxing is his activity of choice.

Not exactly the dog you would associate with a man like Jayden, Mojo's owner. You'd expect something big and powerful

—and a whole lot of scary—like a German shepherd or a Rottweiler.

Mojo gives me a happy *woof*.

I laugh. "You don't say. How about I shower, and then we can head to the office? And maybe the guys will be finished with their mission today." I untie my sneaker shoelace and remove my front door key from it. Then I unlock the door and let Mojo into my house.

As I walk toward the bathroom, my cell phone rings from the kitchen table. Thinking it might be Jayden, informing me that he and the men are on their way to San Francisco, I make a quick detour to the kitchen and answer the phone without checking who it is.

"Hello?"

"Isabelle, darling," Grandma Josephine exclaims.

A smile breaks out on my face. "Morning, Grandma." And because I know she's on speakerphone, and I know her routine, I add, "Good morning, Liza and Henri."

I open the kitchen cupboard and remove a glass.

The three eighty-two-year-olds say good morning back to me, their voices more excited than they typically are for this time of day. And normally their voices are pretty damn happy.

"I'm in a bit of a kerfuffle," Granny says. "Can you come over right away?"

"I have to go to work, but I can visit you afterward."

"Now would be better. It's rather urgent." Her honey-smooth voice, which seduced the trousers off many a man in her younger days, has shifted slightly to the panicked zone.

And panic is not an emotion I associate with my grandmother.

"I just returned from my run, and I'm sweaty. Let me shower first."

"A woman is never sweaty," Liza says in a falsely snotty tone. "She only glows."

"Well, my glow needs to be washed off before I can join you. And just so you know, I have Mojo with me."

"Oh, is tall, dark, and handsome joining us?" Henri's tone is more excited than usual.

"Darling," Granny purrs, "how many times does Isabelle have to tell you Jayden isn't gay?"

"I know that. Besides, even if he were, I'm old enough to be his father."

"More like his grandfather," Liza points out with a snorted laugh.

"No, Jayden won't be joining me. He's away on business."

All three of them release a disappointed sigh.

"Such a shame," Liza says on another sigh.

"I won't be long," I tell them before ending the call.

Forty-five minutes later, I'm in Sausalito, pressing my grandmother's doorbell. After a heartbeat, her housekeeper opens the door and lets Mojo and me inside.

I hug Juanita, who is more like family to me. She's been in my grandmother's employment for as long as I can remember. Because the elegantly furnished estate home is too massive for her to handle on her own at her advanced age, she mostly does the cooking and light cleaning. A gardener and housekeeping company are also on Granny's payroll.

Juanita fusses over Mojo, who laps up the attention like a paper towel. "Now, don't you get fur all over the place, young man," she chastises him with her typical warm and friendly smile.

He whimpers as if to apologize for snoozing on Granny's couch the last time we were here.

"They're on the balcony," she tells me, even though I already know that. Unless it's cold and rainy, the trio always eats their breakfast outside.

Mojo and I step onto the large deck that overlooks the bay. My stiletto heels click against the light, reddish-brown tiles.

Granny and Liza are seated on the wicker sofa, looking as elegant as always in their designer outfits. Henri sits in a matching armchair.

In front of them, the coffee table is loaded with teacups and an assortment of cut fruit and pastries, including my favorite—strawberry-and-cream filled croissants.

Which Granny only has on hand when she knows I'm coming over.

So, this definitely wasn't a spur-of-the-moment request for me to join them.

Henri, being the gentleman that he is, stands. Or at least attempts to stand. It takes him a minute to get to his feet, his movements not as spry as they were twenty years ago. He's wearing an expensive Italian-cut suit, the jacket a checkered camel fabric. He also has on a burgundy tie, dark-brown slacks, a fedora, and leather shoes that are worth a small fortune.

Henri has always had an eye for fashion.

I walk over to him, and he kisses me on both cheeks. "Looking gorgeous as always, Buttercup. I can't believe you still haven't found a beau yet. Those men are nothing but fools."

I laugh because he says that every time.

"There's nothing wrong with our Isabelle being particular," Liza says. I lean down and kiss her powdery cheek. She pinches mine in return, with a teasing gleam in her eyes. "Although if she doesn't hurry up and find herself a man, her eggs will be as old and wrinkly as mine."

"Darling," my grandmother says, "your eggs withered away decades ago. As did mine. But Isabelle has no need to worry about that. Thanks to modern technology, she can freeze her eggs now, so they are still youthful for when she's ready to settle down with Mr. Perfect."

I kiss her on the cheek and hug her. "I'm not interested in settling down with a man. I'm too busy with my career."

Okay, that's not entirely true. My career hasn't exactly traveled in the direction I had envisioned it would when I obtained my political science degree.

Before attending college, I had planned to be a human rights lawyer and follow in my grandmother's humanitarian footsteps. She was a popular film and stage actress in the sixties and seventies and then switched to focus on her philanthropic work.

She never went to law school. It was my father who pursued his law degree—corporate, not human rights. It was my father who strongly encouraged me to follow in his footsteps.

Except, being a lawyer wasn't for me, I eventually realized.

A lifetime of legal talk sounded dull and uninspiring.

"That's true," Liza says. "It can't be easy working for those five hot men." She fans herself.

"Any luck yet convincing your boss to promote you to an operative?" Granny asks.

"Not yet. I know Liam wants to hire at least one female to join the team. Possibly two. But he's been too busy to even consider candidates."

Plus there's the matter of him wanting experienced individuals, which I'm not. Or at least not experienced at the level he's looking for.

"What you need to do is prove you're fully capable of doing the job."

"I know, but it's not like I've had the opportunity to do that." Other than some minor tasks, like interviewing persons of interest who were more likely to open up to a woman than a man.

But I want to do more than that. I want to be involved in the dangerous missions. Like when the government hires the team for operations that require outside assistance, beyond what the FBI and CIA can do.

The side of the company that the general public doesn't know about.

As for the threesome's original discussion about my love life —or rather, lack of one—I'm not looking to find my own happily ever after. My father cheated on my mother when I was a little kid. Mom never remarried after that. Dad did. Four more times. His marriages tend to last as long as a harvest moon. At most.

But I didn't let this jade me against relationships. Not at first, anyway. I've had boyfriends over the years. But none— except for one—lasted long. Richard was a fellow political science major. The love of my life.

Until I found the love of my life going down on another woman. In our bedroom.

He'd never gone down on *me*, so my discovery was a double layer in the brick wall of disappointment.

I guess it was my fault for not kicking his sorry ass through the door sooner. Even before the situation with the other woman, I knew deep down that he wasn't the right man for me.

For one, he hadn't been a fan of the colored streaks in my hair (they were purple back then). And he preferred that I didn't speak my mind when I accompanied him to the dinner parties his graduate school professors had thrown.

He even hinted more than once that I should also go to grad school and become a boring academic.

All right, he didn't use the word boring.

That was all me.

A slight breeze blows a strand of hair into my face. I brush it behind my ear and bite into the yummy croissant. "So what was so urgent that I needed to rush over?"

Last time it was because she needed a fourth opinion on an outfit she was wearing to a gala for the opening of an art gallery. It was exhibiting photos by famous photographers— both alive and dead—that showcased the movie stars of the past—also both alive and dead.

"Urgent" means something entirely different to me than it does for Granny.

She exchanges a glance with Liza and Henri. They both rapidly nod their encouragement. "I've got the perfect opportunity for you to prove to your boss that you'll be a great operative."

"What opportunity?"

"An ex-boyfriend of mine needs your help."

"Do I know him?" There have been a string of casual boyfriends since Grandpa's death.

"No. Bernard Bradshaw and I used to be an item before I became famous. He was a director at the time, waiting for his big break. We dated for a few years, but then he had an offer to work in Europe."

"Okay, but what kind of help are we talking about?"

Henri picks up his teacup. "The kind of help that you and that tall glass of hot stuff can give him, Buttercup."

Granny grins. "He means Jayden. You and Jayden would be perfect for this mission. And Bernard agreed with me when I told him about you two."

"Great, but what exactly does he need help with?"

"Bernard would rather talk to you face-to-face about it—because of the sensitive nature of what happened. But what I can tell you is that some information might've been stolen from at least one guest while they were staying at his resort. Bernard has several security guards employed there, but he wanted to hire someone from the outside, in case it was an inside job."

"What resort?"

"Paradise Springs Resort."

"It's in Huntington Beach," Liza chimes in.

Granny nods. "That's right. You and Jayden would be staying there. You'll love the place. The five-star resort is supposed to be incredible." She's positively beaming as she tells me this.

"Jayden and the rest of the team are away on a mission," I inform her. "But I'll call Bernard, and he and I can discuss what he needs from us."

"He doesn't want to talk about it on the phone. He has kind of grown paranoid in his old age. He wants to talk to the two of you in person about the case. He's willing to fly you both down for the weekend. If not this weekend, then I'm sure he will be happy to wait until Jayden returns home."

"Jayden's pretty busy for the next while." As the firm's office manager and Jayden's best friend, I am more than familiar with his schedule. "But I can easily fly down and meet with Bernard."

She shakes her head. "That won't do. If you two agree to help him, you will need to go undercover as guests at his resort."

"Okay, I can do that. And I don't need Jayden to join me for that."

Henri chuckles. Liza giggles. "Buttercup, Paradise Springs Resort isn't the kind of place a single woman goes to, hoping to find her soul mate. It's a place where married couples go. Together."

"That's right. You and Jayden will go undercover as a happily married couple." For some reason, Granny looks almost pleased by this.

But I can't imagine why.

"Why Jayden? The other men I work with are just as good at their jobs as he is." However, like Jayden, they're also busy with other cases for a while.

"Yes, but from what you've told me, Jayden doesn't want you to advance in your career at the firm. This would be the ideal way to demonstrate to him that you're more than capable of doing the job. Just think about it. But I really do think you'll agree that you don't want to miss out on this golden opportunity to prove yourself to your boss."

She has a point there.

"But what if Jayden doesn't want to come with me?" Which is likely the case if he believes the mission is too dangerous—for me.

Liza giggles again, for a reason only she's privy to.

Or maybe it's just me who's clueless about the cause. The other two appear to be in on the joke, their lips pressed together as though stifling laughter.

"I'm sure, Buttercup, you can persuade him," Henri says with a wink.

2

JAYDEN

A sharp twig on the ground digs into my stomach. Around me, the forest is quiet in the predawn stillness, the June mountain air cool against my skin.

"So, Dragonfly, how was the woman you went out with last week?" Landon asks through the earpiece, his voice low. "What was her name again? Brandy?"

"Bridget," I reply.

There's a moment of silence through the earpiece before Connor's voice comes through loud and clear. "That's all you've got, a name? No other details?" He's back in the van with the surveillance equipment and doesn't need to be quiet like the rest of us.

"What more do you want?"

"Are you seeing her again?" Liam, our boss, asks from the underbrush on the other side of the log house. We're biding our time until we can finally carry out our mission.

The men in the house are part of the Orlov mafia—headed by crime boss Vadik Orlov—but the government hasn't been able to do much about them, especially when it comes to their suspected links to drug trafficking.

That's where Liam's team comes in. We're the independents contracted by the government.

A job description that is notably absent from the company website.

They're not our only clients. We work for all kinds of individuals and corporations, on all levels of security and intel gathering.

"Is that the estrogen side of you asking?" I say to Liam, the only team member who's married. The rest of us are happily single.

I get a grunted reply that causes the other three men with us—including Adam, who's currently on the roof—to chuckle.

"No, it's the side of me who wonders why you dumbasses are still single. Being married is great—always having someone to go home to who helps you forget some of the crap we have to deal with when it comes to our jobs."

"I think I recently saw that sweet sentiment in a Hallmark Valentine's card," Landon says. "Bet that would get your wife all hot and heavy if you gave it to her."

Liam grunts again, knowing he can't win against us happily single guys. That's not to say Liam isn't happy. I served with him in the military, and I've never seen him happier since he reconnected with his ex-fiancée over two years ago.

They've been married for a year and a half now, and Ava gave birth to their adorable daughter eight months ago.

"So I take it that's a no when it comes to seeing Bridget again?" Connor says, the laughter in his tone unmistakable.

"She was okay. But I doubt she's into booty calls, and that's all I really have time for. You know how it is."

The other three single guys are silent, no doubt nodding in agreement. That's the one thing I've learned about my career—both with the military and Liam's team: Women have issues being in a relationship with a man who isn't around as much as they want. Some get suspicious he's having an affair, mainly because there's a lot of secrecy surrounding what he does.

Or they get pissed that the guy isn't available to participate in the normal activities other couples do, or frequently has to cancel because the job comes first, twenty-four seven.

Then there are the women who can't handle the dangerous nature of the career—although in the case of Liam's team, this aspect of the job has never come up. Usually, I tell women I'm a sales representative for a hospital software company.

A boring-sounding job that results in very few inquiries about my day.

And then there are women like my ex-fiancée. While I was serving with the SEALs, she was the one doing the cheating, with a friend of mine. She was my last serious relationship.

There's also another reason for side-stepping relationships like they're land mines. It has to do with my best friend, whom I served with in the SEALs. We'd been friends since fourth grade. He died in my arms while we were on duty. I couldn't save him—hell, I couldn't even protect him.

"My cousin has a friend if you're looking to get laid," Connor says.

"Have you fucked her?" Because I have a thing against screwing a woman who has also been with any of my friends. Some guys don't give a damn about that. I'm not one of those guys.

"Not at all."

"Why not?" Landon asks through the earpiece.

"Because she's not my type."

"You have a type?"

"Not exactly."

"That's code for she's not good enough for him, but she'll do for you, Dragonfly."

"Then I'll definitely pass. And for your information, I don't need help getting laid. I can do that quite nicely on my own, thanks."

"Hate to break up the girl talk," Adam says, his voice coming through the earpiece low and urgent. "We've got movement inside. Looks like they're getting ready to roll."

"Okay, men. You know what you have to do." That's Liam's motivational speech before things kick up a notch.

We're not the law, so we have to ensure we keep to this side of it...most of the time. Our role in this mission is to get the evidence and turn it over to our FBI contact. The rest of it is their problem—including the paperwork that no one likes to do.

I don't envy them that.

I move into position, keeping low to the ground, my dark skin allowing me to blend into the background.

Gunshots echo through the forest.

"What the hell?" Liam says. "I thought everyone was accounted for inside."

I don't have time to respond. The unsettling crack of a twig behind me puts me on high alert. It's the sound a twig makes when someone slowly creeps through the forest, not wanting to give away their location.

It's too close for comfort.

I attempt to shift my position, to escape notice.

I'm too late. The sound of gunfire echoes once more through the forest. A burning pain rips along my arm.

Shit.

3

ISABELLE

I leave Granny's house soon after discovering a potential way to prove I'm capable of being an operative with Liam's team, and drive to work. Mojo sits happily in the back seat, watching San Francisco go past his open window.

"I wonder what kind of information was possibly stolen from the guest at the resort," I say to Mojo. Excitement bubbles inside me like an overly shaken soda bottle as my mind riffles through the possibilities.

Possibilities that range from top-secret, government-level information, to something I'd rather not consider, such as an illicit love letter to a mistress.

Mojo barks his reply.

My phone rings and I accept the call without checking who it is first.

"Are you heading to the office?" Liam's deep voice powers through the car speakers.

"Yes, I had to talk to my grandmother, so I'm running a little late. But I should be there shortly. Are you guys back already?"

"We're in San Francisco, but we had to take Jayden to the hospital. He's been shot."

His voice doesn't sound overly concerned, but that doesn't stop the sudden chill surging through my body. "Is he okay?"

"His upper arm is pretty banged up, but it could have been a lot worse. He's on medical leave—for the next three weeks at least, while his arm recuperates."

I'm sure that news went over well. Jayden has a serious authority complex when it comes to following physician's orders.

"I can take Mojo to him after work," I say, "unless he can't handle being separated from his dog a moment longer."

The dog in question barks at his name.

"Yes, he would like that—but in his words, sooner rather than later, please. I'll drive him home once the doctor's finished with him. The rest of the guys are going home to shower before heading to the office."

I shake my head even though Liam can't see me. I wouldn't be surprised if none of them have slept in over twenty-four hours, yet here they are, eager to get back to work.

Eager to kick someone else's ass ASAP.

"Was the mission a success?" I ask. "I mean, other than the part where Jayden was shot."

"Pretty much. The rest of it is up to the Feds now."

I flip on the left-turn indicator and switch lanes. "That's good. Sooo...it sounds like you'll be short one operative while Jayden's recovering—"

"The answer is no, Isabelle."

"I didn't ask a question."

"The answer is still no. Look, I know you want to get out in the field, do what the guys do. But it's just not feasible."

I stick my tongue out at the phone. Not exactly mature, but I can't help it. It's that or cuss at Liam for being unreasonable. "Why not? I know you want to hire at least one woman to work with you guys in the field. I'm that woman—and deep down, you know it."

"You don't have the level of training the guys and I have. While you were earning your degree, the five of us were overseas, trying not to be killed by stray bullets."

"And clearly that experience worked out great for Jayden." I smirk even though Liam can't see that either, but I'm sure he doesn't miss it in my tone.

"All the more reason for you not to be in the field."

"I could be a major asset."

"You're already a major asset, Isabelle. You keep everyone organized and knowing which way is up. Without you, everything would be a disaster in the office."

He has a point there. Those guys would be like blindfolded chickens if it weren't for me.

And what happens when a blindfolded chicken tries to cross the road?

Splat.

"I've gotta go. The doctor wants to talk to me. We'll see you soon." He hangs up before I can say anything else.

"What do you bet there was no doctor?" I ask Mojo.

He woofs.

I arrive a short time later at the building where Quade Security and Investigations is located. After grabbing a coffee from The Coffee Nut, Mojo and I head upstairs. I unlock the door and turn off the alarm.

Mojo makes himself comfortable on the dog bed in the corner of the reception area, where he can easily see who's coming and going.

I turn on my computer and check the phone messages, then conduct a preliminary search on Granny's mysterious ex-boyfriend. The more information I know about him and his resort before I contact him, the better.

Even though he doesn't want to talk on the phone about what sensitive information might've been stolen, he's willing to talk to me so that we can make arrangements for my stay at the resort.

But before Liam or any of the guys can accept a case, they always make sure the person hiring them isn't hiding anything that will later bite one of them on the ass.

Except, now that Jayden's on medical leave, that's going to put a giant wrench in our ability to accept the mission.

I might have to come up with Plan B: ask one of the other men to pretend to be my husband while I'm at the resort. Because at the end of the day, the important thing isn't who joins me there, it's that we get the job done.

And it might be enough to prove to Liam and Jayden that I'm capable of doing the job. That Liam doesn't have to hire someone else to fill the role of the female operative—I'm the perfect candidate for the position.

That's not to say I haven't been involved in the field, but the one time Liam let me do something beyond office work involved crashing someone's date. Wes Chiasson, a friend of ours, was in love with his roommate, Hannah, and didn't like the idea of her going out on a date with another man.

So Jayden and I showed up on Hannah's date and did some spying for Wes.

That was the first and last time I was in the field. Eighteen months ago.

And the only reason Liam even went along with it was because he figured it would keep me off his back for a while when it came to my requests to work in the field.

I google the resort. Bernard's picture is on the website. He's not bad-looking—if you're into much, much, *much* older men.

Which I'm not.

I spend the next few minutes pulling up whatever information I can find about his resort. It caters exclusively to adults—as long as you're married—and offers an array of couple-focused activities: spa treatments, sports, wine tasting, cooking lessons, marriage counseling.

"Wow, just look at this place," I say to Mojo. He ignores me, happy to continue napping. "Can you imagine what it costs to stay here?" It's a five-star resort and looks every part of it.

I'm *almost* sorry I'm not married in real life. It looks like a great place to stay—when you're not there on a mission.

I keep searching for additional info on Bernard but don't find much more than some stuff about his movies.

There's only one person I know who can find additional intel about Bernard Bradshaw, and he's currently at home taking a shower.

TOP SECRET

FIFTY MINUTES LATER, THE PERSON I'M WAITING FOR ENTERS THE main doors with Adam. Both are casually dressed in jeans and a T-shirt. Both look very badass.

"Welcome back. In one piece." At least *they* managed to return home in the same condition they left in.

Adam folds his arms across his chest. "I take it you heard about Jayden."

"That I did. Any word on how he's doing?" Liam hasn't contacted me since the initial conversation.

"We called Liam on the way over. They gave Jayden a heavy dose of painkillers that has him pretty much knocked out for now."

Connor crouches next to the snoozing Mojo and pets him. "But it'll take more than painkillers to keep him at home for the next few weeks while he recovers."

Adam's phone rings. He answers it and walks toward his office.

"I have someone I need a background check on," I tell Connor. I write Bernard's name on a sticky note and hand it to him.

"New case?"

"Possibly."

"Does he have a known address?"

I tell him about the resort and the information my grandmother shared regarding her ex-boyfriend.

"Okay, give me an hour, and I'll send you everything I can find. If you need anything more than that, it might take me a few extra days."

"Thanks."

The next hour is spent fielding phone calls and emails. I'm the one who gets the general inquiries from individuals interested in hiring the company. Some requests are basic investigations. Nothing too dangerous.

Liam and his second in command, Landon, handle the special-ops-type missions. Those calls never come through me, but I'm the one who ensures the men have whatever they need...no matter how difficult it is to obtain.

The main door to the reception area opens, and Liam's wife, Ava Quade, enters, carrying their eight-month-old daughter, Cassie.

Grinning, I jump out of my seat and rush over to them. "He's not here yet."

"I know. He called to give me his ETA."

We hug, sandwiching Cassie between us. And then I get to work, fussing over the little girl. "Wow, you're growing so big. What's your daddy feeding you?"

Cassie gifts me with a wide toothless grin—and drool.

"I heard Jayden is injured," Ava says. "How are you doing?"

"Me? I'm not the one who's injured. I'm just here doing my job." And figuring out how to prove I deserve a promotion.

"Yes, but this is Jayden we're talking about. It's never easy hearing that the man you care about is hurt."

True.

Also true is how I get antsy whenever the guys are gone on what is expected to be a dangerous mission. There's a reason the offices are dust-free, and it has nothing to do with the cleaning staff.

"I feel that way about any of the guys," I explain. They might not be my best friends in the way that Jayden is, but Landon, Connor, Adam, and Liam are like brothers to me.

Ava nods, a secretive smile on her lips.

Before I can ask her what that's all about, Connor exits his office and approaches my desk. "Hey, Ava." He gives her a friendly nod, and Cassie reaches out for her favorite "uncle."

He passes me the file he's carrying and takes Cassie from Ava. "As far as I can tell," he tells me, "there are no red flags with this man."

The office door opens again, and Liam enters...with Jayden right behind him, his left arm in a sling. Liam rolls his eyes at us. Message clear. It wasn't his choice that Jayden is with him.

He goes straight to his wife and kisses her as though they haven't seen each other for several months.

While my heart sighs longingly at how sweet those two are together, I stalk over to my best friend. "Aren't you supposed to be in bed?"

A dopey yet sexy smile spreads on his face. "Your bed or mine?"

At the suggestion of my bed, an unexpected heat rushes to my lower belly. I open my mouth to say something witty, but an image of him in my bed, poised over me, pops into my head.

Damn. Where the hell did that come from?

Fortunately, Mojo rescues me from my wayward thoughts. He barks, thrilled to see his beloved owner, and ambles over to him.

"Just how drugged up is he?" I ask Liam. He and Ava have momentarily stopped kissing, his arms wrapped around her from behind.

"Not enough so he can't walk—unfortunately. Enough so that he's not responsible for what he says."

"Will he remember anything he says?" *Or anything we tell him?*

Liam shrugs. "I have no idea. And I'm not about to test him to find out. If I had a choice, I would've left him at his house. But I needed to come here, and I had a feeling it wasn't a good idea to leave him alone."

"He's not planning to work, is he?" Connor asks.

"I think he just wanted his dog. I figured since you were going to take Mojo to him," Liam says to me, "you could drive both dog and owner home."

"Sure, not a problem."

"If you want, we can put him in his office and unplug the phone and computer, so he can't get into any trouble in the meantime. We'll have to confiscate his cell phone, too."

"Or we can leave him on the couch." I nod toward the tall, muscular man who is now sitting there, fussing over Mojo. His dog certainly isn't complaining about his owner's attention.

I grin at the goofy man and his equally goofy dog.

"That's always an option too."

"Do you want me to keep looking into Bernard Bradshaw?" Connor asks.

This naturally gets Liam's attention. "Who's Bernard Bradshaw?"

"He's my grandmother's ex-boyfriend from back in the sixties, before she became famous. He asked her to talk to me because some information was possibly stolen from a guest staying at his resort. He wants to hire Jayden and me to pose as a married couple and help him find out if he has a security issue. That's all she could tell me. He'd rather talk to us face-to-face because of the sensitive nature of the information that might have been stolen."

"Which resort?"

Now I also have Jayden's attention. He pushes himself off the couch and lumbers toward me.

"Paradise Springs resort," I say. "It's in Huntington Beach. He wants the two of us to fly down this weekend so we can talk to him. If we agree to take on the case, we would go undercover at the resort as a married couple."

"Your grandmother does realize that you aren't an operative, right?" Liam asks. "You aren't trained for this."

"She does know that, which is why I doubt it will be anything like your recent mission." As much as Granny wants me to prove to Liam that I'm capable of the job, she wouldn't have suggested I help Bernard if she suspected it would be dangerous.

"Given that Jayden got himself shot up," Connor points out, "he's hardly in the position to do anything."

"Hey, it's not like I did this on purpose." Jayden yawns and sways slightly on his feet.

I grab hold of his non-injured arm and guide him back to the couch. Then I give him a gentle nudge on the chest, indicating for him to sit.

"That is a slight problem," I say to Connor. "Especially since it's a resort for married couples. That's why Bernard wants to hire both Jayden and me. But I don't see why I can't go by myself and find out more information. Then we can figure out where to go from there."

Jayden stares at me like I'm completely *loco.*

"What?"

"This is why I don't want you in the field," he says. "You could be walking into a dangerous situation. Like an iceberg. One minute you're cruising across the Atlantic in the lap of luxury, making out in the rear seat of a steamed-up vintage

Ford. And the next thing you know, you're shoving the love-of-your-life's frozen corpse into the icy waters."

"Seriously, man," Connor says. "What the hell did the hospital give you for a painkiller?"

I snicker. "Hey, leave the poor man alone. He's being his usual poetic self." To Jayden and Liam I say, "We're talking about me going to a resort. In the US. We're not talking about me walking into a dangerous situation and being shot at. All I plan to do is talk to Bernard Bradshaw. That's all."

"Okay, I'll think on it," Liam says, taking his daughter from Connor. Except, I have a sneaky suspicion he's just saying that. As soon as he walks into his office, the thought will be pushed aside—and not because Ava and Cassie distract him. "But until Jayden gets physician clearance to return to the field, he's on medical leave."

"Hey, I'm fine to work in the field now. It's only a little scratch."

Liam levels his gaze at him, the way a father would to a wayward son—even though the two men are only a few years apart in age. "That was hardly a scratch."

Jayden shrugs and winces.

Liam shifts his attention to me. "I have a call I need to make. I'll give you my answer tomorrow."

Fair enough.

4

JAYDEN

I hate it when my boss is right.

I can't type the report I'm supposed to be working on. And it has nothing to do with the meds I took a few hours ago.

Typing one-handedly is a whole new challenge.

And if I struggle with typing, I won't be much use in the field—especially if I need to use my gun. Plus with my arm in the sling, I'm hardly intimidating.

But the last thing I'm going to do is waltz into Liam's office and tell him he's right.

A knock at the door pulls me from the report I've barely worked on in the past two hours, painkillers non-withstanding. Before I can reply, the door opens and Isabelle sails in, her long legs eating the distance between the door and my desk.

She's nothing like any other woman I know. Her outfits are classy, a complete contrast to the cool blue chunks in her wavy black hair.

In other words, she's sexy as hell—but I'm not about to admit that to her face.

"You ready to go home yet?" she asks.

"Isn't it a little early for you to be heading home?" It's only two in the afternoon. She never leaves before five.

"Liam gave me the rest of the afternoon off to get your pain-in-the-ass butt home. Where you are to remain for the next three weeks. You are not to show up at the office. At. All. And if you do show up before you get the okay from your physician, Liam will ground you indefinitely. His words, not mine."

I laugh. "You might as well have told me he was putting me in time-out like a little kid."

"Grounding, time-out. Same deal, pretty much. Either way, you're supposed to take time off and recover."

I groan. "What am I supposed to do in the meantime?" I'm not the TV-watching type. I'd rather be doing than sitting.

She considers it for a moment. "I guess none of your extra-curricular activities are conducive to allowing your arm to heal." She's referring to my martial arts training, my love of riding my motorcycle fast, and the recreational football league I'm in.

The only activity that won't be a problem for my arm is walking Mojo. But it's not like he enjoys long walks. A running dog, he's not.

"What are you doing tonight?" I ask.

"Going home. Making dinner. Reading a book." Isabelle shrugs. "Nothing exciting."

"You don't have a big date tonight?"

"I'm still on hiatus after my last date six months ago. I mean, seriously, who arranges a double date with their mother? And what mother discusses her son's date's menstrual cycle and reproductive health?" She shudders dramatically. "And the sad part was, her questions didn't even disturb her son. He was listening as if my answers would solve world hunger."

"That's what you get for dating the son of a gynecologist."

"Good point. I'll add 'Don't make that mistake again' to my dating to-do list."

"Since you don't have any exciting plans, how about you stay for dinner when you drop Mojo and me off at my house. We can work on our jigsaw puzzle." The five-thousand-piece puzzle that we've been working on for a few weeks.

"How are you going to make dinner with your arm in a sling? Or is that your way of getting *me* to make *you* dinner?"

"Something like that." I wink at her, and she laughs. "I can try to help. You'll have to do the cutting and chopping."

"You're just saying that because my knife-wielding skills are legendary. I can out-chop you any day."

That's not true, and she knows it. We're both pretty decent when it comes to cooking.

Her gaze drops to my injured arm. "How's it doing?"

"It's fine. Like I told Liam, it's just a scratch."

"Right. You're a big bad alpha boy. You're hardly going to admit when you're in pain and have a serious injury. To do so would be a major blow to the old ego." She looks down at my dog, lounging at her feet. "Isn't that right, Mojo?"

The traitor barks in reply.

"Are you going to nurse me back to health?" That didn't quite come out as it had sounded in my head, although I wouldn't complain if she did exactly that.

She laughs. "You wish. All right, turn off the computer and let's get going."

TOP SECRET

A SHORT TIME LATER, WE ENTER MY HOUSE. MOJO AMBLES OFF TO visit the furniture he hasn't seen in the past four days. The woman I hired to clean the house once a week was here while I was away, so now he has to redeposit his hair all over the place.

"Keep off the couch," I remind him, which is a futile effort.

He'll be on it as soon as I'm out of view. "I should probably shower first," I tell Isabelle. Liam and I went straight to the office after I was released from the hospital.

"Will you be okay with that?" She nods at my arm.

"I'm sure I can manage." Once I grow another arm.

She squishes her lips together, gaze dipping down my body. "I'm not so sure about that." She points in the direction of my stairs. "I'll help you remove your clothes, but you're on your own when it comes to showering."

"Is this your excuse to see me naked?"

She bursts out laughing, but there's no missing the flush in her cheeks. "Aren't you the funny guy?"

I follow her upstairs and into my bedroom. She goes to my drawers, then studies me like I'm some sort of lab experiment. "How easy will it be for you to put on a T-shirt afterward?"

"It shouldn't be a problem." Or I'm assuming it won't be a problem.

"When was the last time you had your meds?"

I shrug my good shoulder.

"Liam told me you're supposed to have them every four hours, and he said you had some at the hospital. Did you have any at the office?"

"I don't need them." More like I didn't appreciate how they made me feel.

"Are you sure? Because I have a feeling you're going to need them. There's only so far that being a big tough alpha male will take you."

"I don't want to risk getting addicted to them." That happened to some of my former brothers after they were injured in the line of duty.

I'd rather roll in a puddle of honey and be fed to an army of pissed-off red ants than risk addiction.

"Fair enough. What about over-the-counter drugs? Are you willing to have those?"

"Sure. If I need them."

She nods, but I have no idea whether she's nodding at what I said or a question posed in her head.

She pulls open my top drawer, and before I can stop her, she removes a pair of underwear. "Black boxer briefs? Very nice."

"God, woman, do you have no shame?" I yank them away from her. But really, it's me who has no shame. Because the sight of her handling my underwear has my cock tightening in my jeans.

What are you doing, asshole? I mentally chastise myself. She and I are friends and colleagues. Nothing more.

"Apparently not." She walks out of my room and enters the master bathroom.

I follow her.

"Do you need to wear the sling in the shower?"

"I'm supposed to wear it for the next two weeks, but I never asked if that also meant in the shower." It didn't dawn on me at the time to do that.

She looks from me to my large walk-in shower, with the frosted door and the gleaming white tiles. "You're probably not supposed to get the wound wet for a few days."

"That does sound familiar."

"What else did they tell you?"

"I don't really remember."

That doesn't seem to surprise her. "Hold on a second. I want to check on something first." She leaves the bathroom and returns a few minutes later, talking on her phone.

"Okay....Okay....Is there anything else I should know?... Right. Thanks." She ends the call. "According to Liam, who *was* paying attention to the doctor's instructions, you aren't supposed to shower for the next three days. So in the meantime, I'll give you sponge baths."

I feel my eyebrows jump up my forehead. "Liam actually

told you to give me sponge baths?" *Shit.* What was the asshole thinking?

"Of course not. He said that until you're allowed to shower again—and baths, by the way, are banned for now—you'll have to settle with a sponge bath. I just took it upon myself, as your best friend, to interpret that to mean I'll be helping you. It's not like I haven't seen you half-naked before."

By half-naked, she means I was wearing basketball shorts and only basketball shorts. I had stripped off my T-shirt after we had gone for a run together. She had bemoaned the fact that she wasn't allowed to do the same.

"I can leave the room while you clean your boy parts." She gestured in the general direction of said parts.

I snort. "Sweetheart, they're as far from being *boy* parts as you can get. There's no doubt about it, I'm all man."

She flashes me a smug grin. "I'll have to take your word for it."

We tease each other all the time—but this level of sexual innuendo is new. That's not to say we haven't used it before, but it's always been reserved for other people. Like a date or a one-night stand or a random member of the opposite gender.

"What about tomorrow when I need help again?" I ask.

"I'll swing by after work to check on you, and I can reprise my role as your nurse."

I open my mouth to argue, but she beats me to it. "It's your fault for not having a girlfriend or wife. If you did, your poor friend wouldn't have to do it for you. But if you want, I can ask Connor, Adam, or Landon to give you a hand instead." Her mouth moves sardonically to the side, knowing I will never accept sponge-bath duty from one of those guys—and I can't imagine they would be jumping up and down for the chance to do it, either.

"Yes, my bad for not having a girlfriend or getting married just for an occasion like this. Although if I did have one, the moment I was shot, she would've been out the door. So I've saved everyone that headache by remaining single."

"Wow, you really have a low opinion of women, don't you?" She looks in the cabinet under the sink, removes a washcloth, and straightens. "If a woman loves you, she won't bail on you just because you get shot."

Eager to escape the current discussion, I point to the washcloth in her hand. "So, have you ever done this before?"

"What? Give a guy a sponge bath? Nope. But there's always a first time for everything."

"You know it's not in your job description." Or at least I don't believe it is.

"I know. But it *is* in my best friend description. Okay, let's get you out of your clothes." She unbuttons the white dress shirt. The T-shirt I'd been wearing during the mission was covered in blood. Liam had grabbed the shirt from my duffle bag so I could change into it at the hospital after they finished patching me up.

Isabelle doesn't say anything as she continues slowly unfastening my shirt. I swear she's holding her breath, as if the action requires the utmost concentration, her lower lip caught between her teeth.

Her fingers lightly brush my abs as she approaches the final buttons. A tingling spreads from the spot like the zap of static, only more pleasant.

She inhales sharply, the sound so soft, I'm certain I imagined it. And her fingers pause for a brief moment before she resumes her task.

Once the shirt is unbuttoned, she starts to unfasten my sling. "Keep your arm steady against your body with your other hand," she instructs, her attention still on the device.

After she removes the sling, she peels the shirt off my shoulders and helps me slide my healthy arm out of the sleeve. The removal of the shirt from my injured arm results in a fair bit of mental cursing on my part. Isabelle looks unsettled enough without knowing the wound kills like a motherfucker.

She drops the shirt to the floor and releases a hard breath.

"That wasn't so bad," I say between slightly clenched teeth.

It's a good thing I'm not Pinocchio—my nose would be a mile long.

She reaches for the top button of my jeans.

I grin at her. "You're not trying to cop a feel, are you?"

Her cheeks flare bright red, and she grumbles, "You know, you're the worst patient around. I'm sure there was at least one nurse at the hospital who wanted to jab a needle in your ass just to shut you up."

"I'm an awesome patient." Who will be in serious trouble as soon as she pulls down my zipper.

To keep from thinking about her hands so near my cock, I recount in my head the mission. Right down to the part where I was shot.

It seems to work until Isabelle kneels, hooks her thumbs in the waistband of my jeans, and carefully peels them down my legs.

With her head so close to my package, my cock gets the wrong idea and grows harder.

There's no missing the effect she's having on me.

So I take the only recourse left.

I move my injured arm.

HolymotherfuckergoddamnChrist.

But it works. My cock is no longer interested in being on the receiving end of a blowjob.

Thank God for that.

Lines crinkle across Isabelle's forehead. "Are you okay?"

No. "Couldn't be better."

She helps me remove my legs from my jeans and pushes herself to her feet. "Okay, that was the hard part."

I'm not so sure about that. Because the next part involves

her rubbing the soapy washcloth against my body and wiping it clean. Maybe if she were some crotchety old nurse, I'd be fine. But Isabelle's movements are tentative, her touch more like a sensual caress than a sponge bath.

Christ, I'm not sure how many more days of her helping me like this I can survive.

Right now, being shot seems like the easy part.

Surviving Isabelle's touch? Not so much.

5

ISABELLE

It's common knowledge that men are creatures who are readily aroused. It doesn't take much—but it's easy to misinterpret their body's reaction to mean something else.

For example, when Jayden got a hard-on while I was giving him a sponge bath, it wasn't because of *me* specifically. Like the rest of mankind, his body is wired to physically respond that way.

It's biology.

The survival of our species.

No, my body didn't suddenly heat up at the thick outline through the cotton fabric of his sexy black boxer briefs.

Nope, not at all.

I finish bathing him and leave the bathroom to give him privacy so he can complete what he needs to do...and because I require a few minutes to recover. To bring my body under control.

If that's at all possible.

What I really need is a cold shower to extinguish the heat inside me—especially in my lower belly.

Shit. To think I'll have to do that again for the next few days until he's able to shower.

My phone pings with a new text. I read the message from Adam.

Adam: Are we still on for tomorrow?

Me: Yes!

After I help Jayden put on clean clothes, we go downstairs to his kitchen and start dinner. His kitchen is gorgeous and well-stocked, especially for someone who's away a lot and who isn't a gourmet chef.

I don't mean the ingredients. That's kind of lacking in the fresh food department because he was away for several days. I mean the professional-grade cooking equipment. You would think he's a world-renowned chef based on his collection.

"Soooo...exactly how often do you make fresh pasta?" I point at the pasta maker in the open drawer.

"I'd say I've made it maybe four times. Five tops. I love the taste of it but fuck, it's a lot of work to make it yourself."

"You do realize you can buy fresh pasta in the store? Just like you can buy it dry. Then all you have to do is boil the water and cook it."

"Yes, I am aware of that. That's why I've only made it from scratch at the most five times."

"So why the pasta maker?" I remove the saucepan I'm looking for and walk to the sink in the center island.

"My grandmother bought it for me."

I fill the pan with water. "Ahh, so this would be the grandmother who owned a restaurant, right?"

"That's right. Merlot or Chardonnay?"

"Chardonnay, please."

"My grandmother was a firm believer that a real man knows

how to create pasta from scratch," he says, removing a wine-glass from the cupboard and placing it on the counter. "She figured that because I was her grandson, I automatically knew how to make it. It was in the genes. Turns out, she was wrong."

He picks up the Chardonnay bottle and studies it.

I set the saucepan on the stove, cover it with the lid, and turn on the gas.

"Where's your corkscrew?" I remove the wine bottle from his hand.

His shoulders deflate slightly—enough for me to notice.

"My helping you open a bottle of wine doesn't make you less of a man. Besides, it's only for a week or two." Or longer. I really have no idea how long it takes a gunshot wound to heal. All I know from what he and Liam have told me is that it's a minor wound. Jayden's guardian angel was smiling down on him, because it could have been a lot worse if the bullet had been even a fraction of an inch to the right.

For that, his guardian angel deserves a chocolate *soufflé*.

Hmm. Maybe I should attempt something a little simpler. I haven't quite mastered the fine art of making them.

I uncork the bottle, pour myself a glass of wine, and get to work on making dinner.

"Do you have any idea what kind of information was stolen from the guest at the resort?" Jayden asks as I cut up the plum tomatoes he had in the fridge.

"No. It could be anything. But it must be important enough for Bernard to want us to fly down to talk to him."

"Why doesn't the guest just report it to the police?"

I lift my shoulders in a brief shrug. "Your guess is as good as mine. Maybe the guest doesn't trust the police."

"Or they don't want the police to know what was stolen because it deals with something illegal."

"Yes, there's that too."

"Do you have any idea why he wants to hire Liam's firm and

not someone else? It's not like there's a shortage of private investigators close to his location."

"I guess he heard that we're some of the best in the business."

" *'We're?'* You mean me and the guys are some of the best in the business. You're the best when it comes to kickass office managers."

I fold my arms in front of me. "You know Liam is looking at expanding the team and adding at least one or two women. And you also know I would be great at the job."

"Forget it, Isabelle. What the guys and I do is too dangerous. You don't have the training for it."

"I almost have my black belt in karate."

He snorts a laugh. "Real life isn't a movie—where the bad guys are taken down with karate chops to the neck and round-house kicks to the chest."

"I know that. I can also shoot a gun."

Jayden's eyes darken, and his eyebrows scrunch into a single line. "What do you mean you can shoot a gun?"

"Adam has been working with me for the past year." That's not the only thing Adam—who is a certified shooting instructor—and I have been training together for, but I figure one surprise a day is all Jayden can handle right now.

The poor man is injured, after all.

Jayden gives a semi-defeated huff. "Well, it's still not the same," he mutters.

"Why are you so against me being an operative?" I have my suspicions, but I want him to say it out loud.

He squeezes his lips together, as if afraid to put a voice to his fear and make it come true.

Two years ago, when we first became close friends, I'd come home from a rather god-awful date to find Jayden and Mojo sitting on my porch steps, waiting for me.

"Hey, what are you two doing here?" I asked, walking up the path. I was positive I'd mentioned to him that I had a date tonight.

Even in the dim light coming from my porch, I could make out Jayden's fingers tightening around Mojo's leash. "I just wanted to make sure you got home all right."

He hadn't been thrilled about me meeting Damon for drinks. He kept telling me the man was a self-absorbed bore who was only interested in one thing.

How right Jayden had been about that.

The self-absorbed bore part, that is.

I mean, sure, Damon had only been interested in one thing, but it wasn't what Jayden was thinking. It certainly wasn't what I'd been expecting, which was a little activity between the sheets.

Although in retrospect, something tells me the self-absorbed bore wouldn't have been a very attentive lover... unless we were talking about him loving himself.

The only reason he'd wanted to date me was because he'd discovered who my grandmother was and wanted a juicy story to splash on a tabloid.

When he didn't get it, he proceeded to write one anyway, spinning lies about my grandmother and her deceased husband—my grandfather—that you'd have to be an idiot to believe.

That night, after I came home from the date, I didn't want to tell Jayden what happened. So he kept poking me in the ribs, making me laugh because I was ticklish, and he only promised to stop once I filled him in about my date.

And thus, the tradition was born in which we poked the other person in the side whenever he or she tried to avoid opening up about what was really bothering them.

It's our signal that we aren't going to accept any bullshit, that we're there for the other person no matter what.

I poke Jayden in the side and repeat my question. "Why are you so against me being an operative?"

Mojo looks up at him and whimpers as if to further encourage Jayden to tell me the truth.

I pat the lovable dog on the head. "See, he agrees that you should just tell me why you can't stomach the idea of me being an operative."

Jayden lets out an insufferable sigh. "You can't just let it go, can you? You can't just believe me when I say you don't have what it takes for the job?"

I jab him in the ribs again—slightly harder this time, making sure he understands I mean business.

Another sigh. "Because I already lost someone who mattered to me while serving in the SEALs. I don't want to risk losing you, too."

I reach up and kiss his cheek. "I know you don't, Jayden. And you know I hate that you lost your best friend."

He searches my eyes as if looking for something. Unmistakable hope shines in his. "Does that mean you're going to give up your plans of being an operative?" The emotion in his tone mirrors that of his eyes.

I shake my head. "Nope. No can do, mister. No more than you would give up being one if I asked you to."

He bobs his head side-to-side, in a you-have-a-point gesture.

"I'll ask my grandmother more questions about Bernard— then we'll have a better idea who he is. It won't tell us what went missing, but at least we'll learn more about him than Connor could tell me."

"*We'll* talk to her."

"Are you sure you can handle that? She's not like the bad guys you're used to interrogating. I mean, not unless they enjoy ogling your hot bod like it's a piece of meat to a starving dog."

He chuckles. "I'm sure there are a few who would love to rip off my head like they're a starving dog."

"That's not quite the same thing. My grandmother is notorious for the trail of broken hearts she left behind in her younger days, before she fell in love with my grandfather. She loved men and still does."

Even now she goes out on dates, but those men are closer to her age than Jayden's. But as she explained last year, she's eighty-two years old. She's not dead or put out to pasture. She can appreciate a hot man just as much as anyone my age.

Although usually when she's in the same room as Jayden, she tries to encourage him out of his shirt...as do Henri and Liza.

"Don't worry," Jayden says. "I can handle your grandmother."

I add the tomatoes, olive oil, herbs, and spices to the sautéed onions, and turn down the heat. "Keep an eye on this, and I'll call her."

I return a few minutes later. "We're on for tomorrow afternoon. Are you sure about this? You're supposed to be resting at home for the next few weeks. You're not supposed to be involved in any missions. Liam will probably kill me if he finds out you're joining me."

"This isn't a mission. We're just talking to your grandmother."

"Sure, it's a mission. It might not involve guns and being shot at, but it's still a mission. It's not like you guys jump into a situation without gathering the necessary intel first."

"Again, this thing with your grandmother isn't a mission. We're just talking to her. That's all."

I take a sip of my wine.

Jayden grunts. "You're not going to be an operative, so get that thought out of your head, Isabelle."

"So you keep mentioning, even though you know this is something I've wanted to do ever since I joined the firm."

Shortly after joining, I had admitted my plans to Jayden. He pulled the same caveman routine that he's doing now, stomping into each of the guys' offices and declaring an emergency meeting. The meeting in which he went on a mini rant as to why he thought I was nuts.

Fortunately, not everyone agrees with him. He just doesn't know that. Yet.

"Well, I want to fly to the moon," he says, "but that doesn't mean it's going to happen."

I lift my chin. "It might. You just have to want it enough. Why is it so tough for you to accept that I want to do the same job as you?" By sheer will, I keep my frustration out of my tone.

"Because you're my friend, and I don't want to see anything bad happen to you."

"So you've said, but Adam, Connor, Liam, and Landon are your friends, too, and I don't see you preventing them from doing their jobs."

His eyebrow quirks up. If I weren't so damn frustrated with him, I would find it sexy. "Exactly how many days have you spent deployed in a country at war? How many times have you had to defend yourself in a life or death situation?"

"There's more to your job than shooting at people and avoiding being shot at. A large part of your job is going undercover and gathering intelligence. Who better to do that than a woman whose grandmother is a talented actress?"

I can tell he wants to cross his arms in his typical alpha-male, I'm-right-and-you're-wrong stance, but he can't. And that's only pissing him off more.

"That doesn't make a difference. No more than being the grandson of a talented chef means I can create fresh pasta from scratch."

"That's true, but you also admitted that you only tried to

make it four or five times. It's not like you spent years practicing until you could make it like your grandmother's."

Score one for me.

"Unlike you and your fresh pasta, I've had several years of experience as an actress. I might not have starred in any Hollywood or Broadway productions like my grandmother, but I did star in numerous high school productions." I enjoyed acting, but it was never my career goal. Not in the way it was for my grandmother.

"I know how to get into character," I say. "Heck, I even know how to put on makeup to alter my appearance. I can do things none of the guys on the team can. And that's why I deserve a chance to prove myself."

Score two for me.

Just when I believe I'm getting through to him, that he can finally see things from my perspective, he gives me another of his sexy, it's-never-going-to-happen grunts.

And...game over.

6

ISABELLE

The next morning, I drive to my meeting with Adam. Both he and Landon are in the parking lot when I arrive at the old warehouse outside of San Francisco.

To the average person, the building and surrounding area are abandoned, possibly even haunted—if you believe in that kind of stuff. You can't see the parked cars from the road, further adding to the building's abandoned appearance.

Inside? That's a whole different game.

Adam and Landon aren't the only individuals in the parking lot. Four other men and a woman are suiting up in protective gear.

Paintball gear.

What Jayden and Liam don't realize is that I've been training with Landon and Adam for the past year. The property also has a shooting range, which the general public isn't aware exists. It's for law enforcement and ex-military, but thanks to Adam's connections, I've been allowed to train here, too, as long as I'm with him.

"Lewis, you're with Berkshire, Hathaway, and Reed," Joe

Gardner, a retired naval officer, says, voice booming like a cannon. "Kilpatrick, Cunninghan, and Alward, you're with me."

Carl Lewis introduces himself to the three of us. Adam, Landon, and I have trained with Susan Kilpatrick and Pierre Alward two other times. So we know they're damn good.

We don our protection. Gardner's team heads into the building. The layout inside changes once a month, so we never know what to expect. It keeps us on our toes like in real life, when Adam and Landon are in the field.

We give Gardner's team ten minutes to set up position while we read the dossier he handed us when we arrived.

"Suspected terrorists have kidnapped the mayor's daughter. Negotiations have broken down," Landon says, reading the first page. "And now we have to extract the six-year-old. She's being held captive in an amusement park ride."

We load our weapons.

"Good luck," Carl says to me with a nod, his gaze doing a quick but unsubtle sweep of my body. I catch Landon rolling his eyes. Carl misses it.

We cautiously enter the building, Landon leading the way. Carl is in front of me. Adam has my back.

The area is dimly lit, other than the spotlights shining on the different parts of the setting. Shapes that resemble trees and woodland critters had been cut from plywood and painted to appear cute and cheerful.

The only thing that isn't so cute and cheerful is the army of demented-looking dolls. It's like Chucky's family reunion meets Disneyland.

Music suddenly blares through the speakers above us and throughout the area.

"You've got to be fucking kidding me," Carl grumbles.

I don't think it's the loud music, per se, that he's complaining about as much as the selection: *"It's a Small World."*

"Maybe this is the latest in terrorist torture techniques." I keep my voice low enough so the other team can't hear me over the music.

"I'm sure if it had existed back in the days of the Spanish Inquisition," Adam says, "this would have been the theme song."

Now we just have to hope none of us go insane before we take down the other team.

The hallway splits off. Landon gestures that he and Carl will continue straight ahead. Adam and I are to proceed along the other hall. The lighting is dimmer, the spotlights absent.

He and I peel away from them and keep moving forward, doing our best not to betray our location to the enemy. His back is pressed against the opposite wall, which isn't easy to do. Crazy funhouse mirrors cover the walls.

Our paint guns are held at the ready.

And the music plays on.

We're near the end of the hallway when a shadowed figure steps from either a room or passageway.

The protective vest says "terrorist," but I don't even need to see that to know it's Susan. Her blonde ponytail is the giveaway.

She fires at us, but we're quicker. Adam and I dive to the ground and return fire. Her arm is hit.

Our first target is out.

We continue to the end and peer around the corner. This time we're faced with what could be a storage room. Props and naked mannequins fill the space, providing cover for both the opposite team and us.

Adam and I cautiously move from one item to the next, doing our best not to accidentally knock into anything and give away our location.

Without warning, paint bullets rain at us from up ahead. We dive behind a pair of metal file cabinets.

We call out, making sure neither man shooting at us is a

member of our own team. Then for the next few minutes, it's us against the enemy.

Until it's just us.

Adam makes a daring move that wipes out the second terrorist. I eliminated the first one moments before that.

We high-five each other.

If Jayden and Liam could see me now, they would be more supportive of me being part of the team. I mean, sure, paintball isn't the same as being out there for real, but there's a reason these guys use the location as part of their training.

Of course, telling Jayden that I've been training here is about as good an idea as swimming alongside a great white shark while naked.

He also has connections. Connections that might end my days of practicing here.

But while that might be the case with Jayden, I have every intention of telling Liam the truth tomorrow. It's about time he learns that I'm not as incapable of being an operative as he assumes.

The training exercise continues. By the time I rescue the mayor's six-year-old daughter—a kid-sized mannequin in a dress and baseball cap—the only two individuals left are Landon and me. Adam was shot in the leg, Carl in the chest. All the terrorists have been killed.

The other team congratulates us, and we start packing up to leave.

I'm removing my vest when Carl saunters up to me.

"You did great in there," he says, flashing me a dimple I hadn't noticed before. He's good-looking, but I can tell he's not my type.

I love a confident man who knows what he wants and goes after it. He works hard for it but doesn't take anything for granted. He's confident, but not overly cocky.

Carl isn't that man.

"Thanks," I say. I can't really tell him the same. The man was shot, and I never had a chance to see him in action. He was the first from our team to go down.

"I thought that we could go grab a bite," he says. "Just the two of us."

"Are you talking about a date?"

"I'm talking about getting to know each other—and yes, food will be involved." He flashes me the dimple again.

"Sorry, but I have plans." Which is true. Jayden and I are meeting with my grandmother to walk down memory lane when it comes to her and Bernard.

I catch Adam and Landon watching us from next to Landon's jeep, both looking highly amused. I'm not sure if it's because Carl asked me out for lunch or because I shot him down.

Landon says something to Adam, but I can't hear what he said. Adam laughs.

They resume removing their gear.

"I'm busy tomorrow night, but what about Monday?" Carl says, his tone no less confident than before.

"Thanks for the invite, but I'm too busy these days to have time to date."

"It doesn't have to be a date. We can do something else."

He says this at the same moment that I remove the vest and his gaze drops to my boobs. *Nice going on being subtle.*

"Thanks, but I'm going to have to pass."

Landon and Adam join us, saving me from any more awkwardness.

Grinning, Landon slaps Carl on the back. "Shot you down, huh? Don't worry, it happens to the best of us."

Adam snickers.

Carl looks as though I just smacked him in the face. "I'm

sorry...I...didn't realize you're a lesbian. I wouldn't have hit on you if I'd realized we bat for the same team."

That has both Landon and Adam howling with laughter. Carl glances at them in confusion.

Clearly, Carl isn't used to women turning him down.

7

JAYDEN

I take a seat on the wicker armchair on Josephine's deck, which overlooks the bay. Far in the distance, on the other side of the water, the downtown San Francisco buildings are visible, the late-day fog keeping away for now.

Liza smiles brightly at me, with the same mischievous gleam in her eyes I've seen in my four-year-old nephew, right before he gets into trouble.

I nod at her with my own smile. "Did you two also know Bernard Bradshaw?" I ask her and Henri.

Josephine giggles like a schoolgirl, while looking the part of being a classic Hollywood pinup girl from the 1960s. "They're here because they're hoping you'll remove your shirt for the interview."

Isabelle groans. "I told you he's not going to do that. For starters, we're here on official business. Him questioning you while he's shirtless would be highly unprofessional."

"Are you telling me that CIA agents don't remove their shirts while interviewing witnesses and the bad guys, even if it means getting more information from them?" Henri seems disappointed by that.

"CIA agents aren't allowed to use their bodies to entice their subjects to give up information," Isabelle clarifies.

The corners of my mouth twitch at the innuendo that I'm sure she hadn't meant to suggest. And if her reaction a second later is any indication, I'm right about that. Her head dips forward as if she's about to drop her face in her hands but catches herself.

"That's right," I say, "the CIA code of ethics strictly forbids it."

Hell if I know if that's true or not. Although something tells me that what Isabelle said isn't entirely correct. When it comes to collecting intelligence on the enemy, you use whatever strategy works...as long as it's legal.

And even then, under certain circumstances, everyone looks the other way when it isn't. It's not like the other side isn't doing the same...using seduction and illegal means to gain secrets.

My stomach clenches unexpectedly at the thought and the memory of the conversation Isabelle and I had yesterday—the one about her wanting to work in the field. Would she try to seduce a dangerous man just to get information out of him?

Something tells me she would.

I clench my hands...and relax them. She's not an operative or a CIA agent, so there's no point in getting worked up over nothing.

Liam will never allow her to put herself in that kind of danger. She's too important. Only Isabelle can run the agency with the level of efficiency it's currently functioning at. We can't afford to lose her.

"But even if they do," Isabelle says, quickly recovering herself, "I keep telling you that Jayden isn't a CIA agent." She follows this by smoothly putting the interview back on track. "So let's discuss Bernard. What else can you tell us about him?"

Josephine selects a bagel with cream cheese and strawberry

jam from the coffee table. "Can I ask why you're inquiring about him?"

"The more we know about a potential client beforehand, the better prepared the team will be for successfully executing the mission."

True. Typically, before accepting a case, Connor does a background check on the individual interested in hiring us. That saves the team from nasty surprises later, like discovering you've been aiding a criminal instead of assisting a victim as you had initially been led to believe.

"Fair enough," Josephine says and begins to tell us about the man she dated when she was in her early twenties and still an unknown in Hollywood.

"He was such a gentleman," she says after describing how she and Bradshaw first met. Henri and Liza sigh like lovesick teenage girls staring at a poster of their favorite boy band.

"He took me to a vineyard for our first date. We had been driving through Napa Valley at the time, exploring the area. He told me how his grandparents back in Italy had once owned a vineyard. As a kid, he loved running up and down the rows of vines, helping his grandmother tend to the plants while she told him stories of magical creatures."

"So he's from Italy?" I ask.

She shakes her head. "No, he was born in the US. His father was an American who fell in love while working in Italy. When his stay came to an end, he and the girl married, and she moved to California with him. I used to love hearing their story. It was rather romantic."

And so begins what turns into an all-afternoon interview as Josephine tells us about her relationship with Bernard.

"Did you love him?" Isabelle asks at one point.

Josephine reaches for her tea, her hands shaking in the way that inflicts most elderly people. "At the time, I thought I did. But after I fell in love with your grandfather, I realized what I'd felt for Bernard and my first husband was only fondness. When Bernard left to go to Europe, I thought I was letting him go because I loved him and wanted him to achieve his dreams. But in retrospect, it was because I knew deep down that I didn't love him in the way that I thought I had. In the way that I needed to in order to sacrifice my own dreams so I could be with him."

Crinkles form on Isabelle's brow. "Who says you have to sacrifice your dreams to be with a man?"

"That's what was expected of a woman when we were younger," Liza says. "Our goal was to make our man happy."

"Well, that's kind of stupid," Isabelle huffs.

Josephine and Liza laugh. "Fortunately, times have changed. You still want to make sure your man is happy, but it goes both ways."

"And you should never change who you are to make him happy." Henri says it in a way that makes me wonder if he speaks from experience.

"You mean like how Dad expected my mother to be something she wasn't?" Isabelle asks Josephine. Her eyebrow is raised in challenge, but her tone and eyes still portray her fondness for the old woman.

Isabelle's father is Josephine's son.

"Unfortunately, your father was old-school. You can blame that on his grandparents on his father's side." She winks at Isabelle and chuckles. "Your grandfather encouraged me to be true to myself, something that is a challenge for any actress, both now and in the past. Maybe even more so back then, with the studio trying to dictate how I looked and behaved. Your grandfather loved me for who I was, quirks and all."

"Did Bernard want you to be something you weren't during your relationship?" I ask.

She appears thoughtful for a moment. "As far as I remember, he seemed pretty happy with what he saw. But I was still young at the time, fairly inexperienced when it came to the world. It was Isabelle's grandfather who opened my eyes and indirectly helped me become the woman I wanted to be."

"An award-winning actress?"

Smiling softly, she shakes her head. "No, a humanitarian. But he also supported my ambitions as an actress and stood by my side when I needed him. And in turn, I did the same for him. Our marriage wasn't always perfect because of the challenges we faced due to our careers. The long hours. My being away on location. But because we were strong in who we were, we made it work."

"After you and Bernard went your separate ways, were you still in contact with him?"

"If you mean, did I ring him on the phone or write to him, the answer is no. We ended on friendly terms, but we didn't make any attempts to contact each other."

"And then out of the blue, he calls you? Asking for my help?" Skepticism sits on Isabelle's words like a thin layer of dust.

"Oh, no, nothing like that. He moved back to America several years later, and we saw each other at various events in LA over the years. Because we were still very much involved with the Hollywood scene, it was impossible not to bump into each other from time to time. But it wasn't until a few weeks ago, when he was in San Francisco, that we reconnected and had a chance to really catch up.

"That's when I told him about you, Isabelle, and about your job. He called Sunday night and asked for my help in reaching out to you."

"Why not just call Isabelle at the office?" I ask.

"He'd dropped into town briefly for some family business but was due to fly out later that evening. He felt more comfortable connecting with you and Isabelle through me, instead of just cold-calling you. Like I told Isabelle, Bernard is a little paranoid in his old age. I think that's why he'd rather talk about the case face-to-face, rather than on the phone or via email."

Josephine's gaze darts briefly to me, a hint of a smirk on her lips before she returns her attention to Isabelle. "I don't know if you've talked to him yet, but he told me if you agree to spend the weekend at the resort, you're to book the reservations under the name of Moorehead. That way he'll know that you're coming—unless you insist on talking to him first. But even then he won't be willing to discuss what was stolen on the phone."

"Oh, you mean like as in Roger Moore?" Henri claps his hands in excitement. "He and Sean Connery were always my favorite 007s."

Isabelle groans. "Please don't tell me that's why Bernard picked the name."

"Because Henri likes Roger Moore?" Josephine says, laughing.

I look at the two women, confused at what's going on.

Isabelle fills me in. "Grandma had a small role in the first movie, *Dr. No*. It was when she was still an unknown actress."

Her explanation leaves me no less confused. "Wasn't Sean Connery the first James Bond?"

Henri beams. "That's right. You know your James Bond." There's admiration in his tone.

I shrug. I'm hardly going to admit that as a kid I used to pretend I was 007.

Isabelle grins at me as if she can read my thoughts.

"Bernard and I had a discussion last year at a charity event about who was the best James Bond," Josephine says. "I said Sean Connery. He disagreed and said it was Roger Moore, hands down."

Her gaze flicks over to her two friends, then shifts to Isabelle before landing squarely on me. She can barely contain the excitement in her voice when she asks, "Does this mean you two are flying down to see him this weekend?"

8

ISABELLE

The next day, I walk into the office, my brain buzzing like a busy beehive since I left Granny's house.

Jayden is standing at my desk when I enter through the main doors.

"What are you doing here?" I ask. "Aren't you still on medical leave?"

Jayden isn't the only man hanging around my desk. Liam and Adam are also there.

All three alphas turn their attention to me. Whatever they had been discussing before my arrival ended the moment I stepped through the doorway.

Jayden doesn't answer. Adam seems more amused than anything. And Liam is keeping whatever he's thinking off his face.

"Sooo...will anyone tell me what's going on? Or am I supposed to guess?" I don't suppose it has anything to do with Jayden violating Liam's orders and showing up here.

"What are you up to?" The low rumble of Jayden's voice is enough to make a lion tremble with fear.

I, on the other hand, just shrug it off. "My job. Because unlike you, I'm not on medical leave."

The corner of Adam's mouth twitches, but otherwise, he keeps his cool.

"You and I have been friends for the past two years, Isabelle," Jayden says, "which means I know when you're up to something."

"Me? I'm up to nothing. Other than my job."

"True or false, you're planning to fly down to Huntington Beach this weekend and talk to Bernard Bradshaw? Like you're living in some James Bond movie."

"Hey, just because Henri started fanboying over Bernard's code name for me, it does not mean I think I'm a female version of James Bond."

For one, he's fictitious.

I'm not.

"But you do realize the difference, right? This is real life, not a movie. You don't have the level of training needed for this job." Jayden doesn't wait for me to respond. "And you seem to be forgetting the place is a resort for *married* couples. You're not even dating, never mind married."

The tension building in his shoulders from the moment I walked through the door loosens its hold on him. They relax slightly.

Adam and Liam continue watching us.

Even Mojo is riveted by my argument with Jayden. His eyes are wide with confusion as he gazes between us like he's watching a ping-pong match.

And the ball is now on my side of the table.

I turn to Adam. "I know this is short notice. But will you be my husband?"

It's not like Bernard knows what Jayden looks like. And Adam is just as good an operative as my best friend.

My best friend who is on the verge of losing that title if he's not careful.

The absolute look of horror on Adam's face is priceless, and I can't hold back the building laugh.

Like the rest of the men in the firm—other than Liam—Adam has no interest in falling in love and settling down one day. He's as cynical about love and marriage as I am.

Which is why his reaction is so funny. He's forgotten that little tidbit about me.

But Adam is a fixer, a problem solver. So he's perfect for the job—whatever the job might be that Bernard wants to hire us for.

"I'm talking about being my fake husband for the weekend. I'm not expecting you to actually marry me."

"Sorry, I can't. I've got plans this weekend. As does Landon. In case you're forgetting that, too. We're going to San Jose."

Ironically, I did forget that. Me, the person who knows what each man is up to when it comes to their schedules, forgot that neither of those two men will be available to help me.

And the same goes for Connor and Liam.

That leaves Jayden.

And he knows it, judging from the smug expression on his face.

"I can always ask Henri." The words tumble from my mouth, without any thought to what I'm actually suggesting.

Jayden bursts out laughing, also noting the flaw in the hastily thought out plan. He then flinches, possibly because his injured arm is protesting the sudden movement.

Liam and Adam have never met Henri, so they have no idea why Jayden is laughing. They exchange bemused glances.

"You honestly believe anyone will buy that you're married to a man in his early eighties who's obviously gay?" Jayden asks, still snickering.

"No," I grumble. I really hate it when he's right. "So this is why you're here? To tell me my plan won't work? Okay. You've done that. Now go home"—*so I can think without you irritating me*—"and recuperate like you're supposed to."

He slowly shakes his head. "Nope. I'm here to work."

"Oh, no you're not," Liam says. "I was quite specific about that, Jayden. Until the physician clears you for active duty, you're at home."

"I'm fine," Jayden grunts. "It was only a minor scratch."

"It was hardly a scratch."

It's my turn to give Jayden a smug look. Sure, it doesn't solve my current dilemma, but the satisfaction I gain from it is gratifying. "Well, I guess we're even. My plan has been derailed because I don't have a fake husband for my cover, and you have to stay home because you managed to get yourself shot."

Liam folds his arms and gives us the look we're all familiar with. The I'm-the-boss-and-I-make-the-final-decision expression. "I've had a chance to evaluate the information that both Isabelle and Connor gave me regarding the case and Bernard Bradshaw. And I've decided that Isabelle will go down to meet with him to find out why he wants to hire the agency." His gaze shifts to Jayden. "And since you're so determined to return to work and ignore my orders, you'll be her fake husband."

Jayden flinches and then scowls. "I thought I was supposed to take things easy and recuperate."

Sure, Jayden. And I bet if Liam had suggested any other mission, you'd be all over it.

"You are, but I doubt that'll stop you from working, no matter what I say. I know that she's going to the resort—also, no matter what I say. I'm her boss during her working hours but not during her free time. And I know you have no intention of letting her get into hot water without backup."

God, are we really that predictable?

"Does this mean you'll let me work in the field afterward?" A woman can always hope.

Jayden scowls again. All right, the original scowl never left his face. It just deepens.

"I can shoot a gun just as well as any of the guys, and I've been studying martial arts for the past five years," I inform Liam before he has a chance to answer—and tell me what I don't want to hear.

"She's actually a brilliant shot," Adam adds. "I've been working with her for the past year or so, and I know what she's capable of."

"She isn't trained for this," Jayden says to Liam, voice gruff and unbending. "Just because Adam has taken her to the shooting range, it doesn't mean she's ready to deal with real-life in the field."

"That's where you're wrong. Not only is she a brilliant shot, but Landon and I have also been taking her to Paradise to train for the past year." Paradise is the code name for the property where law enforcement and retired military train with paint-ball guns.

For a fleeting second, a *You-have?* expression crosses Jayden's face, which is quickly replaced by a scowl.

I grin at him. "Surprise!"

The scowl becomes scowlier—to the point where I have to choke back a laugh. Liam, however, seems more impressed by the turn of events than anything.

"How come I didn't know about this?" Jayden demands.

"Because we didn't think you would approve." And clearly, we were right about that.

"Great, then how about you just audition for the next Bond movie and call it a day?" Jayden says to me, still being a stubborn ass when it comes to giving me a chance to prove what I can do. "You told me you used to be an actress in high school. Which means you'll be perfect for the role."

I level a chilly glare at him.

That makes Adam laugh. "At least you two won't have to

work hard at pretending you're married. You remind me of my parents...before they divorced."

Liam shakes his head, and I suspect he's barely containing an eye roll. "You'll report to me once you know what was stolen and why the victim doesn't want to go to the police, and then we'll evaluate whether we want to accept the case and the timeline for it based on Jayden's injuries. But I also suggest you book the reservation for a week—because from where I'm standing, it looks like you both could use a vacation. And hopefully, by the time you return, you'll sound less like Adam's parents than you do now. And Isabelle?"

"Yes?"

"Consider this assignment a part of your trial probation period as an operative. Do either of you have any questions?"

He doesn't wait for a reply. He heads to his office.

9

JAYDEN

Three days after Liam told me I would be Isabelle's fake husband for the next seven days, she and I arrive at the resort we're staying at in Huntington Beach. We've spent the past two days getting our cover stories straight:

We've been happily married for two years.

Adam cracked up when he heard that one. I've been cranky ever since Liam came up with the stupid idea that I'll be Isabelle's fake husband. And Adam's comment about us sounding like his parents before their divorce hadn't helped things either. Good thing my acting skills are first-rate.

Okay, back to our cover.

Isabelle and I don't have any kids yet.

Isabelle is an assistant for an art gallery. Fortunately, Henri owns the gallery and was happy to spend the day helping her get her cover straight. I'm a project manager for a small computer software company. One of our friends, Wes Chiasson, owns the building where Quade Security and Investigations is located, and he has his own software company. If I'm asked, he has given me the okay to mention his company's name.

Most of the other details are the same as in real life. The

closer you are to the truth with your cover story, the less likely you'll stumble over part of it and give away that you're not whom you claim to be.

And that includes the rings on our fingers—or more specifically, on Isabelle's finger. Her teardrop diamond engagement ring once belonged to my grandmother. She bequeathed it to me because I was her only grandson. My ex-fiancée has never worn it, and for that, I'm actually grateful. Suzanna wasn't into vintage jewelry and my grandmother died long after the engagement ended, so Suzanna never had the opportunity to reject the ring.

Before our flight to Huntington Beach, I had a checkup with my physician. He gave me the green light to remove the sling in ten days, but I'll have to take things easy for at least two weeks. We even have a story to explain what happened, if anyone should ask—and it won't have anything to do with the takedown of Vadik Orlov and his mafia crime family.

Isabelle turns the rental car into the entrance of the underground parkade. "Wow, this place looks as nice as it did on the website."

The large white building resembles a Mediterranean villa surrounded by palm trees, with red stone-tiled roofs, large archways, and iron balcony railings. The beach property is a considerable step up from where the guys and I stayed during our last mission.

We park the car, and I remove our suitcase from the trunk. With one arm in a sling, the action is awkward at best.

"I've got that." Isabelle grabs the handle from me. I don't bother to argue. I already know I won't win if I try.

My first thought when we step into the resort lobby is that we've walked into a honeymoon convention. I've never seen so many couples in one place, at the same time, who are obviously in love.

"This is going to be a lot harder than I originally thought," Isabelle says, voicing my opinion that she's not privy to.

I reach for her hand, and we walk to the reception desk. Her skin is warm and soft, and an unexpected heat stirs deep down at her touch.

I'm not much of a hand-holder. The last time I held a woman's hand, it was my ex-fiancée's, and look how that turned out. But for some strange reason, this feels different from when I held Suzanna's.

Isabelle's grip is strong, determined. Suzanna's was delicate, wishy-washy.

As we approach the front desk, the receptionist gestures for us to join her. She's a tall, curvy redhead. Pretty. Green eyes that are slightly wider than average. Her frizzy hair is pulled back in a bun.

No, I'm not sizing her up as a potential date. It's a game I play whether I'm working or not. It helps keep my observation skills sharp. You list several things that appeal to you about the person and several things that don't. It enables you to remember the person later, especially when you need to describe them to your colleagues or the police.

She's wearing a Hawaiian dress with red flowers, and her name tag says, "Rachel."

"Hi. We're checking in," I tell her, my arm around Isabelle's waist. "Jayden and Isabelle Moorehead."

She taps away at her keyboard. "Yes, we have you in a room overlooking the ocean. We also have you signed up for the group activity at three p.m. in the Marina Room."

"Group activity?"

"Yes, it's part of your package. It's very popular and is a great way to keep that spark between the two of you for many years to come. Gabrielle is looking forward to working with you. She's one of our best counselors."

"What kind of activities?" Isabelle never mentioned anything about this to me.

Although from the confused expression on her face, I'm guessing this is news to her, too.

"You'll be in a group with seven other couples, and you'll need to wear your swimsuits," Rachel explains. "Don't worry, you'll love it. I've never had anyone complain about the activities or homework assignments."

"Assignments?" Isabelle echoes.

"That's right. To get the most from the sessions, your counselor will assign you nightly homework. I guarantee you'll enjoy the assignments."

Says every high school teacher ever.

"Because you're only here for a week, you won't experience the full benefit that guests who stay for two or three weeks appreciate, but it's a good start."

She explains a few more things about the resort and the amenities and hands us our key cards and an envelope with Isabelle's and my names on it. I don't recognize the handwriting. "This was left at the front desk for you."

"Did you know anything about the group activity stuff?" I ask Isabelle as we walk to the elevator.

"Not really. I saw something about group activities but didn't pay attention to it. I figured it was a regular resort, where you lie on the beach and drink fancy tropical drinks."

"So you had no idea about the homework assignments?"

"Definitely not. I mean, what resort assigns homework to their guests? But I figure it's not going to be anything like writing an essay, so we don't have to put much effort into it. Maybe we can even skip the group activity. I'm sure it's not mandatory."

I glance around. "We'll talk about this in our room." My voice is low, tone full of meaning. We *will* be talking about this, but not at the risk of blowing our covers because someone over-heard us in the lobby.

At the elevators, I push the up button. A few other couples join us while we wait for the elevator.

"Are you two new guests?" an attractive woman in her early thirties asks, smiling. Both she and the man next to her have olive skin, dark brown hair, and equally dark brown eyes. No distinguishable scars…

Isabelle smiles back at her. "Yes. So far, it seems like a nice place."

"Oh, it is. A friend of mine and her husband came here two months ago, and they couldn't stop gushing about the resort. It completely revitalized their relationship."

Isabelle keeps smiling, but it's only because I know her so well that I recognize the slight change in it. Her smile isn't quite as genuine as before. It's more for show. "That's great."

"I'm Virginia, and this is my wonderful husband, Blake." The woman plants a kiss on his cheek. He gives us the typical man-nod greeting.

"It's nice to meet you," Isabelle says and introduces us to the pair.

"What time's your group session?" Virginia asks, her voice smooth like glass in the late afternoon sun. Her silky brown hair is pulled back in a low ponytail, and her long, lithe body is firm and athletic. Maybe a dancer?

Her husband also looks like he embraces an athletic lifestyle.

"Three p.m."

"That's the same time as us. With Gabrielle in the Marina Room?"

"Yes, but we're not sure if we're going or if we're just taking it easy by the pool."

From the expression on Virginia's face, you would have thought Isabelle had announced that she's really an alien from a faraway galaxy. "You can't miss the sessions. They're the reason people come here. Otherwise, you might as well go to any old resort."

I thread my fingers with Isabelle's and give them a meaningful squeeze. "What my wife means is that we had an early flight and she's a little tired. But I'm sure after we've rested up in our room for a few minutes, she'll be raring to attend. We've been looking forward to them."

The elevator dings open before Isabelle has a chance to say anything. The four of us, along with another couple, enter the enclosed space. Virginia continues with the friendly chitchat until we hit their floor. Her husband seems to take it all in stride, not contributing much to the conversation.

Pretty much my MO.

"We'll see you soon." She waves to us as the door shuts behind her and Blake.

It doesn't take Isabelle and me long to locate our room at the end of the hallway on our floor. As expected, the king-sized bed is the only bed in the room. The floor is smooth tile, with an area rug that extends three feet beyond the bed, on all sides. Not exactly conducive for sleeping on.

Otherwise, the room is pleasant. The bedding is white, with a red, chunky blanket folded across the end of the bed. The love seat, upholstered bench, and the cushions are a mix of turquoise and red. The walls are light cream, and the gauze curtains and dresser are a warm honey brown.

But as nice as the room is, that's nothing compared to the ocean view.

"This is gorgeous," Isabelle says, momentarily taken in by the room, and missing one crucial detail: the single bed.

"I'll sleep on the floor," I tell her.

"Why? Because you're the man?" She exaggerates an eye roll.

"If I say yes, are you going to accuse me of being sexist?"

"Probably. I could also remind you that I'm a big girl who's perfectly capable of sleeping on the floor. I have camped before."

I snort a laugh. "When exactly did you go camping?" Isabelle isn't the sort to sleep in a tent. She's more the camper-trailer type.

And even then I wouldn't go that far.

She ignores my comment. "Neither of us has to sleep on the floor. The bed has plenty of room." She pushes down on the mattress as if testing its springiness.

"You aren't a cuddler, are you?" I ask, even though I'm kidding. It doesn't bother me either way.

A mental image of her cuddling me while we sleep pays a surprise visit, and an equally surprising longing stirs deep.

"Nope. What about you?"

"No cuddling for me, either." I push the image away. The longing lingers, but I don't bother to examine what it means.

"I didn't think you were," Isabelle says.

"There are plenty of cushions. We can build a barricade in case you have the urge to cuddle me while we're sleeping." I wink at her, and she laughs.

"You really don't have to worry about that, but if it makes you feel safer, I have no issues creating The Great Wall of Cushions." Chuckling, she walks to the sliding patio window. "I can't believe how amazing the view is."

She swivels back to me as I open the envelope Rachel gave us. "We're not actually attending the group session this afternoon, are we?"

"That's *exactly* what we're going to do. It's part of our cover. You heard what Virginia and Rachel said. Those sessions are part of the reason married couples stay here. If we don't go, it might draw unwanted attention to us because they'll wonder why we aren't there." I remove the message from the envelope and read it.

"And if we decide to pass on Bernard's request for help, then we no longer have to worry about our cover—beyond claiming we're married?"

"I guess." But the chance of Isabelle passing on the opportunity to prove herself to Liam is as likely to happen as me sprouting Pegasus wings in the next thirty seconds.

All I can hope for is that Liam comes to his senses and orders us home.

"It just sounds so boring," she says. "Let me guess, we'll be wasting time playing bingo, or some other lame game."

"It could be worse."

A wry smile curves on her luscious lips. "You mean like being shot at?"

"Exactly. The worst that will happen is we'll be bored and waste an hour or so there. But despite what the phrase claims, no one has ever actually died of boredom."

She releases an if-you-say-so sigh. "All right. We do the group session, then hope Bernard hurries up and makes contact with us."

"You won't be a very good operative if you're going to be so impatient."

For some bizarre reason, she brightens. "That's the first step, admitting that I'm an operative. Now I just have to prove to you that I'm as good an operative as you...or maybe even better."

"Dream on, sweetheart. You'll never be a better operative than me."

Isabelle practically dances over to me and kisses me on the cheek. "We'll see. I bet by the end of the trip, you'll be singing a different tune."

Somehow, I doubt that.

10

ISABELLE

I step out of the bathroom, dressed in my favorite swimsuit: a zebra-print string bikini with pushup bra. But instead of black and white, the pattern is black and light pink.

It's designed to be sexy.

It's not designed to participate in some boring group activity that probably involves bingo or lawn bowling. But like Jayden said, boring or not, I don't have a choice about participating if we plan to maintain our cover of being a married couple.

Jayden is on the balcony, dressed in his swim trunks. His light-brown skin glows warmly in the midafternoon sun. There's no missing his sinewed muscles, the result of his on-the-job physical training.

Nor can you miss the various scars on his body. Mementos from his time with the SEALs and his missions with Liam's team.

A sudden urge to kiss each one shoots through me. To pay homage to the risks he's taken to secure the rights and freedoms for the countries he fought for, for the people he was protecting.

I grab my cover-up from the bed and slip it on. "You ready to get this over with?"

Jayden steps back inside and flashes me a cocky smile. "Don't sound too excited. You wouldn't want to give anyone the impression you can't wait to participate."

I dignify his comment by sticking my tongue out at him.

He laughs.

"I just wish we could meet Bernard now and not later." That was what the envelope was about that Rachel, the woman at the front desk, had given us: a message from Bernard requesting we meet him in his office at 5:30 p.m.

And that was it.

Talk about keeping us in suspense.

I remove my light-pink stilettos from the closet and slip them on. They're simple in design, rich in elegance. The perfect shoe for my outfit. "Okay, I'm ready."

Jayden's gaze sweeps down my body, and he swallows. Hard. "Nice outfit."

"Thanks. I wasn't expecting to play games in my bikini. Otherwise, I would have packed something more practical."

The Marina Room where we're supposed to meet the group is located on the main floor, down the same wing that includes the spa and the entrance to the swimming pool.

We might be a few minutes early, but we're the last ones here. Seven other couples are already sitting on the thick exercise mats.

Virginia smiles at us. The mat next to her and her husband is empty.

The room is nothing like I was expecting. I was thinking along the lines of a conference room or a small gym. It reminds me more of a spa or fancy yoga studio, with an expansive skylight. The floor and walls are composed of large beige tiles, and a waterfall cascades down the wall opposite the entrance.

In addition to the exercise mats, a dozen loungers with red-and-gray pillows are lined up along the walls.

"Hi," a pretty woman in her forties says. "You must be Jayden and Isabelle."

"That's right," I respond, doing my best to ignore the sinking sensation in my stomach. All the couples look lovey-dovey. The women (or the second male partner in one couple's case) are sitting between their spouses' legs. Jayden and I belong here as much as a dragon belongs at a prom.

One of the men whispers in his wife's ear. She giggles, and a light blush colors her cheeks.

"Perfect. Grab the empty mat, and we'll get started." The woman, whom I'm guessing is Gabrielle, smiles and gestures toward the mat in question.

Jayden and I sit on it. The heat from his chest soaks through the gauzy cover-up against my back. And a different kind of heat settles low in my belly.

He leans close, his breath brushing against my ear. "Are you okay?"

"Just wonderful," is my whispered reply.

"Hi everyone," the woman says. "My name is Gabrielle Mendez. I'm a certified marriage and sex counselor. And for the next four days, I'll be guiding you through some fun activities, to help keep your sex lives fresh and exciting."

At her news, my body stiffens like a diving board.

Holy. Shit.

Something tells me we're no longer talking about Bingo and Scrabble.

"There'll also be homework to do after each session," she continues, "but you aren't required to hand anything in. These are activities that you'll practice in the privacy of your room. Some of them involve you being naked, or partially naked, so they aren't appropriate to practice in a group setting such as this."

Partially naked? The guys are already shirtless, and I'm not the only one in a skimpy bikini. We can't get more partially naked than this.

"Some of the activities are the type you might not normally be comfortable doing in public, but this is a safe, judgment-free environment. What we do here will help bring you out of your comfort zone with your partner, so that you can be more sexually adventurous at home."

Jayden lightly brushes his thumb against the back of my shoulder.

I can do this. I want to be an operative with Liam's team. The guys have to do things outside their comfort zones all the time. It's part of the job.

Besides, it's not like they're expecting Jayden and me to have sex in front of everyone.

God, I hope they're not expecting that.

"Let's start by introducing yourselves and telling us how long you've been married." Gabrielle turns to Blake and Virginia.

"Hi, I'm Blake, and this is my wife, Virginia. We've been married for five years now."

The introductions continue. Anthony and Demek have been married for less than a year, which is the shortest time in the group. Everyone else has been married anywhere between two to forty years.

Or supposedly married, in the case of Jayden and me.

"One of the leading causes for the breakdown of marriages is due to a diminished sex life," Gabrielle explains once we're finished with the introductions. "You become busy with your careers and the kids. In time, the sexual passion that you and your partner once shared becomes a thing myths are made of. Once that happens, the frustration seeps in. The love you had between you fades, increasing the risk of the marriage failing."

Or your spouse cheating on you and destroying your faith in love.

That's not to say my mom no longer believed in love after my father cheated on her. But her ability to trust another man was left in ruins—much like the Roman Colosseum.

"So our goal during these sessions is to ensure at least one foundation of a happy marriage doesn't crumble. You will learn how to keep things fun and exciting when it comes to your sex life."

Well, that's unexpected. But totally doable. I can learn some fun new tricks to use with my flings.

A voice in the back of my head busts out laughing, reminding me that it's been a while since I've had a fling, a one-night stand, or a boyfriend. Basically, anything that involves me having sex.

"We're going to start with a simple, warm-up question," Gabrielle says. "There is no right or wrong answer. All right. What gets you in the mood for sex? For example, music, a glass of wine, candles."

She glances around the room, giving us a moment and then randomly calls on Virginia. "What gets you in the mood to have sex with Blake?"

Virginia giggles, the sound strangely smoky and seductive to be an actual giggle.

I wouldn't be surprised if that laugh is what gets Blake in the mood to make love to his wife.

"He has a way of kissing me on the neck that leaves me desperate to have sex with him. He just has to kiss me that way and *bam*, I'm hot for him."

Blake looks proud and slightly smug at the reply. He rewards his wife with a brief kiss...on the lips.

Guess she won't be ripping off his clothes quite yet.

"That's a great answer," Gabrielle says. "There are areas on our bodies that are considered highly erotic. A simple teasing touch may be all it takes to get your partner in the mood for sex." She looks at me. "Isabelle, what gets you in the mood for sex?"

"Chocolate," I blurt. Jayden chuckles behind me. He knows how much I love chocolate.

"Another great answer. Chocolate is a known aphrodisiac, especially dark chocolate. It leads to better sexual arousal and improved sexual satisfaction. Studies have shown that chocolate consumption enhances your sex drive. So men, forget about giving it to your wife only for Valentine's Day. Jayden, what about you? What gets you in the mood to have sex with Isabelle?"

For a second, an image of a naked Jayden leaning over me on the bed flashes in my mind.

I mentally shake it away. Nope, I'm so not going there.

Besides, it was the power of suggestion. Gabrielle was talking about sex and then mentioned his name. The same thing would have happened if she had called on one of the other men.

The voice in the back of my head bursts out laughing, not at all buying that theory.

Everyone is looking expectantly at Jayden and me, and I do my best not to laugh. Because Jayden is a man. And like most men, just give him a willing partner, and he's ready for action. It's not like men need anything to get them in the mood. They're always in the mood.

Which is what led to the downfall of my father when it came to his secretary.

Who later became wife #2.

Until she became ex-wife #2.

"Isabelle only has to smile at me, and I'm in the mood," Jayden says.

I bite my lip to keep from laughing out loud. I doubt in the two years we've known each other, he has felt *that* way about me.

The guys nod in agreement—as if they, too, get horny at the sight of their spouses' smiles.

Gabrielle continues asking each couple, in turn, to tell us what gets them in the mood for sex.

Cooking dinner together turns on Anthony and Demek.

Hell, cooking with Demek would turn me on, too. His Russian accent is hot.

Oh, who am I kidding? Just *talking* to Demek would have me in the mood. No cooking required.

Once everyone has shared with the group, Gabrielle moves on to the activity portion of the session.

The question wasn't bad. Maybe the activity won't be awful either.

"All right, ladies and Anthony," she says, "come with me, and bring your phones."

The eight of us exchange glances and push ourselves to our feet. We follow her into what resembles a changing room, but with comfy armchairs and a mirror spanning the wall above the row of fancy sinks.

Gabrielle asks us how we're doing so far. "For this activity, you're going to take a photo of a sexy part of your body. It can't be X-rated. So no genitals, please."

Some of us look at each other in confusion (or maybe it's just me who's confused). The rest get to work, taking photos of various body parts.

"Only one photo, ladies and gentleman, unless your first attempt is blurry."

I shrug to myself and snap a photo of my ankle with the butterfly tattoo.

Once we're finished, she gets us to show her the photos, and we return to our husbands, who are amicably chatting about something to do with hiking.

I sit next to Jayden. "So far these activities aren't too bad at least," I say under my breath. If all we're going to do is take non-X-rated photos of our body, then I can survive this aspect of the weekend.

If the real reason we're here is that easy, Jayden and I will be finished with this craziness in no time.

"Ladies and Anthony, you're to now show your husband the photo you took in the other room. Remember, if you shot more than one image, just show him the best one."

I hand Jayden my phone.

"Nice tattoo." He grins at me, and I smack him on his good arm. It's not like he's never seen it before.

"Has everyone seen the photos?" Gabrielle asks.

We all nod and answer in affirmative.

"Husbands, you're to now kiss that body part. But I don't want you to kiss it as though it were a child you're tucking into bed. I want the kiss to mean something. Worship the body part. Let your spouse know how much you love her or him."

Jayden looks down at my ankle, and I can tell what he's thinking. With his sling on, it'll be difficult for him to kiss that body part.

Phew. Guess we got out of that.

Gabrielle sashays over to us. "I suggest, Isabelle, that you lie back and lift your leg up so that Jayden can kiss your ankle." She turns to him. "I didn't realize that you're injured. I'll take that into consideration for the remaining activities and home-work assignments."

Gabrielle tells me to lie down. I do as I'm told and hold up my leg for Jayden. Heat sweeps up my chest, neck, and face, threatening to burn me alive.

When I was thirteen years old, I was one of the Pink Ladies in my middle school's rendition of *Grease.* But while singing

"Summer Loving," I tripped on my own feet and went flying, my arms flailing as I fought to regain my balance.

I felt like a colossal idiot.

That was nothing compared to how I feel now.

Good thing Liam's team can't see us. We'd never hear the end of it if they could.

Jayden lifts my leg and gently kisses my butterfly tattoo.

The embarrassment that hit a moment ago swings in the other direction—and the heat that was hanging around my upper body rushes to my core. I swallow back a small moan before it can escape.

Shit. And this is all because a guy kissed my ankle?

Not just any guy, my body points out.

I ignore it.

Jayden releases my leg, and I lower it to the floor.

"That was perfect," Gabrielle tells him. "You're a natural at this."

A snorted laugh tumbles from between my lips before I realize it's there. Too late for me to prevent it.

They both look at me. Gabrielle frowns in confusion.

"You're right," I say, tone sweet and cheery. "He is a natural. That's how he swooned me right off my feet."

Gabrielle's frown transforms into a smile. Jayden's grin is cocky, the irony of my comment not missed on him, considering I'm currently sitting on my ass.

Her attention finally moves from us to the group. "Has everyone completed the exercise?" she asks.

We all nod.

"Now, we'll switch things up..."

11

JAYDEN

Gabrielle smiles at each of us, and I almost dread what the next activity will be.

So far, they haven't been too bad. I wasn't lying when I said Isabelle's smile gets me in the mood for sex.

There's a certain smile that does it for me.

I don't get to see it too often—which is probably a good thing, given the nature of our friendship. But when I do, it's cold-shower time for me.

"Ladies and Anthony, you are now going to pretend your husband's finger is the most decadent ice cream cone you've ever tasted, and lick it."

I can't vouch for the other men in the room, but my dick stirs to life at the image in my head of Isabelle licking my finger.

Because it's not my finger that my dick sees starring in this new fantasy.

Fuck.

"But before we proceed, men, wash your hands in that room." Gabrielle points to the room that the women and Anthony were in earlier.

"I don't suppose while you're in there," Isabelle says, "you can smother your finger with real ice cream."

I grin at her. "Chocolate ice cream, perhaps?"

She shoves my arm.

"No one will believe you and I are married if you keep that up."

"Oh, don't worry. By the time I'm finished, they won't have any doubts." She winks at me, and I groan.

Why do I feel that whatever she's got planned isn't good news for me?

The other men and I go into what looks like a fancy-ass changing room.

"Well, so far this is better than I was expecting," Blake says. "A friend of Virginia's recommended the resort. She and her husband were here last month and couldn't stop raving about it. That's how we heard about the place. It's also how we found out about the BDSM lessons and private rooms. They don't advertise them on the website."

He squirts the soap from the dispenser onto his hands. "What about you, Jayden? Are you and Isabelle into BDSM?"

"Can't say that either of us has tried it." I'm assuming Isabelle hasn't.

Heck, I don't think she has even read *Fifty Shades of Grey* or watched the movie.

"What is BDSM?" Demek asks, his Russian accent coming in stronger than it had earlier.

Blake explains it to him, and Demek nods. "Ah yes, I am familiar with that concept."

"I highly recommend at least taking a beginner's lesson if you decide to extend your stay here," Blake says to the other men and me.

"Thanks for the advice. I'll be sure to mention it to Isabelle." Or not.

"So what happened to your arm?" He nods at my injured

limb.

"A stray bullet hit it."

All seven men look at me with great interest—mentally guessing what I was doing to be anywhere near a flying bullet.

"Are you a cop or a bad guy?" Demek asks.

"Nothing that exciting. My neighbor was drunk and tried to scare away a pesky squirrel. The squirrel outsmarted him, ducked, and the bullet ricocheted off a metal flag post and nicked my arm. I just happened to be in the wrong place—my own backyard—at the wrong time."

The men gape at me for several seconds, some clearly fighting the urge to laugh.

Blake is the first one to give in to the urge. "It's a good thing you don't require two functional arms to fuck your wife, am I right?" The man has several tattoos on his body, including a stylistic golden eagle. The stripes of the US flag form its wings, the stars the body.

There's a good chance he served with the military, but I avoid bringing it up. I don't want to draw attention to the fact that I served with the SEALs. It's not part of my cover.

Unlike Blake, I don't have tattoos that scream out that I was with the military. Mine are more subtle in design. Only I and the guys on Liam's team understand what they mean.

I don't bother to answer Blake.

We quickly finish washing our hands and return to our spouses.

Gabrielle is still standing near Isabelle. I sit next to her on the mat, and Isabelle takes my hand. I barely hear the surrounding murmur of voices above the sound of my pulse thumping in my ears.

"I want you to look into your partner's eyes while doing this activity. The eyes are the windows to the soul, but they also heighten the sensuality of the moment. And that can lead to great sex."

Isabelle runs the tip of her tongue along her lower lip as if eagerly anticipating the taste of the imagined ice cream.

I don't have to ask her what flavor she's thinking about. She might love chocolate, but when it comes to ice cream, she has a weakness for raspberry ripple.

She brings my hand closer to her mouth, her brown eyes locked on mine.

I swallow hard, and my gaze drops to her lush lips, stained with a pale pink lipstick that matches the stripes of her bikini. The bikini that will now star in my dreams tonight.

While Isabelle is sleeping next to me in the same bed.

I swallow again. Harder this time. It doesn't do much to dislodge the lump in my throat.

"Okay now, don't be shy."

Isabelle breaks eye contact with me and runs her tongue along my finger.

I've watched her eat ice cream before. I even mocked her once because she was moaning loudly at the great taste. The erotic sounds she had made—like she was verging on orgasm —resulted in men looking at her, most likely imagining how she would sound if they got to fuck her.

At the time, I thought it was funny.

Now, all I can hear in my head is the sound she made that day.

My cock thickens at the mental image of her licking it and making those same noises. I try telling it that's not going to happen. It doesn't listen.

Isabelle's gaze returns to mine. There's a heat in her eyes that I don't remember seeing directed at me before. Her lips part enough for my finger to pass through them. Her teeth lightly scrape against my skin—and it takes all my willpower not to groan at how amazing it feels to have her taste me this way.

Isabelle pulls away slightly; then she takes my finger farther into her warm mouth, sucking it, running her tongue down the length of it.

"Great job," Gabrielle says, breaking the trance Isabelle appears to be under. She pulls my finger from her mouth, and it instantly mourns the loss.

"How was that?" Isabelle asks me. There's a slight smugness to her tone, but there's also a hint of something else that I can't get a full grasp on.

"It was good." My voice comes out husky. I cough to clear my throat, not wanting her to find out how much the activity affected me. Christ, I'm dreading to see what Gabrielle wants us to do next.

The need to escape the room and accomplish what we came to the resort to do burns hot in my veins. Or at least that's what I tell myself. I'm restless, a sensation that's fairly uncommon to me.

And that's not a good thing. It's when mistakes happen.

Isabelle peeks at her phone, even though we aren't allowed to be on them—other than when she took the photo of her ankle. "Oh God, there's still thirty minutes left."

She shifts about on the floor. To most people, it appears that she's attempting to get comfortable.

But I know better. She's restless, too. She wants to get out of here as much as I do and talk to Bradshaw.

"Welcome to the world of being an agent," I say under my breath.

"What? You usually get stuck in classes about sex while the bad guy is out there, wreaking havoc on the world?"

"Definitely not. But a large part of the job is about your hands being tied, in a figurative sense, when you just want to get out there and take down the bad guys. A major aspect of the job is surveillance."

"Except we aren't surveilling."

"How's everyone doing so far?" Gabrielle asks the group,

interrupting Isabelle's conversation with me. In her hand is a stack of what looks like playing cards. "I'm going to give one of these to each of you. It's the next question that you'll be answering. But unlike the first one, these questions are just between you and your partner."

She starts to hand them out.

Isabelle quietly groans—which might have more to do with the expressions on everyone's faces after they read their card than anything else.

The "What gets you in the mood for sex?" question was clearly tame compared to what's on those cards.

"At least we don't have to come up with an answer to share with everyone," I tell her. "No one will know that we aren't talking about the questions on the cards."

Gabrielle hands us our cards, and I read mine.

"All right, gentlemen first," Gabrielle says. Unfortunately, she's still standing next to us and doesn't appear in any rush to move away.

She gives me a slight nod to go ahead and ask Isabelle my question.

"Which do you think is hotter? Sex standing against a wall or bent over a desk?"

It actually says table, but the image of Isabelle bent over my desk with her fine ass in the air popped into my head at the wrong moment.

She chews on her lower lip for a heartbeat. "Is it even possible to have sex while standing against a wall?"

I nod because I have personal experience in that area. "I take it you've never done it against a wall. What about while bent over a desk?" *Oh, shit.* I hadn't meant to ask her that.

It's one thing to talk about hypotheticals, about what we *think* is hotter. It's another to talk about what we have done. Isabelle and I might be friends, but this isn't the kind of territory that friends of the opposite gender typically venture.

Gabrielle watches our conversation with interest.

"Can't say I've done that either. But it's not like it's possible to use my desk at the art gallery. It's not in an office. It's in plain view of everyone."

I feel a slight tug on one side of my mouth at how smoothly she handled what could have been a crucial mistake in revealing our identity. While it might not have meant anything to Gabrielle, we still can't risk mistakes like that.

"Fair enough point."

Isabelle has a look in her eyes that I recognize all too well. She wants to ask me if I've fucked anyone on my desk, but something is holding her back. And I don't just mean Gabrielle listening to us—although I'm sure that's a deterrent, too.

"Since you haven't done either of them, Isabelle, which do you *think* would be hotter?" Gabrielle asks, and she nods at me to remind her to tell *me* and not Gabrielle. "If you and Jayden were to do one of them now, which would it be?"

"I assume you mean if we could find a desk to bend over." Isabelle glances around the room as if searching for said desk.

"You have a desk in your bedroom. And walls." She flashes Isabelle a meaningful look.

"I'll go with bent over the desk—after everything has been pushed off with a dramatic sweep of the arm."

I can't help but laugh—because Little Miss Organized would never dare make a mess of her desk. Even for incredible sex.

Isabelle's expression is smug for my benefit. It means nothing to Gabrielle.

"All right, Isabelle," Gabrielle says. "What is your question for Jayden?"

"Would you rather lick whipped cream off me or tie me up and have your way with me?"

Or all of the above.

"As tempting as the whipped cream might be, I'm going to

have to say tie you up." What I want to add, but can't because Gabrielle is listening in, is that I want to tie Isabelle up until she surrenders her goal of being an operative with Liam's team.

The job is too dangerous.

"Great, you two." She walks off to join another couple, even though it's clear everyone else has already finished asking their questions.

"What do you think Blake's and Virginia's questions were?" Isabelle asks. "She's blushing something fierce."

"If they're anything like ours, I'm not surprised. Maybe this is the resort's way of figuring out who would be best suited for their BDSM room." I tell Isabelle about the conversation I had with the men while we were washing our hands.

"I'm not sure I want to know if it was Bernard's idea."

"I'm sorry to say," Gabrielle says to the group, "that's the end of today's session. But before you go, I have your homework assignment for you. Well, more like a double assignment."

She walks to a wooden cabinet against one wall, removes a wicker box from the top shelf, and returns to the group. "The first part is for one of you to *slooowly* undress your partner. Both of you will be standing." She removes a travel-sized bottle of mouthwash from the box. "The clothed partner will wet their fingertips with the mouthwash and rub the other partner's nipples, creating an erotic, tingling sensation."

"Oh, good," Isabelle says under her breath. "I forgot to bring my mouthwash with me. Now I've got some for what God intended it for."

Gabrielle finishes handing out the mouthwashes. Each bottle has a tag tied around its neck, with our homework instructions typed on it.

She then dismisses us with an "I'll see you all here tomorrow at ten a.m. Have a great evening." The innuendo in her words is hard to miss.

12

ISABELLE

After Jayden and I return to our room to change out of our swimwear, we go to the main level and casually walk around. Like the proverb says, "When in Rome, do what the Romans do." We hold hands, blending in with the real married couples.

It feels nice.

The hand-holding.

Richard, my ex-boyfriend, was never one to hold hands. And I hadn't been in relationships long enough with the other guys I dated to qualify for hand-holding status. So holding hands with Jayden is definitely new territory for me.

The main level of the resort is like most hotels. It has a classy restaurant, reception area, and numerous high-end stores. There's even a counter for booking excursions organized by the hotel: scuba diving, helicopter rides, paragliding, hiking.

We walk up the stairs to the second level and find several small conference rooms. All are currently unoccupied.

"Hey, what are you two doing here?" Anthony asks, strolling toward us. He and Demek have changed into causal walking shorts and are sporting bright Hawaiian shirts.

Both are the type of men that straight women bemoan are gay, because the guys are hot compared to the majority of straight guys. They look like they're Calvin Klein models.

Or maybe they are, and that's how they met—during a fashion shoot.

"We were just walking around. Seeing what else is in this place," I tell them. We're supposed to meet Bernard in his office soon. We're just getting a lay of the land until then. "What about you?"

"Looking for the men's room because we're too lazy to go back upstairs," Anthony says.

"Have you made reservations for dinner yet at the restaurant?" Demek asks.

"Not yet. We were thinking of wandering around town and seeing what we can find," Jayden replies.

The truth is, we haven't even discussed dinner. We've been more focused on the upcoming meeting with Bernard.

"You're more than welcome to join us. We have a table booked in the resort's restaurant for seven p.m. I can always go ask the hostess if they can accommodate the change."

"Thank you, but maybe another day. We're looking to have a romantic dinner our first night here. Maybe find a place that has a chocolate dessert for Isabelle." Jayden's tone holds an *If-you-know-what-I-mean?* lack of subtlety that makes me want to elbow him in the gut. He's never going to let me forget my answer to Gabrielle's question.

Anthony and Demek laugh.

"If you want a rain check for another night," Anthony says, "just let us know."

They walk away, leaving Jayden and me alone.

We find the main hotel office a few minutes later. Closed blinds cover the glass wall, blocking our view of the inside.

The rest of the wall contains framed nature photos and photos of marine life. Bernard's office—along with the ones responsible for the resort's operations—must be on the other side of the glass door.

Jayden opens it, and we step inside. From the looks of things, the receptionist has gone home, and all the office doors are closed except one. The lights inside both the reception area and the office are still on.

I exchange glances with Jayden. He nods and gestures to the office, indicating to go there.

We casually approach the open door.

A man who reminds me of a storm cloud, with his white hair, gray suit jacket, light-gray knit pullover, and an even lighter gray shirt, is sitting at the desk. Bernard Bradshaw. But his attention isn't on his computer.

He's beaming at us.

He pushes himself out of his chair, studying me like I'm his long lost relative. His office is clutter-free and organized. Unlike the furniture in the reception area, the pieces here are antiques, each with a story to tell. Photos of various celebrities and places around the world adorn the walls and the bookshelf behind him.

He comes around to our side of the desk. "Isabelle. You're the spitting image of your grandmother. I'm so excited to finally meet you. She's told me so much about you." He turns to Jayden. "And you must be Isabelle's colleague and close friend, Jayden Price."

Jayden steps forward, placing himself slightly between Bernard and me. "Josephine said you want to talk to us about a case you need help with."

I step around him because no matter what he might believe, I can take care of myself. He's just too much of a stubborn alpha male to see it.

A photo on the wall of a vineyard and a Spanish-style building catches my attention. In front of the building, gazing into the fountain, is my grandmother.

But this version of my grandmother is one I'm not too familiar with. This version bears a strong resemblance to me, more so than her much older self does. The only noticeable difference in the photo between us is her black hair. It reaches just below her shoulders, the ends curled up. Her long bangs are brushed to the side, and the crown is teased and pulled back. Unlike me, she doesn't have blue streaks.

"Yes, that's your grandmother," Bernard says, noticing where my attention is now.

"The photo was taken in 1960 at the Enchanted Springs Winery in Oakville, California. We went there on our first date together. Wonderful place. They had the best Riesling I've ever tasted. It won the gold medal from the Los Angeles County Fair Association, just two days before your grandmother and I were there. And this one..." He points to a photo that is also several decades old. The couple in it is wearing ski suits, boots, and wool hats. Behind them are a ski slope and pine trees. "This was taken in Squaw Valley, the site of the 1960 Olympics. That was months before your grandmother and I met, but I managed to convince her to join me on a ski trip there. She was quite the adventurer. An adventurer and a deep-down romantic. The best combination."

His eyes glaze over as he reminisces a past long since trodden.

He then shares details about the other photos in his office. Some are places he has traveled with my grandmother. Others are locations he visited with other celebrities from that era.

Jayden and I exchange a glance. Neither of us knows what to make of this. Did Bernard actually fly us down for a particular reason, or is he just an old man with nothing better to do than reminisce about the past with anyone who'll listen?

Just when I think it's the latter, Bernard finally gets back on track about why we're here. "I need your help."

"What kind of help?"

"I'd rather not say here," Bernard says. "The walls might have ears."

I try not to laugh. The old man sounds like he's been marathon-watching James Bond movies, or at the very least, marathoning the ones when Roger Moore was 007.

Oh, boy.

"Then where do you want to tell us?" I ask.

"How about we go for a ride? There's a place north of here, near the ocean, where people tend not to go. It'll be easy for me to spot if someone's tailing us."

Jayden frowns. "Is there a reason someone would be following you?"

"That's what I need you two to figure out. But like I've already said, I don't want to tell you anything else here. As it is, I'm hoping I've haven't given away too much to the wrong person just by meeting you in my office and talking to you on the phone, Isabelle."

"Okay, we'll go with you," I tell him, all the more curious to hear what he has to say.

Jayden's frown deepens. "Can I talk to you for a second?"

Oh, crap. I recognize that look...which is now directed at me.

"Sure." I turn to Bernard. "Can we have a minute? And then I'll go with you."

Jayden makes a noise under his breath, which could be a growl, but he doesn't say anything beyond that.

"I'll wait for you in the hallway." With an easy smile, Bernard nods at Jayden and leaves his office.

No sooner do we hear the glass door click shut, and Jayden's words come out like Nerf balls from a toy gun. "You're not going anywhere with him, Isabelle."

"Give me one reason why not."

"He wants to take us to a place where there are no witnesses."

I feel my brows crinkle under the weight of his suspicions.

But I can't blame him for how he feels. His job can have that effect on you. I've seen it with the other guys on the team.

"You've got your gun on you, right?" Mine is in our room safe after he insisted I leave it there.

He nods.

"Then we don't have anything to worry about."

"Maybe you should try worrying more than you do," he fires back.

I heave a sigh. "Look, I know he hasn't done anything to earn your trust yet. But I do trust my grandmother. There's a reason she wants me to help him."

"Your grandmother would carry an insect across a busy street if it meant it wouldn't be killed trying to cross it."

A rough laugh bursts from between my lips. "She's a humanitarian, not a bugitarian."

"Which means she wants to save the world, no matter whom she's trying to save. Including the bad guys."

I shake my head as if that will help me make more sense of what he's saying. "Don't you think you're being a tad bit melodramatic? In case you're forgetting, Liam sent us here. He wouldn't have done that if there was anything suspicious lurking in Bernard's background."

Jayden answers with a gruff huff, then studies me for a long moment, his eyes narrow slits. "You're going to do this whether I agree to it or not, aren't you?"

I grin, straightening my shoulders. "You better believe it."

He lets out a hard breath. "All right. But I have to fill Liam in on the situation first. If something happens to us, he'll want to have a general idea of where to find our bodies." He pulls his phone from his back pocket and calls our boss.

While he does that, I leave to talk to Bernard. He and I agree to meet at the private garage where he keeps his car.

"Make sure no one is following you when you come." He

shakes his head. "What am I saying? You know better than that."

He walks away, and I return to his office. Jayden is ending his call as I enter.

"Liam's asking Connor to track our movements while we're with Bernard."

"How can he do that?"

Jayden waves his phone at me. "We have tracking software built into our phones."

"By we, do you mean you and the guys?"

"Nope, you have it, too."

That's news to me. "How? Unlike you guys, I don't have a company phone. I only have a personal phone."

Jayden wiggles his eyebrows. "Wouldn't you like to know?"

"Something tells me I probably don't want to know."

"You're might be right about that."

I tell him where we're meeting Bernard, and we head in that direction.

Twenty minutes later, Bernard is driving his BMW north on the highway. I'm in the front passenger seat, and a very grumpy Jayden is sitting in the rear. Old show tunes play through the speakers, loud enough to hear them, but not too loud to prevent us from talking.

Bernard and I get to know each other better while we drive to our destination. Or more accurately, I ask him a million questions about the 1960s version of my grandmother.

"So how come you never got married, yet you own a resort for married couples?" Talk about an oxymoron.

"Do you believe in soul mates?"

"You mean that whole crap about there's only one person out there for me? And after he dies, I'll never find love again?" Not that I've had much luck yet finding love the first time.

I mean two-way love.

Not the kind of one-sided love I had with Richard—because

if I'm looking to fall in love and settle down, it would be a pisser of a deal if my soul-mate lottery ticket has already been wasted on him.

Bernard laughs. "That answers my question. Unlike you, I do believe in soul mates. Your grandmother was mine. But I was too much of a fool to realize it at the time and I put my career first. I lost the great love of my life because of it."

My grandmother didn't believe in soul mates, either. She married one of her co-stars back in the '60s. Divorced him two years later. Then married my grandfather.

He died six years ago, but in all the time they were married, she deeply loved him—and vice versa.

Their marriage was based on mutual respect, friendship, a shared passion for life...and for each other.

So while Granny might have been Bernard's soul mate, he certainly wasn't hers.

I glance at the engagement ring on my finger. The matching wedding bands Jayden and I are wearing aren't anything special. They're simply part of our cover.

The vintage engagement ring is another matter. Tiny diamonds embedded in the braided silver band beautifully highlight the large teardrop diamond.

It's elegant.

It's timeless.

It's gorgeous.

And from what Jayden told me about his grandparents, they were very much in love while they were both still alive. Who knows if they had believed in soul mates. But either way, they'd enjoyed a love that most people dream of.

Jayden laughs from the back. "And that's why you created the resort—because you lost the love of your life?"

"No, I created it because I wanted to ensure that people who have found that special someone to share their life with have a place where they can nurture the flame between them. So they don't make the same mistakes I did. What happens when you deprive a flame of oxygen?"

"It dies out," I say.

"Exactly. My resort is that oxygen. It's making sure the flame between a couple never burns out."

"But why only married couples?"

"Because I'm old-fashioned."

"You're telling me you never had sex with your soul mate or any of the other women in your life?" Jayden asks, not sounding like he believes it for a second.

Bernard chortles. "I said I'm old-fashioned. I didn't say I was a monk."

"So do as I say, not as I do?"

"Pretty much."

Bernard checks the rearview mirror for the tenth time in the past few minutes. The farther we drive from Huntington Beach, the more relaxed he seems to become.

"We're almost there," he eventually says.

"Where's that exactly?" Jayden asks.

13

JAYDEN

Several rules of self-preservation keep me alive on the job. Number one: be aware of your environment.

Are there any dangers—visible or potential?

What is your exit strategy?

Can you maintain communication with the outside world?

Where can you take refuge if shit goes to all hell?

Which is why the moment my phone indicates a lack of cell reception, I'm mentally cussing.

And my body is gearing up for fight or flight—with an emphasis on the former.

Right now, Connor will be contacting Liam to advise him that he no longer has eyes on me. And my boss won't be happy about that.

Especially since I have Isabelle with me.

Bernard doesn't answer my question about where we're going. He turns down a side road and continues until we hit a dirt path.

I recheck the reception. Still nothing.

He drives several more miles, parks, and climbs out of the vehicle. We join him.

An open stretch of beach is ahead of us, with not a single person in sight. Which means if he plans to kill us, he's found the perfect location.

"We're here." He smiles as if a million years of stress have fallen from his shoulders, and he can finally breathe.

"Where is *here* exactly?" I ask again.

"Nowhere special—other than to me." He looks at Isabelle. "I made love here for the first time to your grandmother."

She covers her ears faster than a cheetah chasing down his dinner. "We're not talking about my grandmother having sex, thanks." Her voice is louder than she probably planned. A nearby seagull squawks in protest.

He's right about the place not being anything special. The area is mostly a combination of sand and wild grass.

Chuckling, I wrap my fingers around Isabelle's wrist and pry her hand from one ear. "After the afternoon we had in the sex class, hearing that your grandmother had sex when she was in her twenties has you embarrassed?"

I don't know why, but I have a sudden craving to kiss the horrified expression from her face.

She shrugs, and I turn to Bernard. "Okay, you've had your cloak-and-dagger fun. What's going on? Why drag us to this godforsaken area? Why couldn't you have just told us at the resort?"

"Like I said before, the walls might have ears."

Isabelle and I exchange looks, having no idea what he's talking about.

So he tries again. "One of my guests last week reported that a memory stick went missing from his room. And a few hours later, it reappeared as if it had been there all the time."

"Maybe it had been," Isabelle says, "but he just didn't see it until later. You know, like when you look for something in the fridge and it's right in front of you, but you still don't see it."

Bernard shakes his head. "No, he's positive it was taken and then returned. He had some important legal documents on it that he's worried might've been copied before the device was returned. And he's not the only one who has reported possible break-ins."

"*Possible?*"

"A few guests mentioned items were moved in their rooms, but nothing went missing. Others reported a weird feeling, like they were being followed, but no one was there when they turned around."

"Housekeeping could have moved the items while cleaning the rooms."

"That's what I thought at first. But the areas being searched aren't those that housekeeping normally touches. Like inside suitcases and drawers. The guests who approached me about it are OCD types who would notice if something was slightly ajar. What we don't notice, they would.

"And then the recent theft happened—which has me believing there might be more victims who aren't aware of it."

"And nothing else was stolen?" I ask.

"Nothing else was reported missing. Which is why it doesn't make sense. Why go through people's belongings if you're not going to steal anything?"

The breeze blows a strand of hair into Isabelle's face. She tucks it behind her ear. "Maybe the person was searching for something."

"The question is, what?" I ask. "They could've been looking for something of value, and when they didn't find it, they left the room. For all we know, there was nothing of interest on the memory stick to the person who stole it, but instead of tossing it, the individual developed somewhat of a conscience and returned it."

"Which is a pretty risky thing to do, if you ask me," Isabelle says. "The victim was positive it was stolen, so his guard is naturally going to be up."

Bradshaw shifts on his feet and glances over his shoulder, as if double-checking that we're still alone. "I don't think the person was searching for valuables. All the individuals who came forward told me they had brought their laptops to the resort so they could sneak away to do some work. And none of their other valuables in the room were stolen or touched."

"So if someone has actually been breaking into the rooms, it could be they were interested in what was *on* the laptops. There's a chance the person accessed them. Maybe hunting for passwords to bank accounts or other banking information."

"If that was their goal," he says, "they didn't succeed. Or at least they didn't succeed when it came to those four individuals who came forward with their allegations. They said there were no strange activities associated with any of their accounts, and that goes for their social media and financial accounts. There's not much I can do about guests who leave personal items in their rooms, but I do want to make sure the risks to their belongings are minimal."

"The fact that someone is entering the rooms and touching guests' belongings is disconcerting enough. Do you have any idea who might be involved?" I ask.

He shakes his head. "Prior to the report of the memory stick going missing, the previous reports of the possible break-ins have been going on for a couple of months...or longer. So I don't believe it's a guest. We have several long-term guests, but no one who has stayed there for the entire duration this has been going on."

"So we're looking potentially at staff. They would have access to the rooms."

"That would be my guess, but the individuals I've hired are all good people. I can't imagine anyone being capable of doing that."

"Imagine or not, it's still our most plausible explanation."

"Have you reported any of this to the police?" Isabelle asks.

"I haven't. At first, it was because I didn't have anything substantial. I can hardly file a report without evidence. No one would take that seriously, and the hotel security found nothing suspicious. I suggested to the person who was positive his memory stick had been temporarily stolen that he should report it to the cops, but I think he was too embarrassed to do that. He chose not to."

Bradshaw's right about one thing: the police don't take you seriously when the only "evidence" you have is your gut reaction.

They need more than that.

"What are you expecting us to do?" Isabelle asks.

"I need you two to figure out what's going on and locate evidence I can go to the police with. Because my gut is warning me that whatever is going down is something big." He looks between us, expression hopeful, venturing on pleading. "Does this mean you'll take my case? Your food and accommodations will be covered for as long as you need. And I'm more than delighted to pay your agency fee."

"I'll need to confer with my boss first," I tell him.

"Why do you think the walls have ears?" Isabelle asks.

"I didn't want to take a chance that whoever is doing this has bugged my office."

"Fair enough." I don't really believe that's the case, but as long as he believes it, he's less likely to accidentally mention to the wrong person why Isabelle and I are staying at the resort.

Because despite what he might think, Isabelle's safety is my number one priority.

14

ISABELLE

Two hours later, Liam has given the go-ahead for Jayden and me to investigate the alleged theft and Bernard's suspicions. But this was with a resounding, "Keep out of trouble, or else there'll be hell to pay when you get back."

I assume that was directed more toward Jayden's injury than anything else.

And *possibly* because I don't possess the same level of training as the guys on Liam's team.

We're also to report to him regularly, to make sure we *are* "keeping out of trouble."

Apparently, *Dad* doesn't trust us.

In the meantime, Bernard gave us a list of guests who were staying at the resort while the suspicious activities were going on, the individual who reported the theft of the memory stick, names of potential victims, and staff working during any portion of that time frame.

Now we're waiting for Connor to provide us with the information he's uncovered, especially a potential link between anyone on the list.

"Is there anything else I can bring you?" the waitress asks Jayden and me.

After Bernard dropped us off at the resort, Jayden and I found a restaurant not too close to the hotel.

"No, I'm good." I pop another bite of the chicken enchilada into my mouth and do my best not to moan like Meg Ryan in the infamous *When Harry Met Sally* scene.

I fail.

"God, these are soooo amazing." Why can't mine ever taste this good?

Jayden gives me a weird look, then turns back to the waitress. "I'm good, too."

She leaves us to finish our meal.

I reach over to his plate, scooping some of his burrito filling onto my fork, and sample it. "Yours is delicious, too. But not as good as mine."

He follows suit, tasting my food. His mouth turns into a slight pout. "You're right, yours is better than mine."

"That's because I'm a pro when it comes to ordering at restaurants." I wave my fork around as I talk, punctuating each word as though conducting an orchestra.

Jayden and I return to the movie discussion we'd been having before the waitress approached the table. As much as we want to discuss Bernard and the case, this isn't the place.

"Hey, fancy meeting you two here," a familiar male voice says.

I glance up from my plate.

"I take it you needed to build up your energy levels after completing our homework," Blake says. Virginia's standing next to him, holding his hand.

"Homework? Oh. Right. The homework." The one involving mouthwash and Jayden's or my nipples.

The one that neither of us is planning to do.

"That's right. With all the exercise we did *after* the assign-ment," I say, "I was famished."

Blake and Virginia grin knowingly at us.

"I know what you mean," she says. "After all that post-assignment exercise, I can eat a large steak."

Damn, just how much sex did they have?

And more importantly, exactly what were they doing during sex to burn that many calories? It had to be something athletic.

With a trapeze.

And trampolines.

And whatever else those two are into.

I can guarantee that all the sex I've had in the past—combined—wouldn't burn enough calories to warrant these enchiladas.

But none of my past boyfriends had turned intercourse into a calorie-burning activity. The sex was usually over before I had a chance to even build a tiny bead of sweat.

"I can't wait to see what we'll be doing tomorrow in the group session." Blake pulls out the empty chair next to Jayden. He gestures for Virginia to sit on it. She's close enough to be practically sitting on Jayden's lap.

Jayden smiles at her, keeping whatever he's really thinking off his face.

I follow his lead, squelching down the tinge of jealousy squirming inside me.

Jealousy I have no right feeling—he and I are just friends.

Except she doesn't know that. She thinks I'm his wife.

So maybe I should be instigating a catfight. Pulling her off my man...even though he technically isn't mine.

She's not aware of that, either.

Blake sits next to me and leans toward me, enough to be in my personal space.

The corner of Jayden's mouth twitches down. It's not noticeable unless you're schooled in the fine art of reading his expression.

Except I have no idea why he's reacting that way.

If he were playing the role of my husband—which he is—he wouldn't control his annoyance at Blake's actions to the point of indifference.

Or maybe Jayden thinks it was an accident and doesn't want to make a scene—much like the reason I'm not pulling Virginia off him.

"So, have you thought about our little chat from earlier?" Blake asks him.

"Which chat was that?"

"The special rooms in the resort that most guests don't know about."

"Have you two participated in BDSM before?" The way Virginia says it, you'd think she was ordering a latte from Starbucks—and not discussing my sex life.

A quick glance at the nearby tables tells me that no one is paying attention to what she said. And if they are, they're too polite to reveal that her question has them riveted.

"I can't say that I have."

Virginia leans across the table as if she's about to share a state secret with me. "If you're interested, we'll be happy to show you the ropes. Both literally and figuratively."

"Show us the ropes?" I parrot back. Somehow, that sounds like a whole new level of kink than if Jayden and I use the room with just the two of us.

"Thanks for the offer," Jayden says, "but we'll pass."

"You don't know what you're missing out on, man," Blake says. "Your sex life with Isabelle will be so much richer for it."

Some unnamed emotion flares in Jayden's eyes. "Our sex life is already fucking phenomenal." He keeps his voice low so as not to share fictitious insights about our sex life with the rest of the restaurant.

Virginia glances at me for confirmation. I nod at her, grinning. On the outside, it looks like I thoroughly agree with Jayden's assessment. On the inside, I barely keep from cracking up at her enthusiasm for making sure my sex life isn't lacking.

And also at the reality—Jayden and I aren't having sex. Together.

Or in my case, at all these days.

Virginia's expression switches to happiness for us. Blake appears oddly disappointed.

"Well, if you would like to join us"—her gaze flicks appraisingly at Jayden—"let us know."

And that's when something tightens deep in my belly.

They aren't only interested in teaching us the ropes. They're swingers.

Virginia is hoping to experience Jayden's body the same way I supposedly am as his wife, and Blake is hoping to do the same with me...in the same room, at the same time.

Inwardly, I shudder at the thought.

Jayden's expression darts to Blake and darkens for a microsecond before returning to Virginia.

"Will do," Jayden casually informs her with a smile that I know is forced—only she and Blake won't realize that. It takes a close friend to recognize it.

The pair leaves us to our dinner after that. Neither Jayden nor I comment on the strange conversation once they're gone. We finish our meal, then return to our room to await Connor's call.

Shortly after we arrive, there's a knock on the bedroom door.

Jayden and I exchange glances. "Are you expecting anyone?" he asks.

I shake my head. "Not that I know of."

He walks to the door and cautiously opens it.

"Room service," the man on the other side announces.

"We didn't order any room service," Jayden tells him.

"This was sent on behalf of Gabrielle. She said you would understand."

Jayden opens the door wider and allows the man, who's wearing the standard uniform here—a red-and-white Hawaiian shirt—into the room.

He parks the cart, covered with a white tablecloth and a red satin place mat, near the bed. He removes a plate from beneath the cart and sets it on top of the place mat. "Enjoy."

He then leaves the room.

Jayden lifts the silver dome covering the plate, revealing a single slice of chocolate torte.

And a length of silk rope.

Wrinkles form on his brow. "Why would Gabrielle send us this stuff?"

"Because when she asked us what got us in the mood for sex, I said chocolate. And when I asked you if you would rather lick whipped cream off me or tie me up and have your way with me, you said tie me up."

"So what? If I had picked whipped cream, she would've sent a can of spray whipped cream?"

"Exactly." I toss the rope at him. "Enjoy! I plan to thoroughly appreciate my chocolate dessert."

"What am I supposed to do with this?" He gestures to the rope in his hand.

"Practice your boy scout knots."

I raise a forkful of torte to my lips. Jayden's gaze follows it.

I wrap my lips around the dessert and moan in the same way I did in the restaurant while eating the enchiladas. Only this time the moan is louder, unrestrained. With intent.

"Oh, God. Whoever made this is a saint." I thought the enchiladas were good.

This is heaven.

The downside? I'm now horny.

I take it back. The chocolatey goodness wasn't made by a saint. The devil himself created it.

But since I'm not about to snub it—because that would be a crime in itself—I devour another bite.

And make the sound again.

I can't help it. The dessert is just that good.

Jayden watches me the entire time—which, for some reason, is an even bigger turn-on.

Suddenly the room feels a lot hotter than it did a few minutes ago.

I lift the dessert-laden fork toward him. "You want a bite?"

I expect him to do the polite thing and decline. He doesn't.

He shortens the distance between us and wraps his lips around the fork. There's something predatorily sensual about the move, and I almost moan out loud.

Seriously, what's in that torte?

"That *is* good," Jayden says, voice huskier than it was a moment ago.

"I know! Bernard needs to give whoever made this a pay raise." I take another bite and offer some more to Jayden.

Like last time, he doesn't refuse it.

A few bites later, the dessert is all gone, and I'm in the mood for sex.

Someone shoot me now.

But since room service didn't include someone to help me with that dilemma, I scan the room to find something else to do.

Something to distract me.

Jayden's phone rings and he answered it. "Hey, Connor.... Okay....I'm putting you on speaker so that Isabelle can hear what you have to tell us." He turns up the volume and holds the phone between us.

"I ran the names you gave me through several databases," he says after Jayden gives him the okay to talk. "First, the potential victims are all politicians—including one senator and his wife—or individuals with political aspirations. They weren't the only ones who met those criteria on the guest list. So if they were targeted for that reason, there's a good chance the others were also targeted. They just didn't realize it."

"So it could be politically motivated," Jayden says. "But if that's the case, we don't know why. Nor do we have any evidence of that to pass to the authorities."

"There's more," Connor says through the speaker. "A former guest, who stayed there at the same as the first victim, has known links to the KGB."

"How do you know that?" I ask.

"I have my sources."

I can practically hear the theme music from *The Twilight Zone* playing in the background to his words.

"The FBI doesn't have an issue with the person being in the US?"

"They're monitoring his actions. So far, he hasn't been caught doing anything to raise suspicion."

"Does he have any connections to the staff working here?" Jayden asks.

"None that I can find. That doesn't mean there aren't any. It means it's not showing up on any resources available to me."

"What about the other guests?" I ask. "Any links between the individual and everyone else who was here during the same period as the suspicious activities?"

"Again, there's nothing I've been able to ascertain. But I wouldn't exclude that possibility."

"When did the last politician stay here?" Jayden asks.

"That would be last month. He wasn't on the list of guests who came forward with concerns of suspicious activity. But that doesn't mean whoever's involved didn't target his room."

"What about the person who believes his memory stick was stolen while he was a guest here?"

"Tyler Mathews is the one individual without any known interest in becoming a politician...but the legal firm he's a partner at represents a senator."

"Has the senator stayed at the resort?" I ask.

"He's not on the list that Bernard gave you. But it's feasible he stayed there before the suspicious activity."

Connor gives us the senator's name, and I tell him I'll get back to him after I talk to Bernard.

"There's something else you should know," Connor says. "Another guest checked in last night with her husband. She's running for a seat in the House of Representatives."

"So the person responsible for the break-ins could also be here."

"It's always a possibility," Connor tells us. "I'll keep working on my end to find a connection between everyone, but it will take me a while—if it's even feasible."

"Isabelle and I will see what else we can learn on this end," Jayden tells him. "But we're going to need more manpower. Someone who can interact with the staff without drawing any attention."

"I'll let Liam know. But whoever joins you will need to be hired as a resort employee, so they can uncover intel you won't be able to as a guest."

"That won't be a problem," I explain. "The resort owner will hire him if it means finding out what's going on."

"I wouldn't tell him about the potential KGB link," Connor says. "That might make him jittery and set off alarms for whoever is responsible."

"Good idea."

"All right. I'll inform you if I find anything else." Connor ends the call.

I grin at Jayden—because things are about to get more interesting.

[TOP SECRET]

ALL RIGHT, WHEN I SAID SEVERAL HOURS AGO THAT THINGS WERE going to get more interesting, I didn't mean the dilemma I'm now facing....

"Sooo...which side of the bed do you want?" I ask Jayden as he exits the bathroom, his arm still in its sling. He's wearing his black boxer briefs—and only his black boxer briefs.

Beads of water glisten on his naked chest.

Damn it. No one has the right to be that sexy.

My gaze flicks to the ceiling. It's a lovely ceiling...as ceilings go.

Okay, it's a boring ceiling, but at least the sight of it doesn't leave my lady bits humming with possibility.

I'm standing on the left side of the bed—my preferred side —in nothing more than my black satin cami set.

I clearly didn't think that one through—no more than Jayden did when it came to his sexy underwear.

But really, what difference does it make? Jayden doesn't see me as anything more than his friend. Sexy sleepwear, flannel PJs, it's all the same to him when it comes to what I'm wearing.

Jayden's gaze skims down my cami set, and his warm chocolate eyes go dark. "I'll take the right side."

"Perfect." I pull back the covers.

"What happened to the barricade?"

"I didn't think we needed it."

He's already admitted he's not a cuddler, and I'm sure I'm not going to wake up in the middle of the night with my arms around him.

Well, I'm pretty sure my arms won't be around him.

Jayden studies the bed for a moment, then me, and then the bed again. "I sleep naked."

Yeah, that wasn't what I needed to hear. Now I've got the image in my head of a naked Jayden sleeping next to me.

I grab the small red-and-aqua cushions from the bed and the armchair and arrange them in a single line down the center of the bed.

Not that they provide much of a barrier.

They're more decorative than anything.

Jayden laughs. "Are you worried that you won't be able to keep your hands off me?"

"With you in those boxer briefs, how could I resist?" I wink at him, to hide what I'm really thinking, and climb under the covers.

I turn off my bedside light. He does the same with his, and a few seconds later, climbs under the covers on the other side of the Great Wall of Pillows.

Don't think about how he's naked. Don't think about how he's naked....

Unfortunately, repeating that a million times in my head is about as useful as counting sheep. Thirty minutes later, I'm still staring at the ceiling, watching the pale strip of light from between the curtains sit motionless up there.

The air-conditioning hums from the vent in the wall near the ceiling and prevents me from figuring out if Jayden is asleep yet. I can't hear the slow, even sounds of his breath over the noise.

But this is Jayden, a former Navy SEAL. He's trained himself to sleep anywhere, anytime. I bet he's sound asleep, unfazed by our sleeping arrangement.

Lucky him.

15

JAYDEN

Don't think about the sexy woman sleeping next to you, and don't think about her long, toned legs, barely covered by her satin shorts.

Also, don't think about her perfect breasts, with her taut nipples pressed against her top, the narrow straps, and low neckline that taunted you with a view of her sweet cleavage.

And definitely don't think about what it would taste like to suck one of those tight buds in your mouth.

I flip over in bed for what has to be the fiftieth time in the past two hours, and inwardly bemoan that I can't ride away on my motorcycle from this restlessness....

16

JAYDEN

The best thing about what I do for a living is the variety. No two missions are alike.

With one exception.

They always result in a shitload of paperwork.

And I'm certain this one will be no exception.

Isabelle and I enter the room where the sex classes are held. Sex education in school was nothing like this. I might have paid more attention if it had been.

The same individuals from yesterday are already here—with two new additions.

A couple in their early forties is talking to Gabrielle: Democratic House candidate for Washington State, Caroline Bateman, and her husband, Davis.

Isabelle and I did a Google search on her last night after Connor told us that Caroline and her husband had checked into the resort. She's the last person you'd expect here, given that she's a political candidate.

Or maybe that's why they're talking to Gabrielle. They're telling her that they won't be attending the sessions on how to spice up your sex life and marriage.

Demek is watching the pair with great interest, but he's too far away from them to hear what they're saying.

Gabrielle gestures to the vacant gym mat on the floor, and they sit.

"I hope everyone had an enjoyable time last night." Her tone holds a wink-wink-nudge-nudge attitude. Isabelle and I clearly weren't the only ones who had a visit from room service.

But if everyone's expressions are any indication, the others didn't have *"Take a cold shower"* on the top of their to-do list after their unexpected visit.

Nor did they spend a good portion of their night trying to fall asleep because the sexy woman next to them was off-limits.

And while I don't doubt most of the men woke up with morning wood, they didn't have to use their hand to relieve it.

"Did everyone do their homework assignment?" Gabrielle asks.

We all nod. Lightning doesn't strike Isabelle and me.

"All right, let's warm up with an easy question. You won't be sharing the answer with the class this time. Just with your partner. Which of the following gets you most worked up? A deep kiss, when your partner grabs your butt, or when they push their body against yours?"

Like the last time, Gabrielle is standing next to us, waiting to hear our reply.

"When you kiss me deeply," Isabelle blurts as if she can't say the words fast enough.

I go for something simpler. "I'll admit the kisses are great, but so is the way you brush your body against mine."

The truth is, I didn't have to lie...much. I have no idea how great the kisses would be if we actually kissed, although I can imagine they would be good.

But I have experienced Isabelle brushing her body against mine. She wasn't trying to turn me on. It was an accident, but the outcome was the same.

Gabrielle waits for everyone to finish answering the question. "Everyone stand up."

We do as we're instructed.

"Now, I want you to kiss your partner. But I don't mean a quick kiss. I'm talking about a soul-stirring kiss. That magical kiss you used to give each other when you first started falling in love."

Isabelle swivels her head to me, panic stamped all over her face.

"Don't be shy," Gabrielle says, not noticing Isabelle's reaction. "When you were younger, you wouldn't have thought twice about letting people see how crazy you were for the other person. You wanted the world to know you were in love.

"But over time, you become too busy with the kids, with your separate interests, with your careers, to take a moment to re-ignite the special magic you once shared. The result is the beginning of the end of what you have between you. You become more like roommates than lovers."

This time when I look at Isabelle, she has steel determination on her face. She then smiles at me, and the same reaction I always get when she smiles at me like that stirs beneath the surface. Her smile isn't forced. There's an element of relief there.

"Okay, let's do this," she says, keeping her voice low so her words can't be mistaken to mean something else.

She runs the tip of her tongue along her lower lip, and damned if I don't want to do the same with my own tongue when it comes to her mouth.

"Are you sure about this?" I ask, also keeping my voice low.

"Absolutely."

She places my face between her hands. Her fingertips are soft against my day-old scruff. I lean down, shortening the distance between her lips and mine.

And...we have contact.

I'm only vaguely aware of the sounds around us. I'm too lost in the sensation of Isabelle's mouth against mine to care.

At first our lips touch and nothing more. But then she slowly parts hers, welcoming me, encouraging me to take things further.

And that's precisely what I do.

I pull her against me and worship her lips, her mouth, her tongue with my own. Tasting her. Breathing her in.

My heart beats frantically in my chest; my skin tingles with need.

I always figured Isabelle's kisses would be good. I never imagined they would be *this* good.

"That's great, everyone," Gabrielle says a minute or so later, breaking the spell Isabelle has woven over me.

We step away from each other, but my gaze is still on her face, searching for clues as to how she felt about the kiss, even though that's probably the last thing I want to know.

The kiss was part of our cover, for the job we were hired to do.

Except it felt like so much more than that.

Our cover is fake. The kiss...wasn't.

"I suggest you do that as much as you can while you're staying here," Gabrielle continues, unaware of my inner turmoil. "The more you kiss like that, the more it becomes part of your daily life. Never go a day without giving your partner that special soul-stirring kiss. Your marriage will thank you for it."

The rest of the group nods at her words of wisdom.

"I doubt that was the problem with my parents' marriage," Isabelle says under her breath. "My father couldn't keep it in his pants when it came to other women."

For a second, my heart pinches at her words, having experienced firsthand the pain of infidelity. Although in her case, because she was so young at the time, it clouded her view of marriage. She doesn't believe in happy marriages. They're a temporary farce, easily broken by the careless actions of one selfish partner.

"Our next activity should get things going. Men, I want you to sit in your chair. Demek, Anthony, you can decide which one of you will sit on it. Ladies, you're going to give your partner a lap dance."

Christ. Shoot. Me. Now.

None of the other couples look uncertain about our next exercise. Even Caroline and her husband appear excited.

Blake's and Virginia's reactions don't come as a surprise. They're probably wondering if Gabrielle would care to toss in some handcuffs and whips while she's at it.

"Well, this should be interesting." Isabelle's gaze avoids mine. She's too busy looking at everything else around us.

I almost expect her to be out the door before I can sit.

With a Christ-this-is-going-to-be-a-disaster sigh, I sit on our chair, which faces outward—as they all do—so the men can't see each other or the other wives. That way if things go hard south of the border, no one else will witness it, other than our spouses.

Upbeat dance music pipes through the speakers in the ceiling.

"Okay," Gabrielle says, "I want you to straddle your man's legs and show him your moves."

I might've had a better chance if Isabelle wasn't in her bikini. But I'll give her this...she's doing a good job when it comes to her cover. If I didn't know better, she'd have me convinced we're happily married.

Does that mean I'm going to tell Liam that I believe she has what it takes to be an operative with the team? Hell, no.

"I'm dying to know how this will help us figure out if something illegal is going on at the resort," Isabelle murmurs in my ear.

I can only shrug. "Keep your eyes open. It could be that more than one person is involved—if there is something illegal going on—and we aren't the only fake couple here."

"So basically, hope they aren't very good actors when it comes to this stuff?"

"Yeah, pretty much that."

Isabelle slowly gyrates her hips, barely touching me—and my cock comes to life. I try repeating the Navy SEAL oath in my head...backward.

That doesn't work. Mostly because her hips are making it too difficult to concentrate. At this point, I'll be lucky if I even remember the oath forward.

With her hips still moving and her gaze focused on whatever is going on behind me, Isabelle places her hands on my shoulders. "How am I doing?"

Fortunately for both of us, her sensitive parts don't come in contact with my hard length.

Shit. Spoke too soon.

Isabelle's hips stop moving, and her eyes dart from whatever held them captive down to mine. Her eyes darken, and her gaze drops to my lips...and continue farther south.

"*Oh*." Her eyes return to mine, and the tip of her perfect tongue trails along her lower lip once more.

And that's all I can take before I forget myself.

I cradle the back of her head with one hand and draw her mouth to mine. And then we're kissing like we were a few minutes ago. Damn, I hadn't realized how much I already missed that.

The music comes to an end, and Isabelle and I stop kissing.

I tell myself this is all an act for the sake of our cover. But as much as I try to convince myself of that, I'm having a hard time believing it.

The sexual tension between us has been bubbling under

the surface for a while now. For the longest time, I thought it was just me who felt this way.

But the pull Isabelle has on me is getting harder and harder to ignore.

And now we no longer can.

The kiss has brought down our unstable house of cards.

"You and I need to talk after this," I tell her.

She cringes. "How about we don't and pretend we have?"

That gets a chuckle out of me, even though it's probably not the best response.

"Well, let me tell you," Gabrielle says, preventing Isabelle and me from saying anything else. "That was hot. And your husbands felt the same way. Why don't we give them a few minutes to recover, and I'll tell you our plans for this afternoon."

Isabelle disappears from view. The soft sound of someone sitting on an exercise mat behind me reaches my ears.

"We have a cooking class this afternoon. You'll be making a delicious meal and dessert, which you'll get to enjoy afterward in our special dining room. But things won't be as simple as they sound." She doesn't go into further detail.

Instead, she explains what we can do to keep our marriages healthy, suggestions for keeping the lines of communication open between partners. Fun activities we can do together to remind ourselves why we fell in love to begin with—and so that as the years of our marriages tick past, we're still growing together and not apart.

"There is no *one* magic ingredient to a successful marriage," she says. "And anyone who tells you that marriage is easy is lying to you. It takes work. But I assume since you're all staying at the resort, you're happy to do whatever it takes to get and stay there.

"Of course, having a healthy sex life does make a difference. Research has proved it. Often when one partner feels the need to cheat outside a marriage—either physically or emotionally —it's because those needs are no longer being dealt with at home. That's not to say it's the other person's fault—because it isn't. It means the communication between the couple fell apart, and the cheater didn't know how to state his or her needs.

"For some individuals, they cheat because they're unable to become aroused with their partner. The woman doesn't experience orgasms. The man has trouble getting an erection. So they wonder if these problems will go away if they have sex with someone else. That maybe the problem isn't with them...it's with their partner. They cheat on their partner without talking to them about it first. Maybe if they had addressed the issue head on, things would have improved. But now they'll never know because they assume they can only enjoy sex with someone else.

"That's not to say every relationship that goes astray is due to a lack of communication. Some partners cheat just because they can. It's a thrill, and they don't care about the other person in their relationship. They only care about their own needs. Those are the individuals you want to get rid of like yesterday's trash."

A murmur of agreement ripples through the group as I wonder which category my ex-fiancée fell into: the one who cheated because I wasn't there for her due to my deployment overseas...or the one who cheated for the thrill of it.

I guess that's an answer I'll never know.

I twist around on my chair, wanting to see Isabelle's reaction to Gabrielle's comments.

"Husbands, are you recovered enough for the next activity?"

17

ISABELLE

Jayden joins me on the gym mat. From the quick glance I indulged in before he planted his butt there, it's clear he's recovered from my lap dance.

And I've *almost* recovered from that and our kiss.

Holy shit, the man can kiss.

"How many of you have trouble communicating with your partner what you like when it comes to sex?" Gabrielle asks.

A few people raise their hands. I treat it as a rhetorical question.

"We've been taught from the days of the dark age that while it's natural to have sex—that's how our species survives—it's not acceptable to talk about it with our partner. If there's something we enjoy or don't enjoy, many of us keep silent, hoping our partner will figure it out on their own. That they've developed the ability to read our minds."

Yep, that sounds about right.

Gabrielle smiles knowingly at the murmured words spoken to blushing partners. "Part of my goal is to help you gain the comfort level you need to casually discuss these things with your partner. Once you can do that, it will go a long way toward increasing your sexual satisfaction.

"We won't be sharing our answers with the group, but we will discuss with our partners—in this safe environment—what we enjoy, what we don't enjoy, and what we would like to try when it comes to sex."

Oh, boy. Hopefully, she won't be hovering around Jayden and me like she's been doing for a number of the exercises. Surely, one of the other couples will be just as fascinating to hang around—maybe even more so than us.

I bet Virginia and Blake's conversations will get Gabrielle hot in record time.

"First, you're going to discuss your favorite sexual positions," she says. "But what I want you to do is face each other on the mat and hold each other's hands. And when the other person talks, listen. There'll be no judging. It's all about communicating."

I swivel on my butt to face Jayden and take his hand. It feels large and calloused in mine, his fingers long and masculine. It also feels oddly natural to be holding his hand this way.

"So, what's your favorite position?" I ask in an I'm-just-shooting-the-breeze tone. This is the kind of question you might discuss with your friends—your same-gender friends. This isn't the type of question you ask a colleague.

For once, Gabrielle doesn't wait to hear our answers. She walks over to join the BDSM crew.

Which means I'm not expecting Jayden to actually reply.

So I'm surprised when he does.

"I don't have a single favorite position," he says. "I like variety like the next person."

Except the next person—the one sitting next to him—isn't familiar with variety when it comes to positions.

I'm only experienced with one position.

On my back.

As vanilla as you can get.

"But if you had to pick one, what would it be?" For some reason, I want to know this about Jayden. Don't ask me why.

I take a quick scan of the couples on the floor, trying to determine if any of them are skipping the question because they aren't here for the same reason as everyone else.

Everyone, I mean, other than Jayden and me.

So far, no one sticks out as a potential suspect.

"Well, right now, given my situation," he says, unabashed at the line of questioning, "I would have to say you riding me would be the way to go."

His words jolt me from my task and remind me that he's actually answering the question. That he's doing a better job than me of not looking like we're undercover.

That's not the only reaction his words get. Heat and wetness race to my core. I cross my legs stretched out in front of me, hoping he doesn't notice the impact his answer has on me.

"Me?" The response barely comes out, trapped in a suddenly dry mouth. I cough to clear my throat, even though that's not the problem.

"Yes, you. You are my wife, right?" One side of his mouth tilts up in that sexy grin no mere mortal woman is immune to —most certainly not me.

"That's true."

"What about you? What are your favorite positions?"

"Positions?"

"Right. I'm asking in the plural. You do realize there's more than one position for having sex, right? I know we established yesterday that you've never had sex while standing against a wall or while bent over a desk, but there are still other ways to do it."

"My sexual repertoire isn't as extensive as yours, Jayden." But now that we're talking about it, I suddenly wish it were.

Then I'd have something to compare and discuss.

"What positions have you fucked in?" The odd thing is Jayden appears genuinely interested in my answer.

"I've only done it in the missionary position. The guys I've been with and Richard weren't very creative in the sex department."

"And you didn't think to ask to try something different?" He adds under his breath, "Is anyone acting suspiciously?"

I shrug. "Maybe that's the added perk of being here. I'll now have the confidence to tell my grandmother I want sexy lingerie for my birthday, instead of the granny nightgowns she sends."

Jayden stares at me as if my hair has turned into a cornrow of withering Medusa snakes—mostly because Granny would never give me something like that. She's the kind of grand-mother who *would* send sexy lingerie to her adult grand-daughter.

And he knows it.

"How's it going here?" Gabrielle asks us, now standing behind Jayden.

Realization dawns on his face. My answer to his question isn't so bizarre anymore.

He mouths, *Nice save.*

"We're doing great," I tell her with a smile.

My gaze momentarily shifts to Caroline and her husband. She's blushing, and he's grinning.

I'm not the only one paying attention to her. Demek is also looking in her direction. He notices me watching them both and gives a little wave before returning his attention to his husband.

"Now, I want you to discuss the longest orgasm you've had with your partner," Gabrielle says.

Seriously? She couldn't have asked me something simpler —like solving an unsolvable math equation?

She doesn't say it out loud to the group. She saved the question for Jayden and me and is now waiting for us to discuss it. In front of her.

"I can't say I've ever timed my orgasms to know which was the longest?" Jayden says in a way that suggests they're usually long.

Lucky guy.

"That's my problem, too. All my orgasms with Jayden have been incredible and...um, long." A girl can fantasize, right?

"How about you share what was going on when you had the most incredible sex together? Then you can continue to build on that level of success in the long term."

Shit. Why couldn't my first mission be something more manageable? Like wrestling with a grizzly bear or interviewing Hannibal Lecter.

"We were hiking together," I blurt, mostly because I once read the hottest sex scene that took place while the couple was hiking. It wasn't a busy trail, but the thrill of possibly being discovered made them come hard.

What woman wouldn't want that?

Jayden's cocky smile is back, but Gabrielle doesn't see it. She's too busy nodding, impressed with my answer.

"Jayden, what about you?" she asks him.

"I'll have to say that I agree with my beautiful wife. That's one of my fondest orgasm memories."

I bite my lip to keep from laughing out loud.

"That's good to know," she says. "I'll let you get back to practicing being open with each other. You can also talk about your sexual fantasies, things you would like to try. Let me know if you have any special requests while you're staying at the resort. I was informed this morning that you two have extended your stay here for two more weeks. So you'll definitely want to take this opportunity to explore ways of heightening your sex life."

She beams at us. "Demek and Anthony, as well as Blake and

Virginia, have also extended their stay for another ten days. Caroline and Davis were already booked to stay that long."

The look on Jayden's face tells me he's thinking the same thing as me. They made that decision *after* Caroline checked in last night.

"All right," Gabrielle says to the group, "I've changed my mind about us not sharing with the group. I want you to tell us what you love about your partner. Isabelle, you go first."

Oh, crap.

My brain scrambles for an answer. "He makes the best hot chocolate....He motivates me to push myself harder, especially when I'm working out. He understands when I need space and knows when I need a good laugh." The more I talk, the more the words slip out without any thought. All genuine. "Just seeing him and the way he smiles at me when we're in the same room...makes me feel all warm and tingly on the inside."

My face heats up as the final words reveal themselves.

Gabrielle turns to Jayden. "What about you, Jayden? What do you love about Isabelle?"

He grins at me and my insides grow warmer and more tingly. "The way she blushes when she's embarrassed."

My face turns into a fiery inferno at that.

"I love how she gets excited at the sight of chocolate, and how she motives me to be a better person. And I love that she loves m...our dog, and Mojo loves her."

"Great job, you two." Gabrielle prompts the rest of the group to answer the question.

Jayden and I continue watching each person, waiting for them to let slip that they aren't who they pretend to be.

But to my disappointment, that doesn't happen.

So either they're top-notch actors, or no one here is associated with the reason Bernard hired us.

"It's time to wrap up our morning session," she says after the last couple has finished sharing. "You guys all did a fantastic job. Just remember, when you have rough days, when your partner gets on your nerves, remind yourself of all the things you love about them that you shared with us. And practice your communications skills with each other regularly, and before you know it, being open with your partner will be like a second skin. Be patient and remember the long-term benefits.

"We're going to meet up again at three p.m. for our cooking lesson with the resort's world-renowned chef. He's an incredible teacher, so we're fortunate to have him with us. And for your homework assignment, I want you to keep practicing communicating with your partner about your sexual preferences and needs. Remember, when your partner gives you feedback, it's not to be critical. It's to benefit you both.

"The other assignment is for you to get naked. One of you will take a warm washcloth and gently rub your partner's body, paying special attention to the erogenous zones. And I'm not talking only about the obvious ones. See if you can discover ones you didn't know about."

With that, she dismisses us.

Jayden and I push ourselves to our feet. "We should introduce ourselves to Caroline Bateman and her husband, like everyone else seems to be doing." His breath lightly teases my ear, his body almost touching mine.

She does appear to have gained the attention of a few members of our group, including Blake and Virginia. Maybe they want to find out if Caroline and her husband would like to swing with them sometime...and I don't mean at the playground.

"And after that, you and I need to talk." Jayden traces his fingers down my arm, the gesture intimate.

I shiver at his touch. "About what?"

He shifts his head, his lips trailing against my jaw. Then his teeth gently capture my lower lip between them.

My heart rate spikes, racing like a kid chasing an ice cream truck. And I swear my breath is matching it, beat for beat.

He releases my lip. "About this chemistry between us that we've been pretending doesn't exist."

Ah, that. So I wasn't the only one who had noticed it—or who was trying to pretend it wasn't there.

"All right. First, we do our job. After which, we deal with the pink-and-white elephant in the room." An idea takes shape in my head. It's a gentle nudge at first, telling me it could work. Being at this resort doesn't have to be an exercise in sexual frustration.

We join the group. Jayden's hand rests against my lower back. There's something possessive about it—although it might be more a warning for Blake that Jayden isn't one to share his toys.

Or woman.

Caroline is explaining to the group why she and her husband are here in light of the fact that she's running in the election. "There will be voters who believe the resort is the devil's work...or some nonsense like that. Sex is supposed to stay in the bedroom and not be discussed. They're the ones who are against sex education in our school systems.

"But I'm a strong advocate of a healthy marriage and doing whatever it takes to achieve that—as long as it's moral and legal."

"So you're not worried about your opposition painting you and the resort in a negative light?" Anthony asks.

"If I worried about every little detail individuals dug up about me and spun into a negative light, I wouldn't get up in the morning. Heck, I'd be disappointed if they didn't try. It just means they don't see me as a liable threat. I have more fun when I'm treated on equal ground, rather than someone who can be easily dismissed."

The group nods, impressed by her words. A few more questions are asked. She eagerly answers them before saying, "I do believe we have a homework assignment to do, which I, for one, am excited about. If you're interested in talking some more, we can get together for drinks tonight."

Everyone agrees to it.

Jayden and I introduce ourselves to Caroline and her husband, keeping to our cover. As far as Caroline's concerned, we don't want her to find out the real reason we're interested in her.

Not yet, anyway.

18

JAYDEN

Before Isabelle and I return to our hotel room following the sex class, we head to Bradshaw's office to talk to him for a moment.

Or at least try to. Given his paranoia that the walls are listening to him, who knows what he'll tell us.

"Hello," the receptionist says when we enter the area where the resort offices are located. She's about forty, has long, curly strawberry blonde hair, and is wearing a simple light-pink cardigan over a bright floral dress. "Can I help you?"

I glance over at Bradshaw's closed office door. "We would like to talk to Bernard Bradshaw. Thanks."

"Do you have an appointment with him?"

"No, but he's expecting us." All right, that isn't exactly true. We told him we'd be in contact with him while we were at the resort, if need be, but to keep our cover authentic, our interactions with him would be kept minimal.

She checks something on the computer. "What's your name?"

"Jayden and Isabelle Moorehead."

"He's still on a call. But you can take a seat"—she gestures to the two wingback chairs in the small waiting room—"and I'll let him know you're here once he's finished."

We thank her and do as she suggests. While we wait, Isabelle and I discuss our fictitious plans for the afternoon, keeping up our cover as resort guests.

After five minutes, the receptionist picks up the phone again, tells Bradshaw that we're here to see him, then ushers us into his office.

He's all smiles as we enter, making a big show as if this is the first time he has spoken to us. All for her benefit.

As soon as she leaves, he shuts the door behind her. "Is there something you need?" he asks us, keeping his voice low.

"We just need to know if Senator Wilfred Chase the Third has been a guest at the resort," Isabelle says.

"The name doesn't sound familiar. Let me check." He taps away at his computer. "It doesn't look like it. Why? Did you find something to suggest he was here?"

I shake my head. "No, nothing like that. We were just following a potential lead."

Bradshaw's eyebrows leap up his forehead like two white frogs. "Anything good?"

"Unfortunately, nothing that will tell us what's going on."

A cloud of disappointment drifts onto his face and weighs down his tone. "Is there anything else I can help you with?"

"No, that's everything for now."

"You know, during the second world war, members of the ally resistance would leave messages in designated areas, in case they needed to relay important information along the networks but without raising the enemy's suspicions. If the Germans arrested a suspected spy or a member of a resistance network, the other members wouldn't be at risk of being caught because they were never seen together. The only way the Gestapo would learn the truth was if they tortured the information out of the captured individual."

"Are you suggesting we do the same if we want to ask you more questions?" I ask, holding down the laughter that's hovering beneath the surface.

His head rapidly nods. "I do."

"Okay, what do you propose we use for the dropbox?"

Bradshaw smiles, pleased that I'm going along with his cloak-and-dagger game. "There's an old copy of *Jungle Book* in the small reading room downstairs. We can use that. But if I leave you a message, I'll tell you where to leave the next one, so no one starts to wonder why we both keep checking the same book."

I fight against the corners of my mouth's urge to tug up. "Sounds good."

Isabelle and I thank him for his time and return to our hotel room. We couldn't talk in the elevator about Bradshaw and about what happened in group session. Other hotel guests were also on it.

And to be honest, I have no idea what to say to her when it comes to the kiss. I haven't really thought things through. I only know that after the kiss that left me reeling, we have to talk.

If we were here under any other pretense, we might've gotten away with continually ignoring the simmering chemistry between us. But not here. Not now.

Once the door shuts behind us, I turn around to say something. Anything. But whatever I was going to say gets lost as soon I look at her. Her eyes have gone dark, and she has the same hungry expression that mirrors how I feel.

Before I realize what I'm doing, I push her against the wall, and my mouth is on hers. There's no teasing like there was earlier. No gentle kisses. We're both content to devour each other, the kisses hard and deep.

It's as if we're trying to prove something to each other, to ourselves.

Isabelle's arms go around my neck.

I bend slightly, grabbing the back of her thigh, and hoist her leg around my hip. The heat between her legs soaks through the fabric of my swim trunks. I press my body forward, eager for more.

My mouth leaves hers, and I plant small kisses along her jaw and down her neck. She moves her head to the side, opening herself for me to enjoy.

She tastes as good as she smells. Sweet and wholesome. A contradiction that is Isabelle.

A small moan releases from between her perfect lips, and I can't help myself. I thrust my hips forward, allowing the hard part of me to torment her soft heat.

Or maybe I've got it all wrong. Maybe the only person I'm managing to torment is myself.

"So what do you think would be hotter? Me fucking you like this or with you bent over the desk?" I hadn't meant to say the words out loud. The memory of the question from yesterday sneaked in, unconcerned at how inappropriate this all is.

Isabelle is my colleague, and everyone knows you shouldn't fuck the person you work with. Things will only get messy.

But no matter how much I attempt to remind myself this, my body says screw that.

"Oh God, yes," she pleads.

My body practically trembles at the implication. My brain isn't so easily convinced.

I release her leg and step away, working at slowing my heart rate, slowing my breath.

Shit.

Isabelle's eyes are closed, and it looks like I'm not the only one trying to regain control of their body. Her breath matches mine.

Her eyes open. Dazed confusion stares back at me. "Why did you stop?"

"Because we shouldn't be doing this. We're on a mission. And what we were about to do is dangerous."

"Dangerous? Why? Is your cock going to explode while inside me?"

A laugh erupts from my lungs. "That's exactly what's going to happen, but not in the same way you meant. I just mean we work together. Don't get me wrong. I want to fuck you. Have for a while. But you're important to me, Isabelle. You're important to each of the guys we work with. And they would kill me if I screwed things up with you because I couldn't keep my dick in my pants."

Or swim trunks, as the case might be.

Isabelle moves away from the door and walks toward the drawers. "Why would us having sex screw things up? It would only screw things up if one of us wants something the other one can't give—like a long-term relationship." She opens the drawers, still avoiding eye contact with me. "But that's not the case with either of us. Neither of us is looking for a happily ever after."

She pulls out a T-shirt and slips it over her head, hiding her mouthwatering tits and cleavage. I mentally groan at the visual loss of them.

"What are you saying? You want to have an illicit affair at work? Because you realize we can't tell anyone, right? It's against company policy."

All right, I have no idea if the last part is correct. The topic of a sexual relationship with a coworker has never come up. Why would it when five out of six of us are heterosexual males? And Isabelle is more like a sister to the guys.

It's only me who has never felt brotherly toward her, other than the part where I want to protect her from every asshole out there...and then some.

But she's also my best friend, and I don't want to see that get messed up, either.

"I'm definitely not interested in an office relationship." She pulls a pair of shorts from the drawer. "They usually don't work, and they cause more problems than they're worth. But I'm also not sure how much longer I can endure all the sex talk and the homework that we can't do. Not to mention the activities that remind me how long it's been since I last had sex, and how when we return to San Francisco, I still won't get any." She slips on her shorts and slides them up her delectable legs.

"Do you want to call off the mission?" I ask because that would solve a shitload of my problems. Problems that involve Isabelle and her crazy desire to be part of Liam's team, constantly putting herself in danger.

If she backs out of the mission, Liam will realize she's not suited to be an operative, and she'll resume her job as our kickass office manager.

And I won't have to always worry about her being hurt or killed.

She shakes her head. "How about we have sex while we're here, as part of our cover?"

Okay, not the answer I was expecting.

"But it's only while we're here," she says. "Once the mission is finished, things return to what they were before. Friends without benefits. Colleagues who aren't fucking during or after office hours."

"And you're all right with that? Because I'm not looking for a girlfriend."

"I don't want to settle down, either. I'm not interested in dealing with what my mother went through. I'm a big girl, I can take care of myself, as I keep proving again, and again, and again." A one-sided smile slides onto her face. "But sometimes a girl gets tired of taking care of herself and her needs. Sometimes she would rather a man make her come instead of her trusty fingers."

I groan. "You're killing me, Isabelle." I'm not sure I'll be able to chase that image from my head now. It's permanently rooted there.

"I mean, I get it if you're not interested. I'm not a virgin by any stretch of the imagination. But it's also clear from my answers to Gabrielle's questions that I'm far from experienced at being a sexual adventuress." Her eyes adopt a pleading innocence that puts all puppies to shame. "Show me how to be more sexually adventurous, Jayden."

Those are the last words she says before my mouth captures hers in an all-consuming kiss.

19

ISABELLE

Normally, I'd be that woman who says office romances are a bad idea.

The same thing with colleagues who fuck as a way to deal with work-related stress.

But what Jayden and I are about to do falls into neither of those realms. It's part of the job description of being undercover.

Or so I tell myself.

The truth is, those sessions with Gabrielle, when we're talking about sex, are driving me crazy. Everyone else in the group gets to return to their rooms and deal with their pent-up sexual frustration.

Jayden and I didn't have the same opportunity.

Until now.

This thing between us is only temporary. A way to deal with the post-session itch, if you will. As soon as the mission is over, we'll go back to being coworkers and friends without benefits.

And I will have proved to Liam that I can do this job just as well as his men.

Jayden and I keep kissing, my hands exploring the hard

ridges of his stomach. I've been craving to do that for a while now.

He pauses in kissing me, and my lips cry foul. "Are you sure about this?"

"Absolutely. Are you?" Because I don't want him to have any regrets afterward.

He nods, a languid smile forming on his lips. "Normally, I don't have a problem removing clothes off women, but right now I'm a little short-handed."

"I'm sure one of Gabrielle's upcoming homework assignments will be a striptease. So we'll just be jumping ahead in the lesson plan."

His eyes adopt a mischievous gleam. "I guess this means we need to catch up with the homework assignments we've missed so far."

"That's a good idea. We wouldn't want to be the slackers who never do their homework and are still expecting to ace the class."

I step back. Jayden releases his one-armed hold on me.

My hands go to the hem of my T-shirt, and with imaginary music playing in my head, I move my hips in time to it. I slowly slide the hem up my body, revealing my stomach, teasing him, turning the dance into a sensual game.

Keeping my knees together and my hips still moving, I slowly crouch partway, before returning to a stand. Jayden is practically drooling as he watches me.

I slide the hem of my T-shirt up the rest of the way, yanking it over my head. I toss it toward the love seat. It doesn't make it that far and lands on the floor a few feet from it. Next to come off are my shorts. They end up near the T-shirt.

I undo the front of my bikini top. The fabric falls away from my breasts, and I toss it somewhere near where my T-shirt landed. The music continues playing in my head.

Covering my breasts with my palms, I push them together,

enhancing my cleavage. I'd feel like an idiot if it weren't for the way Jayden is looking at me. He's like a starving wolf, staring at Little Red Riding Hood's picnic basket, eager to sample the goodies.

That alone bolsters my self-confidence.

I release my breasts and slide my hands down my sides, to the string ties keeping my bikini bottom in place. A moment later, that too is no longer covering my body.

And so concludes the dance portion...

Jayden closes the distance between us once more. I reach for his swim trunks. "Let me help you with those."

He doesn't try to stop me. I pull on the drawstring, untying it. His hard length is noticeable through the fabric, and I lick my lower lip in anticipation.

I carefully pull his swim trucks down, freeing his cock.

For a fleeting second, I wonder if maybe this isn't such a good idea. Every time I see him, I'll have this image of him in my brain.

Which will make working with him slightly more challenging.

Sure, I'm not guilt-free when it comes to my unexpected fantasies about him, but now I won't be able to banish them as easily as I could before this trip.

I mentally shrug away my concern, convinced that I've got this covered (excuse the pun), and lower his swim trucks to his ankles.

He steps out of them.

He's also wearing a short-sleeved shirt, but to remove it means removing his sling, so I leave it in place. I do, though, unbutton it. To hide his body while we're screwing would be a shame.

"It'll be easier for you if I ride you," I say. And then I have another thought. "I don't suppose you came prepared and have condoms in your suitcase?"

"I have one in my wallet."

"Only one?"

He nods. "I wasn't expecting to have sex here. But we can always find a drug store in town."

"Can't we just look for them in the gift store? I'm sure they'll have them there."

"Right. We came here but forgot to pack condoms?"

"Or maybe we greatly underestimated how many we'd need, and we ran out of them on day two. We weren't expecting Gabrielle's classes to make us so...horny."

He laughs. "You might have a point there. Okay, we'll check what they have after we're finished the cooking class."

"Maybe they'll have ones that glow in the dark." I'm kidding.

Well, not about them having glow-in-the-dark condoms.

I wouldn't be surprised if they have them—as well as many other novelty varieties.

"I'll pass, thanks." Jayden removes his wallet from his shorts, flips it open, and removes the foil package. He hands it to me.

"Bed or love seat?" I ask. I'm up for either one.

"Bed this time." He walks to it, arranges the pillows against the ornate metal headboard, and leans back against them. His thick cock stands proudly to attention, almost as if saluting me.

I might not have any experience with being sexually adventurous, but at least I do know how to put a condom on a guy. My best friend in high school and I practiced on a lot of bananas.

I'm a pro at it.

I'm also pretty good at rolling them onto a man's penis.

As I demonstrate to Jayden, his sexy moans accompanying my movements.

I straddle his thighs. Before I can position myself, so his

wide tip is against my entrance, his hand is on my hip, keeping me in place.

"Not yet." His hand cups the nape of my neck and brings my head down to his. Then he resumes kissing me.

And there's not a single complaint about that from me.

His hand slides away from my neck, down my shoulder to my breast. He brushes his thumb against the hard bud. I gasp softly against his mouth.

He plays with my breast, squeezing it, kneading it, teasing it, all while we continue kissing.

His mouth disappears from mine, and he leans forward, taking the other nipple into his mouth. He sucks on it, twirls his tongue around it. My breath comes in faster, harder.

His hand leaves my breast and trails south to between my legs. My sex is slick with need, and he spreads the wetness around my clit, pushing me rapidly to the abyss I sense waiting for me.

A finger slips inside me, followed by another. "Oh God," I moan. On reflex, I thrust my hips forward.

Jayden's mouth leaves my breast and moves to my shoulder. His tongue flicks against my skin; his teeth lightly bite me.

Closing my eyes, I groan and rest my forehead against his. My fingers brush over his shaved short black hair, needing to explore every part of him.

I open my eyes, and my gaze goes to his hand between my legs. His fingers continue alternating between burying themselves inside me and spreading the wetness around the sensitive area. Just seeing his sexy, long brown fingers between my legs, and the familiar tribal dog tattoo on his forearm proves to be too much.

An unfamiliar sensation stirs deep, and my inner muscles start to spasm around his fingers, pulling me to where I've craved to go for so long. "Oh God," I groan.

I keep watching his hand until I can't keep my eyes open

another second. "Oh God, *Jaaayden*." The last word comes out as a sustained groan, and my muscles clamp down hard. I'd be surprised if my grandmother and her friends don't hear me in San Francisco.

At least no one in the resort will think we're faking that part of our stay here.

Once I'm recovered enough, I reopen my eyes. Aftershocks continue trembling through my body—which has waited a long time to experience this monumental occasion: my first, and hopefully not my last, man-induced orgasm.

Holy shit. This is what I've been missing out on for all that time?

Wow. Who knew?

Jayden grins at me. "Good, huh?"

I roll my eyes. "As if you didn't know. And thank you, by the way."

"Sweetheart, we're just getting started."

I was hoping he would say that.

I wrap my hand around his still-hard cock and position my entrance against his tip. I lower myself onto him, filling, stretching, mentally singing hallelujahs to myself.

"*Christ*, you're tight." Jayden groans in a way that says that's not a bad thing.

It's a fucking amazing thing.

"You're welcome," I say on a grin.

I rock my hips back and forward, searching for the right rhythm to take us where we both want to go.

Where I wouldn't mind finding myself once again.

"I want you to stroke yourself." Jayden's voice is strained and huskier than the last time, his good hand helping me find the rhythm. "I want to watch you make yourself come."

"Okay," I say on a panted moan.

I move my hand to the juncture between my legs and do as

he asked. My fingers brush against my clit, and I'm back on the edge of the good old abyss in record time.

"Yes, just like that," he says.

And that's all it takes to topple me over—taking him with me.

He releases a guttural groan that is more erotic than anything I've heard in a while.

I thought I came hard last time. That was nothing compared to now. Stars flood my vision, and I'm floating *up, up, up.*

I'm vaguely aware of Jayden guiding me off him. I collapse on the bed while he goes to the bathroom. He returns a minute later with a wet washcloth as I sink back to full awareness.

He gently cleans my sensitive parts, the washcloth delightfully warm. "I know it's not exactly the homework assignment..."

Once he's finished, he tosses the cloth onto the floor and lies down next to me. I roll onto my side, facing him, and prop my head up with my bent elbow. "How's your arm doing?"

"I would be happier if I could remove the sling now."

I shift over to kiss him...just because I can.

"Can I ask you a question?" I'm in no real rush to get up. That's not to say we can stay in bed all day. We've got a job to do. But right now, I have a great appreciation for how cooked spaghetti feels straight out of the pot.

"My favorite color is black, and no," he says, "I didn't have any pets as a kid."

I snort a laugh. "Is that what your one-night stands usually ask you?"

"No, but you get the general idea. That's why I don't often stick around afterward."

"So no post-coital cuddling?"

"Definitely not. What about you?"

"I'll admit I enjoy cuddling after sex as much as the next

woman. But most one-night stands are like you—eager to race out the door before the condom hits the bottom of the trash can. And Richard wasn't into it, either. Once we were finished, he would turn the news back on or go to sleep."

That's what I got for dating a political science major who had aspirations of one day being a senator—possibly even the president. He was glued to the twenty-four-hour news station like bears to honey.

"I can't believe you gave him up. He sounds like a winner."

I chuckle. "Not a day passes when I wonder if I made a mistake. Just like not a day passes when I think I should cut out my spleen and feed it to a river of piranhas."

"Sounds like fun."

"Doesn't it? So what about you? You know why I'm not interested in repeating the mistake of believing a man is capable of being faithful to me. Why aren't you interested in settling down and having a bunch of little Jaydens running around the house, wanting pony rides from Mojo?"

We've never discussed his past dating life. Not like we have mine. He usually avoids the topic when I bring it up.

And usually, I let him get away with it.

Which is why I almost fall off the bed when he replies. "Pretty much the same reason as you. I was engaged at one point. I was in love with her and believed the feeling was mutual. I was already a Navy SEAL when we got engaged, and she understood what the job entailed: that I would be away on missions and putting my life at risk for my country. She told me she didn't care. I was fighting for the right to freedom, and she was proud of me because of that.

"I came home after one mission to discover she had been sleeping with a friend of mine from high school. Not only that, she had decided she would rather not be with a man who might die on the job tomorrow, and who was never around when she needed him. The last two points I could understand.

What pissed me off was that she couldn't wait for me to come home and tell me that to my face before she screwed around with my friend."

I cringe at how similar our stories are, minus the part about me risking my life for my job.

The only thing I was at risk of dying from back when Richard and I were dating was an infected paper cut, which I got while studying for finals.

"So you never met anyone after that who changed your mind?" I ask.

"Nope. Quite the opposite. Because of the nature of my job, I tend to tell the women I date that I'm a sales representative for a hospital software company. It's a good cover for why I'm frequently away, and then I don't have to deal with women getting upset by the dangerous nature of my job. The team can be called on short notice to go on a mission, and a lot of women don't appreciate that. Especially when it means canceling a date at the last minute, and then they don't hear from me for a few days or weeks.

"I even had girlfriend slap me in the face, positive I was cheating on her, and that's why I was away a lot. Apparently, her father was a lot like yours, so she automatically thought the worst of me. She was my last girlfriend. I decided afterward that remaining single was a better idea."

"So you're throwing the baby out with the bathwater," I say. It's not a question. It's a statement of fact.

"Yep. Just like you're doing the same. A cheating father and ex-boyfriend have you swearing off long-term relationships."

I flop onto my back. "We're quite the pair, aren't we? Maybe that's why we're friends. We get it."

"So now that we've bared our souls," he says with a deep chuckle that gets my lady bits tingling again, "we need to figure out our next steps when it comes to the mission."

"Do you usually discuss your cases while lying naked in bed with the guys?"

He laughs harder this time. "Is this your way of saying my nakedness is distracting you from doing the job?"

"Not at all. I'm assuming that once I join the team, these meetings in bed will be a thing of the past."

I roll back onto my side in time to see him visibly cringe, as if he just sat his naked ass on a porcupine. And the porcupine isn't happy about it.

A knock on the door stops me from saying anything more on the subject.

"I'll get it," I say, twisting around to climb out of bed.

"You can't do that. You're naked."

"So we're not going to answer the door and hope they go away?" I lower my feet to the floor.

But not fast enough.

Jayden is already up and walking to the door.

"Hello, you're naked, too," I call after him. He pauses, grabs his swim trunks from the floor, and quickly pulls them on, despite only being able to use one arm.

I walk to the dresser, reassured that whoever is at the door won't see me once Jayden opens it because of the room's layout.

I hear the door click open. Jayden says something I can't make out.

"What the hell?" he says rather irritably as I pull open the top drawer.

"Well, it's about fucking time."

Only the voice doesn't belong to Jayden.

It belongs to Landon.

Oh, crap.

20

JAYDEN

For a second, after Landon barges into the bedroom, Isabelle stands next to the drawer, naked, freshly fucked, and looking like a deer standing on the train tracks.

A train barreling toward her.

She blinks herself out of her stunned stupor and darts to the bed, yanks off the chunky decorative blanket, and covers her body with it.

If she were to turn around, Landon would get to see her glorious naked ass staring back at him.

Goddamn it.

"We weren't expecting you," Isabelle says, her face as red as the blanket.

"Apparently not," Landon replies, laughter in his voice.

"What are you doing here?"

"Liam sent me to help you. You need someone to gather intel on the staff. I'm that man. He spoke with Bernard this morning, and I'm already set up." Which would explain his outfit. The khaki pants and the parrot-print Hawaiian shirt are as far from his usual style as you can get. It's the outfit the maintenance employees here wear.

Bradshaw must have figured we knew Landon was here, which is why he never mentioned any of this when we met him an hour ago.

"So while you two are relaxing"—Landon gestures at the messy bed that wasn't in that state a short while ago—"I'll see what I can learn from the staff. Liam and Connor brought me up to speed with what they know so far. Would you care to bring me the rest of the way? Preferably before I have to go down to room thirty-four and fix the clogged toilet."

"It hasn't been all fun and games." All right, that's not entirely true.

What Isabelle and I were doing before he showed up was a lot of fun.

A smirk slides onto Landon's face, and I have to fight back the urge to punch it off.

"All I can say is that it's about damn time you two did something with that sexual tension between you. It's been off the charts for the past few months and driving us all insane."

"You've got it all wrong." Isabelle's face is still a shade of flustered red. "It's not what you're thinking."

Landon raises his hands. "Hey, it's none of my business what you two do. That's between you...and your latest stylish outfit." He gestures at the chunky blanket covering her.

The blanket that's doing a shitty job hiding her naked body.

He turns serious. "Liam wanted me to tell you the informant who was going to testify against Vadik Orlov is dead. His body was discovered last night. This mission"—he nods at Isabelle—"could be coming to an abrupt halt if the Feds request our help again with the situation."

Fuck. I get shot in the arm by one of Orlov's henchmen, and the Feds couldn't at least keep the informant alive?

"And then Jayden and I will return to finish this mission?" Isabelle asks.

Landon shakes his head. "It doesn't sound like it. We've got some other cases coming up that require Jayden's expertise—once he's recovered from the gunshot wound."

Isabelle does a reasonably good job of keeping her disappointment off her face, but I know her too well not to notice it.

Inside, I'm doing some impressive somersaults worthy of an Olympic gold medal at the news. Now, I just need the Feds to hurry up and request our help, so this ridiculous plan of Isabelle's to prove she should be part of Liam's team will come to an end.

And I'll no longer have to worry about her safety.

"So how about you get me up to speed on what's going on here," Landon says, "and then I can leave you two to your fun and games."

Isabelle groans—and not in the way she was doing earlier, while she was riding me.

I grab his arm and half drag him, half lead him toward the door, where he can no longer see her.

A few seconds later, the bathroom door clicks shut.

"Whatever you do, don't say anything about this to Liam and the team," I say, my voice is a near grunt. "Like Isabelle said, it's not what you think."

Okay, that isn't true. It's precisely what he thinks. But hell if I'm confirming that.

We're on a job—all three of us—and right now we need to focus on the reason we're here.

"Give her a second to get dressed, and then we can plan what to do next." I keep my voice low. It's too easy for anyone to accidentally overhear us while we're standing by the door.

"How are you holding up? I know this can't be easy." There's no innuendo or teasing in his tone this time.

Which means I have no idea what he's talking about.

Realizing that, Landon says, "I understand that you want to put her in a jar to keep her safe. But you're wrong. She's perfectly capable of looking after herself."

That gets another caveman grunt from me.

"I'm dressed now," Isabelle says from the main part of the bedroom.

I flash Landon a warning look, and we join her.

She's wearing a sundress that looks incredibly sexy on her. Although truth be told, I'm already dying to strip her out of it.

But that will have to wait until later.

We get Landon up to speed about what we know. About Caroline Bateman and her husband staying here, and about the individuals in our group sessions who also extended their stay.

The one thing we don't elaborate on is what goes on in those sessions. I merely mention that it's a marriage counseling course, and that seems to satisfy him. He nods at us.

"Because we don't know the motive for the break-ins," I say, "we don't know if Caroline is even at risk."

"We also don't know if the break-ins are still an issue, or if the person of interest has moved to another location." Isabelle is still unable to look at Landon without her face glowing like a red traffic light.

He nods. "The first thing you need to do is talk to Caroline and make her aware of the potential situation so she can take precautions. Maybe find out her link to the other politicians and political candidates who have stayed here during the past six months, as well as Tyler Mathews." The lawyer who reported the stolen memory stick. "It's possible there's a connection between everyone that we don't know about.

"And I'll see what else I can dig up about the staff and the guests without letting anyone find out the real reason any of us are here."

We make plans to meet later in town, and Landon goes off to unplug the toilet in crisis.

As soon as the door clicks shut behind him, Isabelle takes one look at me and covers her face with her hands. "I can't believe he saw me naked." She shakes her head, hands still in place.

She then uncovers her face and smacks my arm. "Why didn't you stop him or at least warn me?"

"I tried. I didn't realize he was going to barge into the room like that. There was no time to warn you."

She goes back to covering her face. "Now he's going to tell the guys, and they'll know you and I are having a fling. While on a mission together. Which is hardly professional."

I reach for her wrist and peel her hand from her face so I can at least see half of it. Her other hand returns to her side.

"Judging from his reaction," I say, "it doesn't sound like any of them will be too concerned. It seems they've been waiting for us to hook up for some time now."

"Which only makes things worse. Did you even know I've wanted to jump your bones for a while now?"

"No more than you realized the same about me when it comes to you. I thought I was doing a good job keeping it from you and everyone else. Guess I'm not as good of an actor as I'd hoped." I grunt at that because being good at pretending to be something you're not is vital in this job.

"You had me fooled." She glances toward the nightstand. "We've got some time before we're expected at the cooking class. Where do you want to start when it comes to talking to Caroline Bateman?"

"We need to get her and her husband alone so we can talk to them in private without her fans listening in. I suggest we go for a walk and see if we can locate them. If we're lucky, they're on their own."

I quickly shower, change into shorts and a T-shirt, and we head downstairs. I automatically reach for Isabelle's hand without realizing what I'm doing. The action feels more natural each time, to the point where it feels strange not holding her hand when we walk together.

Caroline isn't in the lobby, but Demek and Anthony are.

"You two look like you couldn't wait to start our homework," Anthony says.

"Are you telling me you and Demek didn't rush to your room to do the same?" Isabelle asks in what I recognize to be her flirty voice.

Demek cracks up laughing.

Anthony ignores him. "We're going out to the pool to soak up some sun and drink cocktails before the cooking class. Do you want to join us?"

Isabelle lightly squeezes my hand. "That sounds like a great idea. We'd love to join you."

They lead the way to the main pool area, and we locate an empty table with a large green umbrella blocking it from the hot sun. The place is busy with other couples, but Caroline and her husband aren't here.

"I love your accent," Isabelle tells Demek after we've ordered drinks from the waiter, who appeared shortly after we sat down. "Have you lived in the US for long?"

"For about five years. I thought by now I would have gotten rid of it, but so far it has stuck tight. There goes my chance at being a Hollywood star and playing American roles." He laughs.

His husband chuckles. "Right, because your lack of an American accent is the *real* reason you won't be a Hollywood star."

"All right. Not being a convincing actor doesn't help either." Demek winks at Isabelle, and she giggles. The only time I've heard her giggle is when she's flirting with other men.

But that's not what she's doing now. She's working her magic on him.

"What made you decide to move here?" she asks.

"Anthony. I met him when we were both traveling in Europe, and we hit it off. We kept in contact and I came to visit him."

"And like they say, the rest is history." Anthony lifts Demek's hand, showing off his husband's wedding ring.

Isabelle leans forward to look at it. "That's beautiful. Does yours look the same?" she asks Anthony.

Anthony shows her his ring, which is identical to Demek's.

This, of course, leads them to want to see our rings.

"I love your engagement ring," Anthony tells Isabelle, inspecting her teardrop diamond ring. "It's gorgeous. Is it a family heirloom?" he asks me.

"It was my grandmother's." Like with the hand-holding, seeing the ring on Isabelle's finger seems so right—like it doesn't belong anywhere else.

My heart tightens. It's not an unpleasant sensation. Just the opposite.

"What do you two do for a living?" Isabelle asks.

"We're both architects," Anthony says. "And as of last year, we created our own company that is proving to be very successful."

The four of us talk a little longer before Caroline, Davis, Blake, and Virginia join us and order drinks.

The eight of us chat until it's time for the cooking class. Unfortunately, neither Isabelle nor I have a chance to talk to Caroline on her own. But she does charm and entertain the group with stories of her political achievements and amusing blunders.

Her husband adds funny anecdotes, but he also lets her be center stage. The group asks her a lot of questions, especially Demek, who is fascinated by her, if not a little awestruck. Most she answers. Some she gracefully sidesteps.

TOP SECRET

THE EIGHT OF US ENTER A DIFFERENT CLASSROOM FROM THE ONE we were in this morning. A central counter is parked in the middle, a large tilted mirror above it. The remaining space accommodates apartment-sized kitchens, lined up against three walls.

Isabelle inhales deeply. "Please tell me we get to eat whatever they've been cooking in here. It smells sooo good."

She's right; it does smell incredible.

Gabrielle is already in the room, with a man in a chef hat who I can only assume is our teacher. "I'm excited to introduce the resort's esteemed chef, Michael Marchant." She tells the group about his training and accomplishments.

"I always enjoy teaching this class." He chuckles for what seems to be no reason. "And I hope you find it equally as enlightening. I'm going to teach you how to create *flamiche*, which is a French leek pie that is absolutely delicious."

He spends the next thirty minutes showing us step-by-step how to make the perfect pastry and the filling, detailing what to do and what not to do. We follow along with the recipe Gabrielle handed out beforehand.

"He makes it look so easy," Isabelle murmurs under her breath.

Blake leans down to whisper something in Virginia's ear. She swats his arm like he's an annoying bug.

He grins broadly at her, lust darkening his eyes.

"We'll bake it for forty minutes, until it's golden brown," Michael says once he's finished with the demonstration. "Then we let it cool for ten minutes and remove it from the pie plate. You'll want to serve it warm."

He walks to the oven and places it inside. He returns with

another pie from a different oven. "Fortunately, you don't have to wait that long before you get to sample a piece. I made one earlier for you to try." He cuts it into thin slices, and Gabrielle passes us each a plate and a fork.

Isabelle takes a bite of her slice. "Oh, God. This tastes even better than it smells...which is hard to believe. It already smelled like heaven."

I sample mine and have to agree with her there. "Don't tell Landon that. I'm sure he would rather eat this than be unplugging toilets."

She laughs. "You're right about that. I definitely think I got the better end of the deal." Her gaze lazily trails down my body, her eyes dark.

I have to agree with her there, too.

"Because this class is hands-on and not just about you sampling the food," Michael says, "you and your partner will prepare your own pie to eat. And while it's baking, I'll show you how to whip up a simple dessert that will wow your friends and guests."

"But before he does that," Gabrielle says, "I want Jayden, Anthony, Virginia, Davis"—she lists a few other partners in the group—"to come with me for a minute."

Those of us who were listed exchange curious glances and follow her into the hallway.

21

ISABELLE

After a few minutes, Jayden and the others return to the classroom.

"What was that all about?" I ask him. While he and the others were away, I claimed a kitchen space that gives us a good view of the rest of the group, and I skimmed over the recipe.

He loops his arm around my waist and leans in close. "You'll find out soon enough."

His husky voice and warm breath against the shell of my ear causes a delicious tremor to skip along my skin.

If his injured arm weren't still in a sling, I'd lean into him and absorb the feel of his strong body.

But since it is, I just kiss him.

It's that, or reveal my frustration that Jayden, Landon, and I could be yanked from this mission, so they can deal with Vadik Orlov and his fellow crime-family assholes.

Even though I'm more than happy to have that criminal element removed from the streets, I'd rather it didn't happen at the expense of my plans to prove to Liam I'm worthy of the job promotion.

The kiss I give Jayden is nothing like the kisses from before lunch, when we experienced each other in a way I never thought would ever happen.

Neither is it a sweet kiss.

It's somewhere in between.

I pull away, smiling on the inside at his smug expression, and start carefully measuring the ingredients for the pastry.

His arm snakes around my waist again.

Crap. Why do my knees go wonky every time he does that?

Stop it, I command. They don't listen.

He kisses the side of my neck.

Don't even think about it, I warn my knees. *Be strong*.

He nips my neck in a teasing move.

"Hello, trying to work here."

"I know. And you're incredibly sexy when you're working." He kisses my bare shoulder and traces his fingers down my arm, releasing a trail of goose bumps in their wake.

I reach for the curry powder.

His hand moves to my stomach, and two fingers creep below the waistband of my panties, hidden under my sundress.

Even though several layers of clothing are sandwiched between his flesh and mine, that doesn't stop the heat rushing to my core.

I will not moan. I will not moan. I will not...

His fingers inch farther south.

And I moan.

The sound isn't loud enough for the others to hear, but it is loud enough for Jayden to catch. He chuckles in my ear.

Which sets off a small round of fireworks between my legs.

I mentally attempt to extinguish them, and open the curry powder. I don't bother measuring it. I dump what I'm guessing is about a teaspoon into the mixture. If I added too much, Jayden has no one to blame but himself for distracting me.

"Are you going to help me at all?" I ask, grabbing the hand-held mixer from the counter. "Or am I the little woman who you're expecting to cook and clean for you?"

I scan the room and the other couples hard at work—since Jayden and I are supposed to be keeping an eye on Caroline. We're not here to actually learn how to create *flamiche*.

And we're certainly not here for Jayden to distract me from doing our job.

That thought is a hard kick in the gut. Is that what he's trying to do?

But that doesn't make sense. He might not want me to be a member of Liam's team, but he would never do anything to jeopardize a mission.

Caroline is busy mixing her pastry, her concentration one hundred percent focused on that...and not on her husband rubbing against her from behind.

She bites her lower lip as if that's the only thing grounding her—and preventing her from twisting round to make out with him. Even from here, I can tell she's pressing her teeth hard into her lip, fighting to keep her concentration on the task.

Several other couples, like Caroline and me, are attempting to assemble their pies. In the case of Blake and Virginia, both of them are working hard at their task, although she seems to be enjoying subtly touching him as much as possible.

Jayden kisses my other shoulder.

And just like that, the final pieces of the puzzle fit together. "You're trying to seduce me. That's why Gabrielle wanted to talk to you guys in the hallway?" I turn around to face him, eyes narrowed. "You're supposed to distract us while we're making the pies?"

He shrugs, a lazy grin on his face. "She told us couples who cook together stay together, especially when flirting is involved."

"I'll be sure to cross-stitch that and frame it in our kitchen."

"I don't know, maybe she has a point. From what I've heard,

Liam and Ava cook together whenever they can. And I've never met a happier couple than those two."

"True." And if there's one person I couldn't imagine cheating on his wife, that would be Liam.

The man would die for his wife and daughter.

I have no doubt about that.

"Your parents never cooked together, did they?" he asks me.

"I'm not sure my father even knows how to boil an egg, let alone do anything else in the kitchen. It's why his single status never lasts long."

Although if you ask me, he would be better off just hiring a housekeeper. It would cost a lot less compared to all the alimony he's had to pay over the years.

"Maybe Gabrielle is on to something. My parents are happily married, and they do cook together on the weekends."

"What about you and your ex-fiancée? Did you cook together?"

"No. But we weren't living together at the time, either."

"Do you think it would have made a difference if you had cooked together?" For once, I'm not trying to prove a point—much. I really am curious.

"I doubt it. Our relationship problems had nothing to do with whether we cooked together or not. It had to do with me being away the majority of the time, risking my life, and Suzanna being lonely and hooking up with someone who was available."

"How's everyone doing so far?" Chef Marchand asks the class. The amusement in his voice now and from earlier makes sense. He knew about the plan for our partners to seduce us.

He was aware of the challenges we would face—beyond creating the perfect pastry.

There are a few answers of "Good" and "Great," as well as a thumbs-up from one couple, who is busy making out.

As long as she doesn't smack him on the ass with the spatula or whisk—the cooking version of BDSM—all is good.

"Since I've figured out your game," I say to Jayden, "does that mean you're going to help me now?"

"Are you saying I'm not allowed to seduce you anymore?" he asks on a wry smile.

"Will that part be in your report to Liam?" I'm joking. *Mostly*.

He groans. "I have no idea how I'll explain the majority of what we've been doing here in the goddamn report."

I give him a brief peck on the lips. "Just stick to the facts, soldier. Minus most of what goes down in the class and in our bedroom." Unless Liam is interested in bringing Ava to the resort at some point, he doesn't need to know the full extent of our stay here.

I return to making the pie. This time Jayden helps me... minus the blatant seduction.

Which I quickly miss.

"Hey, Landon." Anthony's voice breaks through the chatter in the classroom, and all eyes are drawn to the man standing in the doorway.

The man Jayden and I work with.

The man who's here undercover.

Oh. Shit.

22

JAYDEN

At Anthony's acknowledgment of Landon, Isabelle stiffens next to me. I fight doing the same.

Other than when Landon allegedly came into our bedroom to do his job, we aren't supposed to know who he is. But how the hell does Anthony know him?

Unlike Isabelle, Landon acts as if being recognized is no big deal. He gives a simple nod to the man and joins him, without sparing Isabelle and me a glance.

They chat for a moment. Anthony points to Demek, who shakes Landon's hand.

The other couples return to whatever they were doing before, no longer interested in the maintenance guy and Anthony.

Isabelle and I do the same. "Any idea how Anthony knows Landon?" she asks under her breath.

I wrap my free arm around her from behind, keeping up the pretense of the Seduce Your Spouse game. "I have no idea," I say against her ear and kiss her jaw. "But we'll find out soon enough. Word of advice for next time something like that happens. Don't stiffen if you're not supposed to know someone." I kiss the side of her neck. "Actions like that—no matter how inconspicuous—will get you into trouble if the wrong people notice."

With each tender kiss, the tension visibly drains from her, and she releases a stuttering sigh.

We finish the pie shell with only a small patch job required and fill it with the ceramic beads. While she starts slicing the leeks for the filling, I carry the pie plate to the ovens at the front of the classroom.

Landon is no longer talking to Anthony. He's up front with Gabrielle and Michael. "I'll get on it right away," he tells them. "I'll just need to get my tools."

He turns to leave and spots me with the pie plate in hand. A cocky smile tugs at the corner of his mouth, too slight for anyone to notice but me.

He nods at me. Not in the same way he did a short time ago with Anthony. This is more like the polite nod of *Hi, how are you?* you give a stranger.

I return the nod and pass Chef Michael the pie plate. He slips it into the oven and tells me to come back for it in fifteen minutes.

I return to the kitchenette and help Isabelle prepare the leeks as much as I can.

We flirt, we joke around, we act like we do most of the time when we're together—all the while keeping an eye on the other couples. But something feels different this time, between us. I don't mean different because we had amazing sex before lunch.

Or even that we had amazing sex. Period.

Just different—in a good way.

A sudden urge to kiss her sidles up to me. Any other time I would ignore it. Shove it into a wooden box and throw it out to sea to swim with the fishes.

This time I take full advantage of it.

Call it extra credit.

For the class.

I remove the knife from her hand and lay it on the plastic cutting board.

Her mouth curls to one side. "Is that your way of saying you've had enough of slicing leeks for the day?"

"No, it's my way of saying I want to kiss you again." Somewhere in the back of my head, a voice reminds me that this isn't a good idea. I need to look out for my heart, protect it the same way I'm trying to protect Isabelle from herself.

My heart has already been stepped on, disregarded.

I can't let it happen again.

But I've kissed lots of women in the past, and my heart is still whole from the experience, so I ignore the voice. What the heck does it know anyway?

"You're really taking our being happily married to heart, aren't you?" she says.

"There's a reason I'm good at what I do." I wink at her, and she laughs.

"Are we talking about the job now or your lovemaking skills?"

"Both. Although it would be a lot easier to do either one if my arm wasn't fucked."

Except then *I* would be with Liam on the mission that he and Adam are currently on, and Adam would be the one here with Isabelle, pretending to be her husband.

Kissing her.

Touching her.

Listening to her answers to Gabrielle's sexual questions.

And hell if I want that to happen.

Mine, the voice in my head says. A caveman grunt accompanies it, along with the mental image of tossing her over my shoulder and carting her away.

I cup Isabelle's cheek and lower my lips to hers. I could definitely get used to kissing her like this whenever I want. Too bad that's not the way it's going to be once the mission is over.

We've already agreed that what happens in Huntington Beach stays in Huntington Beach. There will be no kissing or sex once the mission is complete.

There will be no office romance.

We'll go back to being friends...without benefits.

Knowing that at some point this will all end, I take advantage of the moment, stroking and swirling my tongue against hers. She follows suit, driving me crazy with the need to do something more. Something hotter.

Something that isn't suitable for the classroom.

TOP SECRET

CAROLINE IS AHEAD OF US AS THE GROUP WALKS AWAY FROM THE classroom. She's busy talking to Demek and her other ardent admirers. Her husband, Davis, walks behind the group, taking it all in stride.

"Can we talk to you for a moment?" I ask him. "In private."

Welcome to Plan B. Since it's next to impossible to talk to Caroline without everyone else listening in, Isabelle and I figured we'd have an easier time approaching Davis about our concerns when it comes to the mysterious break-ins.

"What about?" This is a man who is used to being the backup plan when people want to talk to his wife. The leery expression on his face is the dead giveaway.

"The owner of the resort asked the firm we work for to do extra security work after several guest rooms were allegedly broken in to. We have reason to believe your wife could be the next target. We need to talk to the two of you about what to keep an eye open for, and we need your help so we can identify the culprit."

"Why aren't the police talking to us about this?"

"Right now there's not enough evidence for the authorities to look into it. That's why Bernard hired the company Isabelle and I work for."

"You can confirm this with Bernard if you'd like," she says. "But we do ask that you and your wife be discreet. We don't want to alert the individual that their activities are under investigation."

"But if it means my wife's safety—"

"Right now we're under the belief that this goes deeper than your wife. It could have serious political implications and implications for national security." All right, we don't have actual proof of that, but if the KGB is involved, then it's likely true.

"Is this because my wife is running for a seat in the House?"

"We don't have that answer yet. It could be she's not a target at all. We need to figure out if she is and the connection between her and the previous victims."

"What did they steal? That way I'll know if she's at risk."

"Other than a memory stick, nothing has been reported missing. And we're not even one hundred percent certain it was stolen. It went missing but then turned up again. It could be the device was in the bedroom the entire time. So other than that, we have no idea what the unknown suspect is hoping to find. But whatever it is, they believe it's in the targets' room."

"What do you need us to do?" he asks.

"Be vigilant. Don't leave anything in your room with valuable information on it. With your permission, we'd like to set up a camera in your room so if anyone breaks in, we'll have a recording of it to hand over to the authorities."

"You want us to sleep with a camera watching us?"

What he doesn't say but I can hear in his tone is, "You want to videotape my wife and me having sex?"

Thanks, but no thanks.

"You would turn it off when you enter the room and back on before you leave. Make sure the door is locked from the inside when you're in the room. The unknown suspect has only entered the rooms when no one is in them."

"I'll need to talk to my wife first, but I don't believe it will be a problem for her. National security is as important to her as it is for the next person."

Isabelle passes him our business card. It doesn't give away much information about the nature of our company. It also doesn't have either of our names listed. For security reasons.

The last thing you want is for the wrong people to get ahold of the card and realize it doesn't jive with your cover.

That never goes well.

Davis leaves to catch up with his wife.

Since we have time before we're due to meet up with Landon, we head outside to check who's by the pool. Caroline and her husband aren't there, but Anthony and Demek are, along with Blake and Virginia.

Mildred and Keith, a couple in their sixties, who are also in our sex group, are sitting with them.

Demek waves us over.

"I was telling everyone how I know Landon," Anthony says to Isabelle and me after we sit down.

"Landon?" Isabelle asks, doing a great job of looking clueless. "Who or what is that?"

"The man who came into the classroom while we were making the leek pie."

"You mean that tall, delicious drink of a man?" Virginia asks. Without waiting for Anthony to answer, she says to her husband, "We should see if he's seeing anyone. They might be interested in double-dating with us."

I almost snort a laugh because I can guarantee Landon is neither dating anyone nor is he into swinging.

At least not in the way they're thinking.

"So how do you know him?" Isabelle casually asks.

"The company I used to work for hired him and the security firm he works for to do surveillance on an employee they believed might be stealing company secrets."

Fuck.

"Did he catch the thief?" Blake asks at the same moment Demek says in his sexy Russian accent, "Why do you think he's pretending to be a maintenance worker at the resort?"

"Maybe he's not pretending." Isabelle's casual tone matches her cool-as-a-sliced-cumber expression. "Maybe he really is a maintenance worker now."

"I don't know." Virginia smiles as though she's having impure thoughts about him. Thoughts that would cause even a sailor to blush. "I like the idea better that he's a spy."

She traces her fingers up and down Blake's arm. "Don't you think it would be fun if we role-played with him? He could be an international spy and you're the bad guy. And you both want me."

Isabelle's nonchalant expression switches to a wince.

I have to agree with her there. When it comes to our colleague, that's an image neither of us wants.

"So why do you think he's here?" Demek asks his husband.

Anthony shrugs. "He said he left the company he worked for because the job wasn't as interesting as you would think."

"And you don't believe him?" Demek asks. "Do you think he's here to spy on the guests?"

My stomach clenches to the size of a shriveled pea.

Double fuck.

23

ISABELLE

Oh, crap!

That's the first thought that enters my mind after Demek asks Anthony if he thinks Landon is a spy.

Okay, not so much a spy—like CIA—than a guy snooping around.

"You guys have watched way too many James Bond movies," I say with what I hope is a convincing laugh.

"Ooh, now we're talking," Virginia says. "Daniel Craig is definitely *the* hottest 007." She looks at me for confirmation.

"I personally think Sean Connery is the sexiest Bond," Mildred says.

"You would, yea young lass." Her husband's fake Scottish accent is on the sorrowful side of things.

She giggles and takes his hand. He beams at her.

And my insides melt into a sticky, marshmallowy goo. Their interaction is too adorable for words—like cute fluffy puppies being playful in a video. You can't help but keep watching.

And want one.

"What's your secret to such a long and happy marriage?" I ask Mildred and Keith because one, I really am curious to hear the answer and two, to distract everyone's attention from the conversation about Landon.

He can't do his job if everyone is spying on him, waiting to destroy his cover.

"They're not so much secrets as things people easily forget once the honeymoon period ends. Communication is key. If you don't calmly talk through your problems and listen to what the other person says, how are you supposed to solve the issues before it's too late?

"But you also must spend more time together as a couple than most couples do. It's easy to become busy with our careers, our kids, our individual hobbies, and before you know it, your partner is no longer an important part of your life. Not like when you were dating and pretty much inseparable. Back then, you shared the same interests and opinions on important topics.

"We all grow as individuals as we get older. We're not the same person we were when we first dated. That's the beauty of it. The more we experience life, the more we grow. But when you're both growing and no longer spending time together, it's easy to grow apart. Eventually, you get to the point where you no longer have anything in common."

Keith nods. "Everything Mildred said is true. We were one of those couples. We were no longer doing things together like we were when I was courting her. If we had continued down the path we were heading, we might not have lasted this long. But we realized our mistake and rectified it before it was too late."

"And in the end, we discovered that we enjoyed creating whimsical ceramics together."

"Which we turned into a fun small business."

Mildred removes a small photo album from her oversized beach bag and passes it to Jayden and me.

We open it and leaf through the pictures of handmade plant pots that resemble colorful little trolls.

"Oh, those are adorable." I pass the album to Virginia, who has the same reaction.

"We've been making them for the past ten years." Mildred puffs out her chest and practically glows like a nightlight. "The tricky part was making sure what we loved doing together didn't overshadow why we began making the plant pots to begin with. We could've easily let the business side swallow us up. And then we would've been back where we started—except now as business partners instead of lovers."

"We made a decision early on to keep things small and manageable," Keith explains. "We even have a picture on the studio wall that says '*Couples who play together stay together.*' That's our motto for a happy marriage."

"What about you two?" Mildred asks. "Do you and Jayden have something you love doing together? And just to clarify things, sex and watching TV together doesn't count. Sex and intimacy are definitely important for a happy marriage, but they are only part of the equation, especially when you're older."

"We love to do jigsaw puzzles together," Jayden says.

They all look at me for confirmation.

I nod. "It's true. It's a great time to talk and share about our day. And we love hiking and cycling together." All this is true.

Actually, when I think about it, there are a lot of things we do together—other than the one that I probably shouldn't have kept from him for the past year.

If I had been honest with him about my practicing at the shooting range and Paradise, the paintball training center, maybe Jayden would have more faith in my abilities.

Maybe then he wouldn't worry about my safety as much. He would trust that I can take care of myself.

Unsurprisingly, Blake and Virginia list BDSM as the thing they enjoy doing together.

"Isn't there anything else you two enjoying doing as a couple?" Mildred asks.

They exchange glances. "Why isn't that enough?" Blake asks.

"Because there comes a time in a man's life when things don't work as well as they used to," Keith says, a knowing, enjoy-it-while-you-still-can smile on his face.

The image of Blake and Virginia as seventy-year-olds still doing BDSM pops into my head, and I choke down a laugh.

Jayden's phone rings. He checks the screen and pushes himself out of his chair. "I'll be back in a few minutes," he tells me. "I need to answer this."

Mercifully, the conversation doesn't return to the previous one about Landon being a spy.

Instead, Mildred and Keith share some hilarious stories about their marriage. Like the one when Keith was fifty-eight years old and he scaled the tree outside their bedroom window as if he were a teenager sneaking into her room at night.

"Luckily for me, the fire department also had a sense of humor," he says as we wipe the tears from our eyes from laughing so hard. "None of the crew laughed when they rescued me, but I could tell they were fighting it."

Jayden returns to his seat. "Sorry about that," he says to the group. "Work emergency."

"Didn't you tell your job that you're away on vacation?" Keith's tone mimics the one teachers adopt when a student disappoints them.

"I did, and I promise it won't happen again." He reaches for my hand and gives it a meaningful squeeze.

Too bad it wasn't in the spy manual as to what it means.

"Our plans have changed," he tells me. "Looks like we're free for dinner sooner rather than later."

"There's a great little restaurant not far from the resort that we've been dying to try," Virginia says. "Does anyone want to join Blake and me? Especially you two." Her gaze shifts to Mildred and Keith. "I would love to hear more about your marriage and all the tricks you've learned over the years to ensure it's a long and happy one."

"That sounds like a wonderful idea," Mildred says. "I'll ask Caroline and Davis if they'd like to join us."

We agree to meet in the front lobby in twenty minutes and retire to our rooms to get ready.

As soon as the bedroom door clicks shut, I ask, "What happened to Landon? Are we still meeting up with him?"

"I already have."

"What do you mean you already have?"

"The call I took while we were chatting with the others at the pool was Davis Bateman. He and Caroline wanted to discuss the suspected break-ins. I called Landon to join us, and he's currently installing the cameras and security devices in their room."

It takes a full thirty seconds for the meaning behind his words to hit. "And you didn't bring me with you because...?"

Well, doesn't that just fuck rotten tomatoes? He still doesn't believe I'm capable of doing the job.

Which is rich given his arm is in a sling because he was shot while on a mission.

"Because we needed you to see what else you could learn about the group," Jayden says. "None of them were staying here at the time of the reported incidences, but that doesn't clear them from being linked to the potential crimes. Some of them are highly interested in Caroline, and we don't know yet if that's because they're genuinely interested in what she has to say, or if there is some other ulterior motive."

"You mean like Demek?" I frown. "You don't think he could possibly be linked to the KGB, do you?"

"There's always that possibility, but I doubt it. He hasn't hidden the fact that he's Russian born. KGB agents don't typically broadcast that they're from the motherland. But that doesn't mean we can totally disregard him. No one is above suspicion until we can rule, without a doubt, they aren't involved."

I slip my arms around Jayden's neck—and ignore the twinge in my heart at how natural this feels. "Okay, you're forgiven." I lightly press my lips to his.

The kiss was only supposed to be a quick one. But our mouths have different plans. He gently pries my lips apart—which don't need much coaxing if you ask me. My tongue is the welcoming committee, delighted to be reacquainted with his.

And just like when I wrapped my arms around his neck, kissing him also feels natural. This time I don't ignore the twinge in my heart. Instead, I point out to it that he and I would be a mistake.

Do I believe Jayden is capable of cheating on a woman whose heart he owns? No—not after what he went through with his ex-fiancée. He understands what it feels like to be cheated on.

He would end the relationship with the woman *before* taking up with another.

At the mere thought of having a relationship with him, I mentally shake my head. There's no doubt about it; we don't have a future together once this mission is over—beyond our friendship and being colleagues.

For starters, long-term relationships aren't his thing, especially after what happened with his ex-fiancée. And then there's the issue of him not being fully supportive of my career goals.

As long as he doesn't believe I belong on the team, we don't have a chance for anything else to happen between us.

If I ever give my heart to another man again, it'll be because he trusts that I know what I'm doing. He trusts my choices and decisions—or at least respects them.

He trusts me to be the person I need to be.

24

ISABELLE

The next three days go by in a blur.

But Jayden, Landon, and I are no closer to figuring out why someone targeted the individuals who came forward to Bernard—or if the unknown suspect is still a problem for the resort.

For all we know, the identified victims were the only targets who visited the resort that the individual was interested in.

We also have no idea if he stalked them or made contact with them after they returned home. It's even possible that he moved on to a new location to find fresh victims.

Jayden also spoke with Tyler Mathews, but he still couldn't shed any light on the situation. He had no idea if any of his files on the memory stick were copied, and if they were, for what purpose.

"There're just too many unknowns here," Jayden says as the three of us walk along the path, next to the lake in Huntington Beach Central Park. A dozen or so ducks peck at the dirt forming the bank, searching for food. Ignoring us.

We decided to meet here because the location is far enough away from the resort to avoid bumping into guests from there.

We don't want to raise questions as to why two guests are hanging out with a resort employee.

The only people we've seen so far are the occasional dog owners.

A man walks past with a German shepherd, and I instinctively reach for Jayden's hand, knowing he's missing Mojo. I certainly am.

As if sensing my reason for holding his hand, Jayden gives it a light squeeze in gratitude but doesn't release it. If Landon thinks the hand-holding is strange—because Jayden and I don't have to keep up the pretense of being married while we're here —he doesn't show it.

"We need to interview the known victims," I say. "All we've got to go on is what Bernard and Tyler told us. Which isn't a whole lot."

"I, for one, would like to check out Bernard's computer and see if there's something we're missing," Landon says.

Jayden stops walking. "You think he might be hiding something?"

My best friend's leeriness toward Bernard hasn't lessened any since we accepted the mission. Although I suspect it has more to do with Jayden not being thrilled that I'm here instead of behind my desk back in San Francisco, than for any other reason.

If it weren't for Bernard, that's exactly where I would be.

I wouldn't be here, trying to prove to Liam that he should promote me as an operative. Proving that I'll be a valuable asset to the position.

"I don't know," Landon replies. "I just have a feeling he might be covering up something."

"Like what?" I ask.

"That's the problem. I have no idea. But while I was casually asking an employee a question, he suddenly got antsy for no reason. When I turned to see what the problem was, I spotted Bernard walking away."

"You think Bernard was worried the employee would say something he doesn't want us to know?"

"That's exactly what I believe."

"But why ask for my help if he's hiding something?" Why pull Granny into this…whatever this is? "And why hire us if he doesn't want us to discover anything?"

This all makes as much sense as dipping curly fries in vanilla ice cream.

"That's what I'd like to know," Jayden says, a sudden tension rolling off him in waves.

His hold on my hand tightens. Not enough to crush bones, but enough for me to notice.

"I'll attempt to access his computer tonight and see what I can find," Landon says. "And then one of us should fly out to interview the alleged victims. Maybe they can shed more light on what's been going on. And by one of us, I mean me. You two are busy with whatever you're doing in those mysterious group sessions you've been attending." The corner of his mouth tugs up to one side.

"They're classes to ensure the participants have a long and happy marriage," I say, my tone slightly defensive, surprisingly.

Even though the focus of the sessions is still on having a healthy sex life, there's been a slight shift in them during the past two days. Yesterday, Gabrielle talked about respecting your partner for who they are, not trying to change them.

To which one wife had asked if that meant she should give up trying to get her husband to put down the toilet seat.

"All right," Gabrielle said, grinning. "I give you full permission to keep working on that." Her comment resulted in snickers from the rest of the women.

"Glad to see you find the classes so enlightening." Landon winks at me, and Jayden chuckles. "But either way, unless you're both planning to bail so you can talk to the victims, it'll make more sense if I'm the one interviewing them. People will wonder what's going on if one of you stays at the resort while the other one leaves. Could cause quite the scandal."

A duck waddles up to us and quacks.

Jayden laughs even harder, but I have no idea if he's laughing at what Landon said or at the bird. "I'm sure Bradshaw wouldn't appreciate that. It might hurt the resort's reputation more than if news of the alleged break-ins went public."

He's got a point there.

I move to the side as a jogger approaches and wait until she has passed before risking saying anything more. "It would help if we knew what the victims have in common, beyond their political connection. If Caroline doesn't share that commonality between them, that might be why no one has attempted to break into hers and Davis's room."

"The only way we'll know for sure is by interviewing each of them." Landon's body jerks as if he stepped on a thumbtack. Scowling, he looks at the duck pecking at his leg but continues talking as though it's not there. "You two can start with Caroline." He steps to the side, covering a wide distance thanks to his long legs. The duck waddles after him. "Maybe she can give you some insights. I'll make arrangements to fly out tomorrow morning to meet with Wiseberger in Colorado."

The duck pecks at his leg again. Landon glares at it. "Do that again, buddy, and we'll be eating duck liver *pâté* for lunch."

Jayden and I both crack up laughing.

The bird gives him one more loud quack and waddles back to its companions.

"Are you telling Bernard about the plan, so he can let the senator know you're hoping to talk to him about the case?" I ask. "Or maybe it would be better if we keep the plan to ourselves, just in case your gut feeling about him is correct. But if there's more to this case than he's told us, then the question is, what exactly is he after?"

"That's what I'd like to know, too," Jayden says. "Why drag us down here if there weren't any break-ins, other than the missing memory stick—which might not have actually been stolen. On the other hand, if what he told us is true, we might not have much time before all shit goes to hell."

Landon resumes walking again. "If only we knew what kind of hell we're dealing with."

TOP SECRET

AT THE RESORT, JAYDEN AND I LOCATE CAROLINE AND HER husband sunbathing by the pool. For once, her fan club is noticeably absent, but who knows how long that'll last?

She smiles at us as we approach their loungers. "You didn't join everyone else on their excursions today?"

I laugh. "Me and heights aren't a good combination. So that would be a no when it comes to paragliding with Demek and Anthony. And I have no idea what Blake and Virginia are up to. The last I heard, they were heading into town to do some shopping."

"If you two don't have plans before group session this afternoon," Jayden says, "would you be interested in having lunch with us? We'd like to ask you some questions."

"I'm assuming this has to do with why you're at the resort?" Davis's tone is friendly and optimistic, but not enough to distract from the underlying concern in his eyes.

I nod. "That's right."

Both Caroline and Davis agree to lunch, and we decide to go to a cafe near where we're staying. At our request, the hostess seats us on the patio, where it's not as busy due to the hot summer temperature. Not even the large orange umbrella and ocean breeze are enough to cool it down.

"So, you two aren't really married?" Caroline asks while we wait for the waitress to take our order.

I shake my head. "No, but we're best friends," I say, feeling the need to explain.

"Well, that's too bad." She chuckles, shaking her head. "I don't mean it's too bad you're best friends. It's just that you really had me fooled. I thought what you two have between you is real. You really are good actors."

"Thanks. I guess it's in my genes. My grandmother was an actress, and I did some theater in high school." It also doesn't hurt that what I feel for Jayden is real, too. Not all of it is acting.

But I'm hardly admitting that to any of them—including Jayden.

"Rumor has it," he says, "that we're up for an Academy Award for our brilliant acting."

He grins at me, but there's something slightly off about it. The smile isn't the same one that causes my heart rate to speed up whenever I've seen it lately.

But my heart does hiccup at the sight of *this* smile, unable to ignore the impact he has on me.

We place our orders with the waitress, and then the four of us talk about all things related to Caroline's campaign promises, and what she hopes to accomplish if elected. Fortunately, if anyone on the patio overhears the conversation, Jayden and I sound like two reporters asking her questions.

No one would guess the real intent of the conversion.

"I would like to see more being done to protect our kids when it comes to drugs," she explains as we finish our meal. "I'd like to see stiffer penalties for repeat offenders when it comes to drug trafficking. So many kids miss out on reaching their potential because they get pulled into that unhealthy life-style—both as users and sellers. Too many kids die because of drugs, either directly or indirectly." The more she speaks, the more conviction there is behind her words.

But she doesn't have to do much to convince me of that. Jayden was shot when he and the team were dealing with Vadik Orlov, the mafia family suspected of, among many things, drug trafficking.

Drugs might not have almost killed him, but the bullet from one mobster's gun came close to it. Drugs could have indirectly caused his death.

"And of course," she adds, "I want to see more done about terrorism, to ensure our country and its citizens are safe, and to ensure healthcare is available to all and not only to those individuals who can afford it."

By the time we return to the resort, Jayden and I have a lot more to go on than before when it comes to Caroline. But at the same time, it still feels like we're looking for a needle in the ocean.

Until Landon has a chance to talk to the other victims, we don't know if what we learned about Caroline is the missing element that links them to each other, or if we need to spearfish an entirely different needle.

25

JAYDEN

"**B**efore you go," Gabrielle says at the end of class, "I've got your homework assignments for tonight. Each of you will get a different activity card. You aren't to share what's on your card with your partner. It'll be a surprise." She grins at us—the way a cat does before pouncing on a chubby mouse.

And that sets off the *Mayday, Mayday, Mayday* sirens in my head.

She hands out the envelopes, each with our names on them.

I remove my card and read it:

You and your spouse will go out for dinner in a public setting. While there, you will please her with your hand under the table, fondling her to an orgasm. No one is to know what you're doing. Only you and your wife will know.

My dick twitches, turned-on by the unexplored possibilities. The voice in the back of my head groans...and pretends it's not turned-on by the assignment.

I return the card to the envelope so Isabelle can't read it.

Now the question is, will I actually go through with the

homework? Before Isabelle and I traveled the friends-with-benefits route, the answer would've been no.

But since the class is currently part of the job, I can't see why we shouldn't do the assignment—as long as it doesn't interfere with the mission.

A quick glance at Isabelle, as she reads her card, has me curious what's on it. She's blushing something sweet and fierce.

Not as much as you will be soon, I mentally tell her.

Gabrielle dismisses us.

Most of the group has already made plans to meet up for dinner with us in two hours. So we head back to our room to contact Connor, and hopefully have a chance to talk to Landon. We need to fill him in on the conversation Isabelle and I had with Caroline, for when he talks to Senator Wiseberger.

"So what was on your homework card?" Isabelle's voice has a teasing lilt to it, her face a shy smile.

We walk toward the elevators. The group has already dispersed like dandelion fluff in the wind—eager to get to work on their assignments.

"I can't tell you. That's like telling someone what you wish for when you blow out your birthday candles. The wish becomes null and void." I smirk at her. She rolls her eyes.

"This isn't quite the same thing. I doubt if you tell me your homework, it will make it null and void."

I don't know about that.

Especially in the case of what's on *my* card.

She tries a different tactic. "Don't you want to hear what my card said?"

I grin at her. "Nope. I like surprises."

My phone pings and I read the text. "Landon is waiting in our room," I tell her, keeping my voice low. I don't need to broadcast that one of the maintenance guys is meeting us there.

Never mind the real reason he's waiting for us, thanks to the BDSM rooms here, some guests might put two-and-two together and figure we've got a kinky threesome planned with him.

Thanks, but no thanks.

I rest my hand on Isabelle's lower back, a move that's also becoming second nature, along with hand-holding. It feels nice, but not in the caveman "This is my woman, keep your eyes and hands to yourself" kind of way.

Every time I touch her, I feel more alive.

Which is odd—it's not like I was dead inside before the mission. It's more like the kind of nice you experience when you discover a six-pack of beer in the fridge on a hot day. The difference is, my fingers don't usually tingle with need when I reach for a beer the way they do when I touch Isabelle.

We enter our room to find Landon at home on the love seat, studying his phone.

His attention shifts to us. "Sandra's confirmed my flight reservation to Denver for tomorrow at ten a.m. Depending on what I learn from Wiseberger, I'll decide what I do after that."

Isabelle and I sit on the padded bench at the end of our bed.

"What did you find out from Caroline?" he asks, and we spend the next few minutes catching him up on everything she told us.

"They're both democrats," he says, "as are all the alleged victims except for one. But we don't know if he's the only republican who was targeted."

"It would be more helpful if they at least came from the same political party," Isabelle says. "It would give us more to go on."

I shift on the bench, itching to remove the sling. "True. Maybe the link has something to do with a policy they all agree with. A policy the unknown suspect doesn't want to succeed. Not every democrat agrees with the rest of their party on some issues. Same deal with the republicans."

"You think that might be the missing link?" she asks. "That some members of both parties agree on a specific issue, and it's why the individual targeted them? But if that's the case, isn't it a little strange they all ended up at this resort at one time or another? Why this resort? Is word of mouth about the place that big in Congress? It's on their list of resorts to visit?"

"Yes, the coincidence does seem a little odd, especially if the link is due to an issue they all agree on," Landon says. "Is the unknown suspect only targeting the individuals who stay here? Or is the person also traveling to other targets' homes, and this whole thing is bigger than we realize?"

I nod. "There could be more than one person involved, too. There could be a network."

"I'll have a better idea of what's going on after I talk to Wiseberger tomorrow."

"Let's hope he's willing to talk to you," Isabelle says.

"If he isn't, then I'll call in a favor with one of my government contacts. But I'd rather wait to see if he'll talk to me first before we involve the government just yet. We still don't know what we're dealing with and what kind of connections the unknown individual has."

"Do you suspect any of the staff is involved?" she asks him.

"It's still a possibility. But so far I haven't found anything that sets off warning bells. If it's an inside job, I have no idea who might be involved."

"Are you still planning to hack into Bernard's computer tonight?"

He nods. "He might not be aware there's a link between one of his employees and the alleged crimes. If I'm lucky, I'll find the connection somewhere on his hard drive."

"Or discover that he *is* the connection between the alleged break-ins and the victims," I say, "and he hired us to throw the scent off him. What better way to move suspicion from him than by being the one who reaches out for help investigating the crimes?"

"Do you think he started to feel the heat from somewhere, and that's why he involved my grandmother in convincing us to help him?"

"That's always a possibility. Maybe I'll be able to answer that once I'm on his computer."

"*If* you get into his computer."

Landon shrugs in the easy manner of his. "Don't worry, I'll find a way."

"We still can't exclude any of the guests—both past and present," I remind them. "Isabelle and I have only gotten to know a few individuals." We've had a chance to spend time with the people in the sex class, but we're still a long way from learning their dark secrets.

And they're just a small fraction of the guests staying here.

During the five days we've been at the resort, we've had the opportunity to talk to more guests and observe others, but we're no closer to eliminating any of them when it comes to the alleged break-ins.

"Is there anyone who seems suspicious?" Landon asks.

Isabelle and I exchange glances and shake our heads. "If any of them are guilty," I say, "they're doing a damn good job of looking innocent."

"Blake and Virginia were ten minutes late for the group session this afternoon," Isabelle says. "But judging from their slightly disheveled appearance when they finally showed up, I'd have to say the only thing they're guilty of was fucking each other senseless somewhere and losing track of time."

I'm not so sure about that.

Not the part about fucking each other senseless—although I have no doubt there was some of that involved at one point today. Now that Isabelle has mentioned it, something else about their appearance seemed out of character for them. Like they had been chasing after something...or been chased.

The difference in them was subtle, as if they had quickly straightened themselves moments before entering the class, breath still a little fast, eyes slightly wild.

But at the time, I just chalked it up to them being late and not wanting to miss anything.

Which could also be true.

26

ISABELLE

The restaurant where Jayden and I are meeting members of our group is relatively busy when we arrive. The hostess leads us to a large table, and we take our seats. Virginia and Blake are already here, as are Anthony and Demek, and several other couples. They're all chatting animatedly.

They greet us and ask Jayden and me what we thought of class today.

"I didn't realize there were so many different ways to tie a person's hands to the bed frame," I say.

Everyone nods in agreement.

"My favorite has to be the one with the giant red bow like a Christmas present," Mildred says, which makes me and the other women giggle. Mildred is in her sixties. But given her and her husband's escapades—including the tree incident—none of us are too surprised by her comment.

A few minutes later, Gabrielle approaches the table, along with Caroline and Davis.

Jayden groans, the sound too quiet to be heard by anyone but me.

"What's wrong?" I ask.

He flashes me the sexy one-sided smile of his that gets me wet in record time. "Nothing."

"Oh, okay." I open my menu and study the food and drink choices. My stomach rumbles softly at all the delicious-sounding options.

Jayden ignores the menu on his plate and leans over to read mine. His hand shifts under the table and lands on my knee.

I startle.

"What are you in the mood for tonight?" His voice comes out deep and husky, and my body instantly sits up and takes notice.

"I'm not sure yet. Everything looks good. What about you?"

"I might go for a steak." His fingers slip under the hem of my dress, his calloused skin rough against the inside of my knee.

My body jolts as if lightning hit me, and I gasp softly.

His hand remains in place.

I glance around the table, but no one seems to have noticed my reaction—other than Gabrielle. She's sitting across from us, so unless she has supersonic hearing, there's no way she could have heard me.

The corners of her mouth tug up slightly, and she goes back to studying her menu.

Jayden's fingers keep moving along the inside of my thigh.

"What are you doing?" I whisper.

He inches his chair closer to mine. "My homework."

"Your assignment is putting your hand up my skirt?" *Wow.* He got the easy card. Mine's the AP version of sex-class homework. I'm supposed to masturbate in front of him.

"That's only the beginning."

"There's more?"

"There's definitely more." He leans even closer—and the farther he leans, the higher his hand travels.

"Hi, I'm Susan, your waitress for tonight," a young woman says. "Is everyone ready to order their drinks?"

I order a glass of Chardonnay, Jayden a beer.

And his hand continues wandering up my thigh.

In anticipation of his touch, the heat that lingered low in my belly migrates south to between my legs.

"Just how far are you planning to go?" My tone is a mixture of lust and panic. Part of me wants him to keep going. The other part worries about what I'll do if he doesn't stop—if he touches the part of me that longs for him.

Will I be able to keep a straight face and keep quiet? Or will we be busted for Jayden groping me under the table?

As if my body has a will of its own, my legs spread a little wider, allowing him better access.

Jayden's fingers reach the elastic edge of my panties, and it's all I can do to not gasp again.

His fingers trace over the fabric and along my seam. I suck in a sharp but still-soft breath.

"Here's your wine." The waitress sets it on the table, along with Jayden's beer.

"Thanks," I somehow manage to say.

I spread my legs a little wider still...and bump my knee against Blake's thigh. *Oops.*

"Sorry," I say on a choked moan as Jayden's fingers do another sweep of my core.

"Not a problem." Blake eyes Jayden with an air of amusement before turning back to his wife and the discussion they're having with Demek and Anthony.

I half listen to the conversation between Caroline, Davis, Mildred, Keith, and Gabrielle...but don't quiz me on what they're talking about. Jayden's fingers are too distracting.

"Right now," Jayden says, maintaining the illusion that we're having an intimate conversation. "I wouldn't be opposed to taking you out into the alley and finishing this off, but I don't want to risk missing any of the conversations."

I bite my lip to keep from moaning out loud and nod. I have no idea which part I'm agreeing to. Or maybe I'm just nodding for the sake of it. My brain isn't functioning enough for me to know for sure.

He asks about one couple who was planning to join us but isn't here yet. I'm glad at least one of us has their head in the game.

"Maybe they're busy doing their homework assignment." Or they were reserving one of the BDSM rooms. I heard Virginia gush about it to them this morning. In her words, it's a real marriage changer.

That's the last coherent thought I have before Jayden's fingers push my panties to the side and plunge into me.

A small moan escapes my throat, drowned out by Blake's thunderous laugh at whatever his group is talking about.

Jayden's mouth tugs into a smug grin. "Not much further."

"You're enjoying this, aren't you?"

His smile widens. "More than you can possibly imagine."

"You better stop before I come and everyone at this table hears me."

I won't be able to face them again after that—which will make this mission a lot more challenging.

"I have no intention of stopping now. I'm having too much fun." He winks at me.

"I mean it." Kind of.

He angles his head and covers my mouth with his. And as my inner muscles clench hard around his fingers, he swallows my moan.

27

JAYDEN

I sit back in my chair, mentally congratulating myself for pulling off the homework of giving Isabelle an orgasm without getting caught.

Everyone else is distracted by their conversations. Except for Gabrielle. She soundlessly applauds Isabelle and me. Her actions go unnoticed by the others.

The waitress serves our food, and the conversation at the table switches to how we met our spouses.

"Wow, that really looks good," Isabelle says, eyeing the pasta I decided to go with in the end. She reaches over and spears a shrimp with her fork, then pops it into her mouth. "Oooh, that *is* really good."

I sample her spicy Thai chicken rice bowl. It's just as tasty as my pasta.

After the first three couples finish sharing their stories, Virginia turns to Isabelle. So far, the stories have been a little dull, which might explain the hopeful expression on Virginia's face.

"I work at a gallery in San Francisco," Isabelle says after a moment's hesitation. "Jayden came in one day looking for a store that sold high-end designer items for pets. You know, like doggie sweaters by famous designers, diamond-encrusted collars for cats, glamorous pet food. Stuff like that."

Okaaay. This version is news to me.

"He was trying to impress a woman he liked and figured it would be the perfect way to woo both her little dog and her. Except, being the typical alpha male that he is, he couldn't be bothered to ask for directions when he got lost. And boy, did he ever get lost.

"So he comes into the gallery, confused because the pet store was supposed to be there and it wasn't. He sees the art on the wall and starts to explain why it's not art. The woman's dog could do a better job. He was probably right about that. But the way he described each piece was hilarious, and I couldn't stop laughing."

"She was laughing so hard," I say, taking over the story, "tears were rolling down her face, and she was getting odd looks from the people in the gallery. They were all staring down their pretentious noses like she was beneath them. That's when I knew right there that she was perfect for me." I wink at her.

"But their I-just-stepped-in-doggie-pooh expressions made me laugh even harder and—"

"She reversed into a statue made out of garbage welded together, and a pointy piece jabbed her in the ass. She stumbled forward, but her stiletto heel got caught, and she went flying—"

"Right into Jayden's arms. And I knew in that instant it was love at first sight. Not only was he tall, strong, and handsome, we shared the same opinion about the artwork." She bats her eyelashes at me, and I choke back a laugh.

"So what happened to the woman you wanted to impress with the high-priced pet supplies?" Mildred asks me.

"I was so taken by Isabelle's beauty and grace, I forgot all about the woman." I stroke my thumb against Isabelle's cheek, and my breath catches at the raw, unexpected emotion in her eyes.

Ignoring the part about being in a busy restaurant, I lower my lips to hers. It's not a hungry, dominating kiss. It's a slow kiss that gives as much as it takes.

My heart stirs, and it feels as though something has finally woken up inside me. Like I'd been half-dreaming, half-awake until now—vaguely aware of the truth but not completely certain what it is.

Without realizing it, I've been falling in love with Isabelle. But unlike in our fictitious story of how we met, there was no lightning-bolt moment. No neon sign telling me what was going on. It had been subtle, happening a bit at a time for months now, easy to overlook.

Uh. Oh.

That's not good.

Maybe if I ignore it, it will go away.

Like an itch.

A voice in the back of my head cracks up, reminding me: the more you ignore an itch, the worse it becomes.

Until you get to the point where you can't stop dwelling on it, can't stop scratching it.

But that's precisely what I'll have to do. Even if I want to confront the truth, I can't while we're on a mission. Our focus has to be on our job.

My phone vibrates in my shorts pocket. I remove it and check who sent a text.

Connor: Decided to do a more in-depth background check on Blake and Virginia. Spidey alert warned that something is off about them. Looks like they aren't who they claim to be. Am only able to find limited information on them.

Me: Witness protection?

This wouldn't be the first time that has happened. It just makes our jobs harder. The last thing you want is to storm into the wrong castle because you're chasing after erroneous leads.

Connor: Possibly. If they are, then the agency who has them under protection is doing their job. I have to be careful about how I tread if that's the case. I don't want to piss off the wrong people.

Connor: I'll tell you if I discover anything else on them. Otherwise, please be advised.

Me: Will do. Thanks.

For a moment, I consider keeping the information to myself. But as much as I want to barricade Isabelle in a safe place, we're still partners on this mission. And as her partner, I have the responsibility to share everything pertaining to the case with her.

I hand her my phone, and she scrolls through the messages. Without looking at Blake and Virginia, she nods and gives it back to me.

Her fingers thread with mine on my lap, and she gives them a light squeeze. Message clear—she won't take any unnecessary risks with them until we know who they are and why they're staying at the resort.

I don't text Landon since the three of us are meeting in three hours, after he hacks into Bernard's computer.

We finish eating our meal, and the waitress checks if we want anything else.

"I'll have the chocolate cake, please." Isabelle hands her the menu.

"I'll have a bite of yours," I tell her.

She pokes me in the chest. "There's no freaking way that you're"—poke, poke—"eating mine." Poke. "You want some"—poke—"then you order your own, mister." Poke.

The last poke is given with a little more oomph than the previous bunch.

Blake chuckles. "I take it your wedding vows included that you won't steal any of your wife's dessert. Or is that just chocolate cake specifically?"

Isabelle grins at him. "Just chocolate cake. Everything else I'm happy to share."

I order Tiramisu.

The faint sound of music plays from the floor between Isabelle's chair and mine.

She removes her phone from her purse and answers it. "Hi, Grandma....What's that?" Her voice raises a few octaves. "I can't hear you. Give me a moment. I need to go outside, and then I'll be able to hear you better." She pushes her chair from the table and walks toward the entrance.

The conversation moves to a discussion about our careers. Fortunately, one of the husbands is an entertainment lawyer, so everyone wants to know all about his famous clients—which means no one is in a rush to hear about my fictitious life as a project manager for a computer software company.

By the time the waitress serves our desserts. Isabelle still hasn't returned.

I'm half-finished with mine when a nagging feeling bitches at me that Isabelle has been gone for too long—even for talking to Josephine on the phone.

I excuse myself and walk out the main doors. Isabelle isn't outside the front entrance. I scan the area. Nothing.

I call her phone.

It goes straight to voice mail. I leave her a vague message, then call Landon. He doesn't answer his phone, either. But that's not surprising if he's currently hacking into Bradshaw's computer. The last thing he's going to do is have the ringer on.

His voice mail message clicks on.

"Landon, I've lost eyes on Isabelle. Have you heard from her in the last few minutes?"

I end the call and walk around the building, searching for her or signs that she was here a few minutes ago.

Still nothing.

Maybe she returned to the resort.

Without telling me first?

I push down the panic that's threatening to erupt like Mentos dropped into Diet Coke.

I step back inside the restaurant and head to our table. On my way there, I ask the waitress if she's seen my wife in the past few minutes.

"I saw her leave the restaurant, but that's the last I saw of her. Is everything all right?"

"I need to settle her bill and mine. Can you do that?"

A concerned frown wrinkles her brow. "Yes, come with me, and I'll do it right now. Are you sure everything is okay?"

Again, I avoid the question. "I'll need to talk to the hostess, too."

She nods and escorts me to the main entrance. "Tammy, this gentleman has a question for you," she tells the petite brunette in a black dress. To me, she says, "I'll get your bill now."

She leaves.

"What can I help you with?" Tammy asks me.

"Have you been here for the last ten or so minutes?"

"I've been here for the past hour. The other hostess seats the guests while I remain here."

"Did you see my wife leave?" I describe Isabelle.

"Yes, she went out through those doors a few minutes ago." She points to the doors in question.

"Did she return?"

"Not that I noticed. But a few customers came in after she left, and she might have returned while I was talking to them or checking the reservations app."

"Did you see her talking to anyone?" The question is a long shot, but I have to ask all the same.

My heart starts pounding to the rhyme of *fuck, fuck, fuckity, fuck.*

Tammy shakes her head. "She was talking on the phone, but that's all I remember."

The waitress returns with the bill, and I hand her enough cash to cover the amount and a large tip on top of it.

"Is there anyone else who would have seen her?" I press.

"Several customers came in during that time, and there were several others who left. They might have seen her. Is something wrong? Do you think someone took her?" There's an odd excitement in her eyes like she's a Nancy Drew wannabe, eager to solve the mystery of some fucking missing sparkling cat.

I still avoid the question...because it means they will call the cops and right now, that's the last thing I need if something *has* happened to Isabelle.

It's not that I don't trust cops to do their job.

It's just dealing with them will waste time.

Time Isabelle might not have.

"Do you remember which customers came in while she was out there?" I ask the hostess.

She nods.

"Can you take me to them? I want to ask them the same questions I asked you."

She hesitates and looks at the waitress, who shrugs.

"I'm not sure if I'm allowed to."

"This is extremely important." Life and death important.

But again, I can't tell her that—not at the risk of her calling the cops.

After what feels like several centuries, she nods and checks her device. "Okay, this way."

I ask the waitress to tell my group that I've paid for our meals, and ask her if she can collect Isabelle's purse for me. I also request that she pack up Isabelle's cake. I'll bring it back with me.

Because no matter what's happened to her, she'll kill me if I don't remember her cake.

Hell, if someone *has* fucking killed her, she'll haunt me for the rest of my life if I forget her chocolate cake.

The hostess leads me to a table with six people. Four of them are adults. The other two are young kids.

I can feel the occupants of my table watching me, curious and wondering what the heck is going on. I don't bother to look over at them.

Loud laughter and talking, and the clinking of metal against ceramic assault me from all corners of the restaurant like fingernails against a chalkboard.

"Sorry to interrupt," the hostess says to the family. "This gentleman has a question for you."

They all peer at me, their expressions bright with curiosity.

"When you entered the restaurant, did you notice a woman with blue chunks in her hair?" I ask.

The adults exchange glances and shake their heads. "Sorry."

The little girl bounces in her chair. "The fairy princess? Mommy, I want blue hair, too." She looks hopefully at the woman who I assume is her mother.

I crouched to her level. "You saw the woman I just described?"

She nods emphatically. "She was talking on the phone and she laughed like a fairy princess."

I have no idea what a fairy princess's laugh sounds like, but she could be describing Isabelle. I always thought her laugh was sexy, but what does the kid know about that?

"Do you remember what color her dress was?" I ask.

"White with lots of blue flowers."

That was definitely Isabelle.

"Was there anyone else with her? Or was she just talking on the phone?"

"Just talking on the phone."

"Did you hear any unusual sounds? Maybe a car engine or a car door banging shut..."

She fidgets in her chair, the way kids do when they can't sit still any longer. Or they have to go pee. "A fairy bell?"

"A fairy bell?" What the heck is that?

"Sweetie," the older woman, who could be the little girl's grandmother, says. "Do you mean a bell like Fairy Dust wears?"

The little girl nods again. "Yes, like Fairy Dust's bell."

"Fairy Dust is our cat," her mother explains.

"Did you see the cat?" I ask the little girl. If the adults don't remember seeing Isabelle, it's doubtful they noticed a cat wandering outside.

She shakes her head, pouting. "We had to go inside the restaurant."

Even though the question is pretty pointless, I still ask the adults if they noticed anyone else outside or heard anything unusual when they entered the restaurant. They admit they were too busy talking to notice much of anything.

I thank the family. The hostess then escorts me to another group of customers. They arrived at the restaurant after the family. All agree that there was no one standing outside the restaurant when they entered.

Shaking my head to myself, I walk to the entrance, reining in the need to sprint there.

Blake approaches me, cutting across the restaurant. Virginia is right behind him. "Is something wrong?" he asks.

Given what Connor texted earlier, I'm not interested in telling them anything. I have no idea who they really are and if they have anything to do with why Isabelle and I are staying at the resort.

"No, everything's fine. Excuse me, I need to catch up with my wife. She had to go back to the resort to check on something."

That's possible. It could be that Landon contacted her about whatever he found on Bernard's computer. Or maybe he just needed her help to distract the old man so that Landon *can* check his computer.

Seeing me, the waitress comes over, carrying the cardboard takeaway box and Isabelle's purse. "Here's the chocolate cake." She hands them to me.

I thank her, and she walks away.

"Hold this a moment." I pass the box to Blake and remove my sling. A sharp ache bites me in the arm.

Goddamnfuckinghell.

"Don't you need that?" Blake nods at the sling in my hand.

"I'll survive," I say with a grimace.

At least I'll survive until Isabelle sees that I've removed it prematurely.

But I'm sure she'll forgive me once she sees the cake.

"Tell us what's going on," Virginia says. "Maybe we can help."

"I doubt it." I don't give them a chance to say anything else. I walk away.

As soon as I'm out the door, I shove the sling into the nearest trash can.

I phone Isabelle's number once more. Again, I get her voice mail. "Where the hell are you? Call me as soon as you get this."

I end the call and try Landon again. Still no luck with him. I text him, telling him that Isabelle has gone missing.

Then I speed-dial Connor.

He answers on the third ring.

"I need you to put a trace on Isabelle's phone." I practically bark into the phone, like a Rottweiler whose prized bone has been stolen.

"Give me a second…"

I begin pacing along the sidewalk. I don't want to go too far, especially since I have no idea in what direction I need to go.

But I'm also unable to stand still.

I'm like the Energizer Bunny with fresh, high-energy batteries.

Connor gets back to me a moment later. "I'm not getting a signal from her phone. Where is she?"

"I have no idea." I briefly tell him what happened.

"Could she be with Landon?"

I explain what Landon might be currently doing—if things have gone according to plan. "I called him, but he's not answering his phone. I've just texted him to see if he's heard from her or seen her. Can you do a trace on him, too, and check to see if he's still at the resort? I'm going to look for them there."

Connor does as I request. "Nothing. Their phones have either been turned off or they're out of range."

"That makes sense for Landon. He's not exactly going to want the phone to go off and give away his location if he's hacking into Bradshaw's computer. And the same for Isabelle if she's helping him." I pick up my pace. "I'm going back to see if I can find them. I'll let you know what's going on as soon as I have some answers."

I don't give him a chance to respond. I end the call and stalk toward the resort, cake box and purse in hand, cursing that Isabelle and I walked instead of taking the rental car.

Cursing that I don't have my beloved motorcycle.

A white sedan pulls sharply to the curb ahead of me and stops. My inner stranger-danger sirens blare, flashing red lights and all.

My body tenses, prepared for a fight or flight response.

Heavy on the fight.

The passenger door opens, and Blake climbs out. He slowly walks toward me, holding up his ID, the letters unmistakable.

"FBI? Are you telling me that you and Virginia are undercover?"

Well, Damn. That explains a lot.

He nods. "We're with the departments of Organized Crime and Civil Rights. We've identified a drug trafficking ring operating in Huntington Beach, with links to the resort."

"And you're telling me this because...?"

"Your legal name is Jayden Price. You're an operative with Quade Security and Investigations. Isabelle is Isabelle Berkshire, the office manager, and *not* your wife."

Double damn. They are good.

At least they haven't figured out that I'm in love with her.

I get to keep some secrets.

So I guess Isabelle was wrong after all. Blake and Virginia weren't fucking each other senseless before class. Their tardiness might've been related to the real reason they're in town. Possibly chasing down the bad guys.

Damn, they have all the fun.

"Can I ask why you are undercover at the resort?" he asks as Virginia joins us.

I tell them about Bernard's connection to Isabelle's grandmother and the alleged thefts. And how one of the former guests has been identified as potential KGB.

"That's classified information," Blake says. "How the hell did you find that out?"

"We have our ways. We thought there might be a link

between that and the politicians who reported the alleged break-ins."

"I doubt it. He was killed a month ago, shortly after his stay at the resort."

"How come we didn't know that?"

"I guess Sinclair doesn't know everything." He's referring to Connor.

"Any idea who killed him?"

"That's still under investigation, but right now the speculation is that it was a mafia hit. Seems our boy was dabbling in all kinds of illegal activity. That or the KGB wasn't impressed with his connections to the mob and did him in themselves."

"Have you located Isabelle yet?" Virginia asks.

"No, I'm just going back to the resort to see if I can find her and Landon." If Blake and Virginia know who Isabelle and I are, I can guarantee they know about Landon.

"Okay, let's go." Blake starts walking to their car. Virginia joins him.

"Go where?" I follow behind.

"The resort. We're heading there anyway. We can give you a ride."

At the resort, Virginia drops Blake and me off at the main entrance. I bring Isabelle's cake and purse with me.

We stride through the main doors. Blake's going to see if he can locate either Isabelle or Landon by the pool. I'm going to check my room.

"I'll meet you down here in a few minutes," I tell him. He splits off for the pool. I continue to the elevator.

As I approach it, the door pings open and Bradshaw steps out—and my heart comes to a screaming halt against my ribs like a crash-test dummy slamming into the dashboard.

He's wearing a suit like he usually is whenever we've seen him during the past five days. But I don't know if Bernard only wears it when he's working or if that's his standard outfit.

I also have no idea if he just came from his office...where Landon was supposed to be.

A wide smile stretches onto his face, and his eyes shine with pleasure. "Nice to see you again, Mr. Moorehead. Are you and your beautiful wife having a pleasant evening?"

He then glances around the lobby. "Where is she?"

Good question.

"Waiting for me upstairs. We're looking forward to putting into practice some of the things that Gabrielle has taught us during the past few days."

His smile wavers for a second, as if he's not sure what to believe. Whether Isabelle and I really are doing the homework, or if I just said that as part of our cover.

"I'm glad to hear it. Well, if you'll excuse me, I'm ready to call it a day. But I think tonight I'll just skip on reading Jane Austin's *Emma*."

Translation: he didn't put any messages in today's secret drop location.

"Have a good evening," I tell him, then stride to the elevator.

Upstairs, I check my bedroom, but there are no signs that she's been here since we left two hours ago.

I take a chance that Bradshaw hasn't returned to his office and check there. But the outside door is locked, and I have no idea if Landon and Isabelle are inside.

Fuck. Where are they?

28

ISABELLE

The lingering haze of unconsciousness gradually fades, and I take inventory of the dimly lit, red-and-black decorated room. My pulse rushes loud and rapid in my ears. "What is this place? Some kind of Count Dracula theme room?"

I look at Landon, who's in a similar predicament. He's shackled to what looks like a giant medical exam table, with black padding, attached to the wall. I'm lying down on the same type of table.

"Never seen *Fifty Shades of Grey*, have you?" he asks.

"I can't believe you're admitting to having watched the movies. Did you read the books first...or *after* you watched them?"

He doesn't say anything, but I imagine him rolling his eyes.

I pull on the shackles again. God, how could I be such a freaking idiot? Did I *really* have to check where the tiny bell sound came from after ending the call with my grandmother?

Apparently, yes.

Good thing Jayden can't see me now. I'll never hear the end of it when we get out.

If we get out.

"You still haven't answered my question," I say when it becomes apparent the shackles have no intention of letting me go.

"Jayden mentioned there are two BDSM rooms in the resort. My guess is this is one of them."

I snort a disgruntled laugh. "Can't say I'm as impressed with it as Blake and Virginia seem to be. But they probably have a lot more fun in here than you and I will be having."

I have a strong suspicion sex won't be on the agenda for whatever our captors have planned. Or at least not enjoyable sex from Landon's and my points of view.

A shudder skittles through me, and my gaze searches the room for a way to escape. "Any idea how we ended up here?"

"Not a clue. I was searching through Bradshaw's computer files when two men in militia gear entered his office. They turned their rifles on me before I had a chance to grab my gun."

"Militia? Any idea who they are?"

"Not your typical hotel security, that's all I can tell you."

"What did they look like?" He describes them. Basically, big, bad, and ugly.

With shaved short hair.

"I haven't seen anyone who fits that description," I say. "Certainly not at the resort while Jayden and I have been staying here."

"There was something familiar about them, but I can't place where I've seen them."

"Is there a chance you were deployed with them at some point while in the military?"

"Maybe. A long time ago. But I don't believe it's that. Not that it matters. Knowing who they are won't get us out of here."

"Did you find anything on Bernard's computer?"

"As far as I can tell, he's involved in money laundering, but he's working for someone else. He's not the brains of the operation."

"If he's doing something illegal, then why risk it all by having Jayden and me come down to the resort?"

"He probably wasn't expecting me to hack his computer. As far as he knew, none of what he's been up to would come under our scrutiny. But that's not all. Turns out Tyler Mathews wasn't just a resort guest. Bradshaw has records of legal dealings with the man."

I shift my body, trying to get more comfortable. If that's even possible. "What kind of dealings?"

"That part I didn't get to find out. The armed men picked that moment to barge into his office. All I caught was that Tyler was involved in the transfer of a large sum of money into one of Bradshaw's bank accounts."

"So it's possible that the alleged theft of the memory stick had to do with that?" I continue searching for something to help us escape—which would be great if I could levitate said item over to me. And then use the magical powers I don't possess to unfasten myself from the shackles. "If there was something on it that revealed Bernard was participating in money laundering or some other crime, he certainly wouldn't want the contents of it to go public. That would also explain why he hired us instead of going to the cops." Except he didn't realize one crucial element...whenever Liam's team suspects criminal activity, they turn the evidence over to the police—or the FBI, as the case may be.

The room is quiet for a moment as I ponder our current dilemma. "Jayden will find us," I say with a heavy dose of optimism. It's all I have on me right now.

Too bad I can't unlock these shackles with it.

That would be more helpful.

"I'm not so sure about that," Mr. Optimism Killer says.

"They took our phones and destroyed them. Connor has no way of tracking us."

"Aren't you like the equivalent of James Bond's Q? Don't you have one of your nifty inventions on you?"

"Sorry to disappoint, but no. What Q creates goes well beyond Liam's budget. Plus Q has a huge staff of researchers and designers. Or did you miss that part in the movies?"

I grunt an unladylike sound. "You're not very helpful."

"Be sure to tell Liam that when it comes to my annual performance review."

I might not be able to see his expression, but I can't miss the if-we're-lucky-to-still-be-alive smirk in his tone.

"Now that I've shared how I found myself in this predicament, why don't you tell me why you're here and not having dinner with Jayden? I thought that's where you two were headed."

I wiggle my wrists in the shackles, attempting to restore the circulation to my arms. "We did have dinner, and if we ever get out of here alive, the three of us really need to go back there. The food is to die for."

I inwardly cringe at my choice of words.

"You have yourself a date. Assuming Jayden doesn't have an issue with it."

"Why would Jayden have an issue with the three of us going out for dinner together? Is it against a company policy I'm not aware of?"

"You really have no idea, do you? Hell, probably neither of you has any idea."

"No idea about—"

The sound of the door being unlocked halts the rest of my words. And my heart, which was trying to convince itself every-thing will be okay, decides *Fuck that.*

I can barely hear the door opening over the thundering pulse in my ears, which has quickly grown in intensity.

Please be Jayden.

But even before the door opens, I know it isn't. Why would he even think to look in here?

As far as he's aware, I went missing at the restaurant—which is true. Why would the kidnappers risk bringing me here instead of taking me to a location that isn't right under his nose?

That's assuming, of course, Jayden has realized by now that I have gone missing.

Two men enter. One fits Landon's description of the man who attacked him.

The other man is significantly older and less muscular, with short gray hair. Even though it's hot outside, he's wearing a business suit. "Looks like Bernard was right. We get two for the price of one."

I want to say something witty, but in moments like this, wit prefers to hide under the bed with the more desirable monsters.

Instead, horror freezes in my veins, reaching down to my bones. "Bernard? What does he have to do with this?"

He taps the side of his nose.

Great. Now we're back in elementary school again when that was the sign for "None of your business."

Fine, if he won't answer that question, how about this one? "What are you planning to do with us?"

The truth is, I don't give a rat's ass what his goals are when it comes to us. I'm just hoping for some sort of long-winded monologue that villains always do in movies...but aren't as obliging to do in real life.

"Where would the fun be if I tell you that now?" he asks with a chuckle that is closer to a giggle than a manly laugh.

His sidekick—who reminds me of a brick wall—doesn't so much as crack a smile. Which is just as well. It would probably be more on the menacing side than the one that is warm and cuddly.

"I don't know about that," I say. "I'm sure the anticipation will only add to the excitement." For him, anyway.

Keep talking, I mentally command him.

The gray-haired man—who I'm assuming is the boss of the duo—nods at The Brick Wall. "Okay, remove her from the table. Gently. No roughing up the merchandise."

Merchandise? I don't need a translation for that.

My eyes go wide at the meaning, and my heart rattles the bars of its cage.

A weird motorized sound starts up from somewhere under the table. The head of it begins raising until I'm upright, my arms stretched above my head, my feet on a platform.

The Brick Wall unfastens the shackles around my feet.

He stands and reaches to free my arms.

The moment the second metal cuff clicks open, releasing me, I bring my knee up between his legs. Hard.

29

JAYDEN

Blake is waiting for me in the lobby. I don't even have to ask if he's seen Isabelle or Landon. I can see the answer on his face.

He nods at the box. "Is there any particular reason you're still carrying that?"

"It's Isabelle's cake. She'll kill me if anything happens to it. And I figured she'd want it as soon as I find her." Plus that might distract her from sharing a huge piece of her mind when she notices I'm no longer wearing the damn sling.

"She loves her chocolate cake that much?"

"What do you think?"

That gets a snicker out of him. "Women!" he mutters.

We head out to the small building at the back of the property where some of the staff lives. And more specifically, where Landon is staying.

I knock on his door. He doesn't answer.

We return to the lobby. Virginia arrives the same time we do, after doing her own search of the area. She shakes her head.

Shit.

The panic from earlier revisits, not at all interested in being contained this time. I try Isabelle's and Landon's phones again, then check with Connor to see if he's had any luck tracking them.

He texts a moment later.

Connor: Nothing yet.

"I have an idea." Blake strides straight to the front desk. "Hi, I was wondering if anyone is using the Gray or Red rooms, or if there have been any cancelations for today." His tone is eager, as if he's hoping one of them is available now for Virginia's and his enjoyment.

The woman smiles. "We do have a cancelation for tonight in the Gray room. Unfortunately, the Red room is out of commission for a day or two due to renovations."

"Thanks." And with that, Blake hightails it out of there without booking the room, leaving the woman looking confused.

"I guess he changed his mind," I say on a shrug, before Virginia and I rush after him.

He doesn't slow down. "I might know where she is," he says as soon as I catch up. "The Red Room was renovated not long ago. Virginia and I thoroughly searched both rooms for signs that they were being used for drug trafficking." He opens the door to the staircase, pulls out his gun from the holster hidden under his shirt, and enters with Virginia and me behind him.

We rush down the stairs, taking care that our footsteps are silent in the enclosed space. At the bottom, we exit through the door.

He presses his finger to his lips in the universal sign of "Don't fucking make a sound," and nods in the direction we need to go.

I pull out my gun from my concealed holster, which I grabbed from the safe when I checked my room.

We quietly stalk down the empty hallway. Near the end of it, a faint strip of light from a partially open door illuminates the carpet. A murmur of voices comes from the room, one belonging to a female, but I can't make out if it's Isabelle.

As we draw closer, Blake's suspicions are confirmed. Isabelle is in there, sounding less-than-thrilled with her current situation.

But that's not what causes the emotions to churn inside me—the pride mixed with a healthy dose of fear.

It's her inner fight—the reason she'd be good at the job even though I don't want her to be part of the team.

"Okay, remove her from the table," a male voice commands from inside. "Gently. No roughing up the merchandise."

A motorized sound, barely more than a whisper, comes from the room.

The three of us get into position, hidden from the individuals inside.

Blake raises his hand and counts down with his fingers. *Three. Two. One.*

He shoves the door open, gun raised, and we enter at the same moment that Isabelle's knee makes contact with some oversized gorilla's nuts.

And like all men do when they witness another man's gonads being assaulted, we cringe and mentally groan in sympathy.

But the sympathy is short-lived.

Because I don't care how much the asshole is doubled over in pain—it's clear he would've hurt Isabelle if she hadn't acted in self-defense.

"FBI, hands where I can see them," Blake barks.

"There seems to be a mistake," the man, who is still standing, hands raised, says.

I don't bother to listen to the rest of his excuse. I shorten the distance between Isabelle and me in several quick strides.

Before she has a chance to say anything, she's in my arm, and I'm kissing her. My injured arm, still holding the cake box, aches something fierce, but I don't care. I just need to ensure she's okay, and kissing her is the best way to do that.

I'm vaguely aware of Blake telling the gorilla to stay where he is and of Virginia's voice.

"Hey, once you two have finished kissing, would you care to release me?" Landon's tone isn't impatience. It sounds like he's trying not to laugh.

I'd been so focused on Isabelle, I hadn't noticed him. Even though my mouth and body are happy kissing her, I turn to see what he's talking about.

A half smile plays on the corner of my mouth. "I didn't realize you were so big into *Fifty Shades of Grey*."

"Yeah, yeah, very funny. Now that you've had your fun, would you get me down from here?"

Blake and Virginia are busy with the two men and aren't paying attention to us. Isabelle helps Landon down.

I hand her the box. "Here, this is yours."

"What is it?"

"The chocolate cake you ordered for dessert."

She squeals in gratitude, which makes the ache in my arm worth it. "I can't believe you brought it with you."

Landon chuckles. "Shit, you do have it bad for her if you made sure you didn't forget it. But the way, what are the Feds doing here?"

"Helping me save both your asses."

"Are they really FBI?" Isabelle asks, eyes wide.

"Well, I didn't actually do a background check on them with the agency. Once I discovered you were missing, Blake revealed their real identities. They already knew ours; they just didn't know what we were doing at the resort."

"So they're not married?"

I shrug. "I guess they're pretending to be married like we are."

"But why are they here?" Landon asks, "And how the hell did you find us?"

I explain what they told me about their investigation, and how Blake was the one who figured out where Landon and Isabelle might be.

"This whole thing is beginning to sound more and more like a setup," Landon says, explaining to me what he found on Bradshaw's computer. "I'm betting my left nut that when I talk to Senator Wiseberger tomorrow, he'll have no idea what I'm talking about. He never reported an alleged break-in to Bradshaw."

"I'd like to know why Bernard manipulated my grandmother into convincing me to come here," Isabelle says. "What was the point in that? He knew I couldn't stay in the resort on my own. I would need a fake husband. Did it matter who that was? Did it have to be Jayden, or would anyone do?"

My blood boils like an overactive volcano, threatening to spew hot lava at anyone who dares harm her. She's right. Why the hell did he want her at the resort?

The real reason, not the fucked-up fictitious one.

"That's something your friends over there"—Landon gestures with a jerk of his chin toward Blake and Virginia—"will have to ask him."

He's right. It's out of our hands now that the FBI is involved. They're the ones who will be interrogating the men. We don't have the authority to do it.

Two cops enter the room, and Blake and Virginia hand off the two men to them. The police leave with Blake. Virginia joins us.

"Blake is going to see if Bernard is still on the resort property," she says after Landon fills her in on the money laundering information on Bradshaw's computer. "Then we'll take him and these guys in for questioning. But we also have some questions for you three. And I'm sure you have your own for Blake and me."

"So you guys aren't really married?" Isabelle asks. "Because you had me fooled."

Virginia grins. "Some of what you heard over the past five days is true...and some of it isn't. Yes, Blake and I are married. We've been happily married for the past five years, but we work in different programs. Our cases happened to be linked this time. And no, we're not into BDSM, nor are we swingers. We didn't think you were, either. Thank God, we weren't wrong about that." She laughs. "It would've been a little awkward if you had been."

She hands me her business card. "Come down to the police station as soon as you can. Hopefully, we can get answers for you as to the real reason Bernard wanted you two at the resort."

30

ISABELLE

Virginia departs the room, leaving Jayden, Landon, and me alone.

"What happened to your sling?" I happen to know Jayden isn't close to being ready to abandon it just yet. His doctor was clear about that.

He shrugs. "I guess it fell off and I didn't notice."

Landon snorts, buying the lie as much as I do.

I don't get to say anything else about the topic. Jayden gestures wildly at the contents of the room, his gaze locked on mine. "This is why I don't want you to be an operative with the rest of us. It's too fucking dangerous."

That fire in his eyes usually gives me chills, in a good way.

Right now, I want to dump a bucket of cold water on his head.

"But it's not too dangerous for Landon? Is that what you're saying?"

"No, because he's a man."

Oh, damn. He did not just say that.

If I were a fire-breathing dragon, smoke would be unfurling from my flared nostrils. "Oh, really? Because in case you didn't notice, when you and Blake came charging in here on your white *ponies*, Landon was still tied up and I wasn't. I was the reason one man was out of commission."

"Christ, I really hate it when Mom and Dad fight," Landon says, barely holding back a laugh.

Neither of us turns to look at him.

We're in standoff mode.

Ready to circle one another. Each ready to bring the other down.

"Maybe I should leave so you two can rip off your clothes and fuck yourselves silly," he says.

Neither of us responds. We continue glaring at each other.

I'm vaguely aware of Landon walking toward the open door. "But you might want to skip on the toys in this room," he says. "I wouldn't want to be responsible for the damage they might inflict. Text me when you're ready to go to the police station." The door clicks shut.

And opens again. "I don't suppose you need a condom?"

"Get the hell out of here!" Jayden's gaze still doesn't leave mine.

This time when Landon closes the door, it stays shut.

"Look, I get it," Jayden says with the growl of an unreasonable caveman. The tension between us is like a live wire. Sizzling. Crackling. Ready to burn.

Or be burned.

He steps closer, the heat between us intensifying. "You wanted to do something different, something dangerous. Well, you've done it. You almost got yourself killed in the process. Now it's time to go back to your regular job."

I let out a hard breath. "You don't get it at all, do you, Jayden? This is what I'm supposed to be doing. Being on this mission with you feels more right than anything else I've done before. You assume I'm incapable of doing the job because you refuse to see beyond the walls of the box."

"It's not that I refuse to see it. I don't want you to get killed. I'm fucking in love with you, Isabelle, and I can't bear the thought of watching you get killed. Because *that* will kill me."

For a second, the world goes completely still, the air in the room sucked out. The meaning behind Jayden's words, even though they were spoken in anger, in the heat of the moment, sears our thoughts. Renders us speechless.

Double damn.

We look at each other for a long moment, our breaths heaving from our hurled words. Then something clicks inside us.

I start undoing his shirt, impatient to get it off him—refusing to fully examine his words for now.

Or ever.

He fumbles with the buttons on my dress, equally impatient to get me naked. Before he has a chance to rip my dress open, I take over for him while he shucks the shirt off his shoulders and tosses it to the floor.

Our clothes are removed in record time...and we're kissing.

Kissing like there's no yesterday, no tomorrow.

Kissing like every word that sears us to the core is revealed with each demanding kiss.

Jayden pauses long enough to sheath his cock with the condom from his wallet. One of the few remaining condoms we'd bought in the resort gift shop the other day.

His teeth gently bite my neck, marking me as his.

But at the same time, I get the feeling that despite what he said about being in love with me, this will be our last time together.

I can't be with a man who isn't supportive of my career choice.

Can't be with a man who wants me to be less than who I am.

His fingers shift to between my legs, and he strokes me,

teases me, drives me utterly insane with need. I can't remember the last time I was this wet, the last time my legs threatened to buckle under me from sheer pleasure.

"I need you inside me!" is all I'm capable of saying.

Jayden bends slightly at the knees, wraps his hands behind my thighs, and hoists me up, so my legs hook around his hips. He flinches, the pain in his arm bothering him, but not enough to lower me to my feet.

The expression in his eyes warns me not to say anything because no matter what, it's too late to stop this fire burning between us.

He positions his thick tip against my entrance and thrusts inside me.

I cry out, my head falling back on the padding behind me.

Jayden keeps going, pushing his hips against me, his hard length filling me. His body slaps again and again into the most sensitive part of me, taking me closer and closer to the edge.

Until I have nowhere left to go.

My inner muscles clench down, sending me to a new stratosphere—and I scream out.

Jayden flexes his hips several more times, burying himself deeper inside me.

Aftershocks sweep through my body, begging Jayden to join me. The last thrust of his hips is met with a guttural grunt.

And I melt into liquid heat.

He stays still, my head on his shoulder, as we wait to regain our breaths.

To regain all awareness.

I don't want this moment to end, but it also can't go on forever. It's time I move on when it comes to my feelings for him.

But as those words take shape in my mind, my heart cracks from the pain of them. Because when it comes down to it, I'm in love with Jayden.

I have been for a while.

I was just too stubborn to admit it to myself until now.

He removes himself from me and lowers me to the ground. I collect my clothes. He deals with the condom.

Both of us ignore the white elephant in the room, watching us with great interest.

Or maybe it's eyeing the provocative array of sex toys and paraphernalia.

"We need to talk," Jayden says, gathering his clothes.

I pull my dress on and begin buttoning it. "No, what we need to do is go to the police station." Because that's more important than discussing what Jayden said before we tore off each other's clothes.

Jayden stands in only his shorts. His skin glistens with droplets of sweat—and for a second, I imagine running the tip of my tongue along those ridges. Tasting him. Loving him.

But that's not possible. Not now. Maybe not ever.

Instead, I drag the tip of my tongue across my lower lip.

And shake the image of him from my head.

"I don't know about you," I say, "but I'm interested in finding out why Bernard really wanted us at the resort if it's not for the reasons we were led to believe."

"Then we go home, and you forget about being an operative?"

"No, we go home, and Liam makes me part of the team."

Jayden grunts. "I already told you that I can't watch you risk your life again."

I cross my arms. "You won't have to. I'm sure Landon or Adam will be more than happy to work with me instead."

"So the fact that I love you and don't want to see you get hurt means nothing?"

I shake my head. "You don't love me, Jayden. Not the real me, anyway. You want to love a china doll that sits at her desk, organizing your life and the lives of everyone else on the team. But that's not the real me. The real me wants to make a difference. She wants to do *this* job." I spread my arms, gesturing to the room.

A one-sided grin cracks on his face. "You want to teach BDSM?"

I roll my eyes and smack him on the chest. "You know what I mean."

"Is this your way of saying you don't love me?"

An ache pinches in my chest at the question—a question I don't want to examine too closely. There's really no point, especially when it comes to Jayden.

Because with love comes disappointments. Between my parents' marriage and my ex-boyfriend wanting me to be something I wasn't and then cheating on me, I've had a lifetime of experience in that department. Deep down, I know the reason for those failed relationships was due to a lack of respect. My father didn't respect my mother enough to stay faithful.

My ex-boyfriend didn't respect me enough to not cheat.

What Jayden wants—for me not to do the job that he loves —means that he isn't able to respect me, either.

Not in the way I need him to respect me beyond our friendship.

"I'm saying that I want to keep being your friend. I'm saying I want to fall in love with someone who can accept me for who I am."

The ache in my chest grows wider, deeper.

Jayden shakes his head, but I have no idea why. "Let's go hear what that sonofabitch has to say about why he dragged us down here." He jerkily pulls on his short-sleeved shirt and attempts to button it.

But it's clear from the slight tremble to his normally steady hand and the grimace he's trying to keep off his face, his arm is causing him pain.

"Here, let me do it," I say softly.

I brush his hands away. He doesn't argue.

[TOP SECRET]

AT THE POLICE STATION, JAYDEN, LANDON, AND I ARE DIRECTED to a room set aside for Blake and Virginia. Blake is pacing. Virginia is studying a map on the dry-erase board.

"So how did Bernard take the arrest?" Jayden asks them as we enter the room. We only know that he was taken into custody shortly after Jayden, Virginia, and Blake rescued Landon and me.

Blake pauses his pacing. "He quickly lawyered up, and we haven't been able to get anything from him. He's still sticking to his story about why he lured you two down and claiming innocence when it comes to drugs and the kidnapping."

"Have you found any drugs on the premise?"

"We're waiting on the search warrant now. We weren't exactly prepared for how things played out. We needed more solid evidence first. You and Landon getting kidnapped threw a wrench in everything. So far we've got zero leads as to who those two men are that we arrested. Their fingerprints aren't on file, and they aren't exactly cooperating. But thanks to what Landon told us about what he found on Bernard's computer, we might have something on him when it comes to illegal activity. We're waiting on the warrant now to seize it."

"The only thing they're saying is that they have no idea what we are talking about when it comes to drugs," Virginia says.

"Do you believe them?" I ask.

"Until we have evidence linking them, we have no idea what to believe. But they will be charged for kidnapping and holding you and Landon captive. They're not getting away from us that easily."

"What about Bradshaw?" Jayden asks.

"Other than the comment about getting two for the price of one that Isabelle and Landon heard, they haven't said anything else on the topic."

"And because they didn't mention Bernard's last name," Blake says, "their comment holds no weight. They could have been referring to another Bernard. It's not exactly an unusual name."

"Can we talk to them?" I ask.

"That's not a good idea. It could end up hurting our case. The best we can do is keep trying, but I don't think any of you talking to them will make a difference.

"My suggestion is to go home. Let us worry about those two. We'll do whatever we can to find out why they kidnapped you and what they were planning to do once they had you. We'll be in contact with you, and you have our information in case anything else comes to mind."

I nod—but my thoughts are already racing ahead to what I plan to do once I return to San Francisco.

Maybe my grandmother unwittingly knows something that can help solve the case.

Because when it comes down to it, she too was duped by Bernard.

31

JAYDEN

The next day, I drive to Josephine's house.

As soon as Isabelle, Landon, and I left the Huntington Beach police station yesterday, we grabbed our stuff from the resort and drove back to San Francisco in Landon's vehicle.

Because Blake and Virginia have taken over the mission, they've arranged for FBI agents to interview the alleged victims Bradshaw told us about, and that includes Tyler Mathews.

Isabelle's car is in Josephine's driveway when I pull up. Isabelle is leaning against the closed driver's door, studying her phone.

My heart races at the sight of her long, toned legs barely covered by her sundress. The same legs that yesterday were wrapped around my hips as I pounded into her.

A memory I won't be forgetting anytime soon.

I park next to her and climb out of my SUV. Mojo barks from the back seat, his tongue lolling to the side.

I open the rear door. He jumps down and bounds over to her. She crouches next to him and wraps her arms around his thick neck.

Never before have I been jealous of my drooling dog until now.

I won't say things have returned to normal between us since my big declaration yesterday. We spent the drive home ignoring the white elephant sitting next to her in the back.

"How's the arm?" she asks, noticing it's in the sling again, which I had to replace after tossing the old one.

"Last I checked, it's still attached."

"That's good." She says it in a distracted way, and at first, I'm not sure if she's talking to Mojo or to me.

She gives him another hug. My goofy dog doesn't complain. "God, I've missed you."

"You saw him only a few days ago."

"I can still miss him." She pushes herself to her feet and strides up the path to the front door. Mojo and I walk alongside her.

The cool ocean breeze ruffles her hair. She brushes a wayward strand behind her ear and presses the doorbell.

The door opens a moment later, and Juanita waves us inside. Mojo barks his greeting.

"Yes, Mojo," she says, laughter in her tone. "You're an adorable dog who plans to shed over everything right after I vacuumed."

He gives her his best doggy grin, proud of such high praise.

"Your grandmother never mentioned you were planning to visit her," she says to Isabelle. "But fortunately, I just made your favorite croissants. I'll bring them onto the balcony as soon as they're ready."

"You don't have to go to all that trouble," Isabelle tells her, which is the opposite of what the gleam in her eyes says.

"For you, *chica*, it's no trouble." She scurries toward the kitchen. Isabelle, Mojo, and I head for the balcony door.

Isabelle slides it open. Mojo pushes past, eager to visit with Josephine. Henri and Liza are also sitting outside with her.

The moment Josephine sees us, her eyes widen. "What are you two doing back so soon? The last I heard, you were extending your stay a few weeks. Did you already solve the mystery?"

Maybe it's just me, but she seems awfully disappointed to see us. The same expression is mirrored on her friends' faces.

"You could say that." Isabelle walks to an empty chair.

Henri exchange glances with Josephine. She gives him the universal gesture for "*Move over.*" Grinning, he can't move fast enough—well, it's more like a fast shuffle—to the other empty chair, allowing me to sit next to Isabelle.

"We have some questions we need to ask you," Isabelle tells her grandmother.

"Ask away."

"Have you and Bernard been in contact much with each other since your breakup?"

"Not really. We would bump into each other from time to time after he moved back to LA because we attended some of the same Hollywood events. We met on friendly terms, but that's about it."

"So before he told you that he needed my help, you hadn't had much contact with him, other than at those events?"

"That's right. A few months ago, we were at the same charity event and started talking. I might have mentioned that you work for a high-level security and investigation firm. You know, in the way a grandmother likes to do when boasting about her grandchild..."

She pauses, and we both nod for her to continue.

"There's a chance I mentioned how you seem disillusioned by long-term relationships because of what happened with your parents, and that I was disappointed there will be no great-grandchildren in my future because of that. I might have also mentioned Jayden."

For the first time since I've known Josephine, she looks uncertain.

"What exactly did you mention about Jayden?" Isabelle asks.

Josephine exchanges glances with her friends. They, too, nod for her to continue. Only this time it's a we've-got-your-back nod.

"That you two would make a great couple if you ever got over your phobia of marriage and long-term relationships."

Isabelle sits a little straighter. "I'm not afraid of marriage. I just don't want to waste time in a relationship if the man will end up ripping my heart out when he cheats on me, or if it turns out he's unwilling to accept me as I am."

"Yes, but Jayden's not the kind of man who would cheat on a woman," Henri says. "He's the kind of man who would cherish the woman he loves. Warts and all."

Isabelle rolls her eyes in the melodramatic manner her grandmother is known for. "He's also a man who is sitting right here. And just so you know, I don't have warts."

Henri grins at me, his dentures glowing in the midmorning sunlight. "Am I not right? You would cherish the woman you love?"

"That's right…as long as I know she won't spear my heart with her stilettoed heel. And that includes taking stupid risks with her life." The last part is directed at Isabelle with a raised eyebrow.

Because I know she would never cheat on me. But if I lost her because something happened to her, that would gut me worse than when my ex-fiancée proved to be unfaithful.

"I didn't plan to get kidnapped. And I certainly didn't expect that gorilla to grab me after I finished talking to Granny on the phone."

A collective gasp rises from the other three individuals, Henri's being the loudest.

"There's a gorilla running loose in Huntington Beach?" he asks.

"I meant figuratively, not literally."

"Oh."

Isabelle laughs. "Try not to sound too disappointed."

"You were kidnapped?" Josephine looks at Isabelle; then her wide-eyed gaze sweeps to me. "You let my baby get kidnapped?"

"It wasn't his fault," Isabelle says at the same time as I tell her grandmother, "This is why I don't want her involved in any more dangerous missions."

There's a chance I might have ended it with a caveman grunt.

Liza and Henri are one step away from clapping their hands in glee at the reality show playing out in front of them.

Isabelle heaves a heavy breath. "Look, I get it. Your best friend died while you two were deployed together, and I'm really sorry about that, Jayden. But you've got to stop trying to protect me like I'm an easily broken tea set."

Another grunt from me. "I'm not trying to protect you. I'm trying to keep you from getting killed."

"Same thing. But that's what you do, Jayden. You protect everyone. Me. Your country. Your colleagues. The clients you're hired to help. That's why you're so good at your job.

"But when it comes down to it, you're no different than those women you've dated. They expected you to give up your job for them...and you're expecting me to give up the job I want to do because it makes *you* uncomfortable."

I gesture at Josephine with the wave of my hand, my eyes not leaving Isabelle's. "What—you think your grandmother wants something bad to happen to you?"

"You can keep me out of your lovers' spat, young man. You're on your own with this one."

"You're actually okay with your granddaughter risking her life?"

"No, but it's not about what *I* want. It's about what *she* wants. Because if it were about what I want, you two silly hens would have already admitted to yourselves and each other that you're in love."

"I told her I love her. She's the one who's not in love with me."

Isabelle lets out another heavy breath. "I didn't say I don't love you—"

"Yes!" This time Liza does clap her hands and grins like a little girl on Christmas morning.

"I'd say this is the perfect occasion for champagne," Henri says, also grinning. "Josephine, I don't suppose you still have the bottle of *Dom Pérignon Vintage Rosé*? We need to celebrate."

Both Isabelle and I stare at him with what have to be "*Huh?*" expressions.

Seeing this, Henri clarifies, "The reason she didn't say that she doesn't love you is because she *is* in love with you."

My heart stumbles over itself at his words, and hope lets out a sigh of relief. "Is that true?" I ask her.

"It doesn't matter if I'm in love with you or not, Jayden. I'm not interested in being with a man who doesn't respect me enough to let me do the job I'm good at. The job I've proved I'm capable of doing."

I ignore everything she's saying because she just reminded me of why we're here. Whether I like it or not, we still have a job to do. Together.

"You told Bernard about me," I say to Josephine, quickly setting the train once again on the tracks. I'll circle back to the love thing once Isabelle and I are finished with our questions. "What exactly did you tell him?"

She considers it for a moment. "Not a whole lot. Mostly your name and how you two are close friends." A frown crinkles across her brow. "Now that I think about it, I didn't tell him about your job or that you work with Isabelle. But when he contacted me two weeks ago, he seemed to know what you do for a living.

"He was the one who suggested that you could help him with his dilemma since the police weren't interested in the case."

"He told you that he had spoken with the police?" Isabelle asks, catching the same discrepancy between that and what Bradshaw told us.

Josephine nods. "He said they weren't smart enough to solve the mystery themselves. And that he needed someone with the brains to puzzle it out."

"And you suggested that Isabelle could help him?"

"No, he did. It was his idea that you both go to his resort to help him."

"Why us both? Why not just me or Jayden?" Isabelle asks.

"Because he said the resort was the perfect setting for you to finally admit to yourselves that you're in love."

Isabelle narrows her eyes at her grandmother, but then her voice goes soft, almost chiding. "Admit it. That's the real reason you agreed to his scheme, isn't it?"

Josephine grimaces. Henri mournfully says, "I guess we won't be having champagne after all."

Liza pats him on the knee, her voice sympathetic. "I'm sure we'll find an occasion to use it soon enough." She smiles sweetly at us.

"Did he say anything that raised alarms when you and he talked about the plan?" I ask.

Josephine gasps, her face suddenly pale. "Alarms? Do you think he was responsible for Isabelle being kidnapped?"

"We believe there's an excellent chance he was involved. Unfortunately, the men who did the actual kidnapping aren't talking."

"Oh, heavens. If I had realized he was capable of something like that, I would never have agreed to the plan. I really thought he was helping me get you two together."

"Had you seen Bernard recently—before he called you to ask for our help?" Isabelle asks.

"He came up to San Francisco a few days before he asked me to contact you. He said he was in town for business but would love to see me before he returned home."

"So you met him here at the house?"

"No, at a restaurant. *Le Pierre*."

"By we," Henri says, "she means that *she* met with Bernard, but Liza and I tagged along. Only he didn't realize it."

"We wanted to make sure Josephine was okay. That he wasn't trying to take advantage of her." Liza spreads her arms, gesturing to the grand house that screams money.

I smile at the two friends. "I'm glad to hear that." God knows what else the asshole would've tried—or could still try—given he had arranged to have Isabelle and Landon kidnapped.

"Did you notice anything suspicious while at the restaurant?" Isabelle asks.

Josephine shakes her head. Liza and Henri exchange questioning glances.

"There was a table with three men not far from where Josephine and Bernard were sitting," Henri says. "They kept looking over at their table. One of them was older. Not quite as old as us, but definitely up there in years. There was also a much bigger man. Like a wrestler. He didn't really say much. It was the older man and the younger one who did all the talking."

"We thought the older man might have recognized her from back in the day," Liza adds. "He was old enough to have seen her movies. It wouldn't be the first time people recognized her and stared at her or approached her for an autograph."

"Did they talk to her or go near the table at any point?"

They both shake their heads.

Henri leans forward, hands clasped between his knees. "No, but at one point Bernard gave a barely perceptible nod in their direction. Josephine wouldn't have seen it because she had just looked down at her plate."

"Did he do anything else to acknowledge them?" Isabelle asks.

"No. Other than that, his focus was fully on Josephine."

"What happened after you two finished eating lunch?" Isabelle asks her grandmother.

"He paid for the meal and walked me to my car."

"And then?"

"Are you asking if he kissed me? You know a lady never kisses and tells." A familiar one-sided smile—the one I've seen numerous times on Isabelle—slides onto Josephine's face.

"No, they didn't kiss," Liza says, not living by the same rule when it comes to her friend. "Josephine drove away, and Bernard did the same in the opposite direction."

"But the three men left the restaurant a minute or two after that," Henri says. "We were outside watching Josephine leave, which is why we saw the three men. They got into an SUV and turned the same direction Bernard had gone."

"Can you two describe them?" I ask.

"The older man was bald," Liza says, "with a white goatee and bushy eyebrows, and he had wire-rimmed glasses. Like that boy who's a wizard and goes to the school that looks like a castle."

"You mean Harry Potter?" Isabelle asks.

"That's the one."

Henri nods. "The younger man could have been his relative. He had the same eyes and nose. But he was at least thirty or forty years younger, didn't have a goatee, and still had his hair, which was black."

"And he had a tattoo on the right side of his neck," Liza says.

"What did it look like?"

"I could only see part of it. Like the older man, he was wearing a dress shirt, which covered most of the design, but from what I could tell, it was a picture of a pocket watch, and there were some words above it."

"Do you remember what they said?"

"He was too far away, and the letters were too small for me to make out the words."

"What color was the tattoo?"

"Black and white?"

A sinking sensation takes root in my stomach.

"Did you see any other tattoos on him?"

"Not that I remember."

"He had some on his fingers." Henri lifts his right hand and points to the back of the middle three fingers.

And the sinking sensation drops to the ground like an elevator whose cable has been cut.

Fuck.

I don't even need to hear the third man's description. The one that Henri had referred to as beefy.

It's Rasputin Zadorov. Vadik Orlov's henchman.

The man with the watch tattoo on his neck is Nikolai Orlov, Vadik's grandson.

I can feel Isabelle's eyes on me, studying me. "Do you know who he's talking about?" she asks.

I speed-dial Liam as I nod. He answers on the second ring.

"We've got a problem," I tell him. "I might know who is responsible for Isabelle's and Landon's kidnapping. And who was responsible for Isabelle and me being in Huntington Beach to begin with."

"Who?"

I relay everything that Henri, Liza, and Josephine told me.

"Fuck almighty," is his response. Along with a few other curses. "Do you have a positive ID on them?"

"No. I have the two witnesses who described them."

"Are you still with the witnesses?"

"Yes."

"I'll get Connor to send you photos of the three men. See if your witnesses can confirm if it's them or not."

A few minutes later, my phone pings with incoming texts. I open up the photos and show them to Liza and Henri.

"That's them," Henri says. "I'd recognize those tattoos anywhere."

The tattoos that say, "Respect the Past," "Create the Future," and "Protect What's Yours." Those last three words are the ones Henri saw on Nikolai's fingers.

Liza also confirms they were the three men that day in the restaurant, watching Bradshaw and Josephine.

"Who are they?" Isabelle asks me.

"Vadik Orlov; his grandson, Nikolai Orlov; and Vadik's bodyguard, Rasputin Zadorov. Vadik Orlov's the crime boss the team was hired to take down prior to you and I going to Huntington Beach."

"You mean the ones who shot you?"

I nod. Those would be the bastards.

32

ISABELLE

After we finish talking to my grandmother and her friends, Jayden, Mojo, and I head out. We've barely left the house when my phone pings with a text...as does Jayden's.

It's a group text sent to the entire team.

"Hell no," Jayden growls.

And I grin. "Sorry, buddy. Looks like you don't have any say in this."

Usually, I'm not part of their team meetings when it comes to their missions. Hopefully, this isn't a one-time exception.

Sandra, my temporary replacement, is sitting at my desk when we arrive at the office.

The warm, bubbly brunette smiles at us. "Liam and the others are in the conference room."

We enter the room and take the two empty seats next to each other at the table.

Jayden grabs a donut. "Christ, I've missed these. Connor, have I told you lately you're the best?"

The way he gazes lovingly at the donut, you'd think he's

going to bite the heads off anyone who dares mess with it. But then he sinks his teeth into it and moans his satisfaction.

Poor donut never stood a chance.

Liam gets everyone up to speed on the situation with Vadik Orlov and his less than savory associates. Jayden and I also fill them in on what we have learned.

"The Feds are desperate to bring in Orlov and his family," Liam says. "They've unofficially asked for our help. Which means you've all been temporarily pulled from your current assignments."

"That's great—but what does that have to do with Isabelle?" Jayden might be successful at keeping what he's thinking off his face, but there's no missing the scowl in his tone.

Liam levels his gaze at him. "She's part of the team. She proved that she's a valuable part of it, beyond what she was doing before, and will be a good operative."

"Does anyone else have any objections to me joining the team?" I ask the rest of the guys, already knowing the answer.

"Hell, no."

"I'm good with it."

"I'm all for it."

They might be good with it, but that's not enough for Jayden. The scowl moves from his tone and takes up residence on his face.

"Glad we've got that settled," Liam says, ignoring Jayden's reaction. "Landon, you and Isabelle are partnering up."

A grunt rumbles deep in Jayden's chest. "Hell, no. If you're insisting on her joining us, then she should be partnered with me."

"You're still on medical leave."

"Really? Because you had no trouble letting me go to Huntington Beach with her."

"That's because I didn't anticipate you ripping off your sling well before you were supposed to and playing her knight in shining armor. Although in retrospect, I should have known better."

"I didn't have a choice. You would have done the same if it were Ava."

"You're right. I would have. Because she's my wife, the mother of my child, and the woman I love."

Four knowing smirks are leveled at Jayden. I pretend to be busy inspecting the donut I have no intention of eating.

"You can stay with Connor and be our communications guy." Liam's tone bars all further argument.

Jayden throws him an *oh-goodie* glare.

[TOP SECRET]

MY DOORBELL RINGS AS I'M FOLDING MY LAUNDRY IN MY bedroom.

For a second, the idea that it's possibly Jayden, coming to apologize for being an idiot, pops into my head. But that hope crashes and burns when I open the door to find Ava standing on my front stoop. Her adorable, eight-month-old baby is jabbering away in her arms.

"Hey, how's my favorite little girl doing?" I ask Cassie. The ends of her short blonde hair peek from under her pink sunhat.

She gurgles in reply.

I open the door wider to let them in.

It's not the first time Ava and Cassie have visited my house unannounced. Even though Ava has her group of mommy friends she spends time with—the wives of Liam's buddies, who are also his little sister's friends—she and I have a different bond than what she shares with those women. Their husbands' jobs aren't considered dangerous.

Even though until recently I hadn't admitted to myself that I love Jayden, it was still tough to watch him leave for missions when I knew there was a chance he might not come home alive.

It's that deep-rooted uncertainty with each mission that strengthened the friendship Ava and I share.

"Are you busy?" Ava asks.

"I was just putting my laundry away. Nothing exciting." Especially after the past few days.

After I grab some drinks for us, we sit on the living room couch. Cassie plays on the pink baby blanket on the floor, examining a squishy block that was also in Ava's oversized bag.

"Liam told me what happened at the resort," Ava says. "How are you doing?"

"Fine. Better than fine. I did what I set out to do—prove to your husband that I'm capable of doing what he and the guys do." I grin, unable to hide my excitement at my new promotion. "And now I'm a member of the team. I'm their first female operative."

She squeals and flings her arms around me in a tight hug. "Congratulations! Liam told me a while ago that you wanted to be one."

I laugh. "Let me guess, he was grumbling about it at the time."

"You might be right about that. He didn't think you were qualified to do the job. *Blah blah blah*. But I knew that once given a chance, you'd prove him wrong."

"Thank you." At least one of my close friends is supportive of my decision.

Too bad the one who counts the most isn't.

"So what's going on between you and Jayden?" She says it so innocently, but there's nothing innocent about the gleam in her eyes.

Two can play at that game. "What do you mean?"

"Oh come on, Isabelle. You don't think for a second that I don't know what happened at the resort, do you?"

"Let me guess, Liam told you." The question is, what exactly did he tell her?

I mean, sure, Landon pretty much put the pieces together when he found me naked with Jayden.

But this is Landon we're talking about. He's not one to gossip.

"That Jayden's in love with you? I pretty much guessed that for myself a while ago."

I open my mouth to deny it, but she doesn't give me a chance. "Don't even think about lying to me. While it might not have been obvious to you and Jayden—and probably the other guys, too—I've always suspected there was more simmering under the surface between you two than you were willing to admit. And for the record, I think you make a great couple."

"I hate to disappoint, but Jayden and I aren't a couple. And we can never be one."

"Why not? I know your history when it comes to men hasn't been spectacular." She knows about Richard. The cheating part, that is. "But you're so afraid of a man hurting you like your father hurt your mother, you've closed yourself off to love."

"For good reason. I've been there. Done that. Maybe I've inherited some sort of gene that makes me prone to being cheated on."

Ava shakes her head as if she's talking to a small child. "What happened with your ex-boyfriend isn't on you. You can't give up on love just because of one idiot's mistake."

"It wasn't just the cheating that was the tipping point for my mom when it came to my father, and for me when it came to Richard. They were never happy with who we were. They were always trying to change us. My mom wanted a career, but Dad wanted her to play the good little housewife. To be his trophy, to show off to other men of his status. My ex-boyfriend was the same. He wanted me to be someone I wasn't. Someone more fitting for his career ambitions."

Ava tilts her head to the side. "But that doesn't sound like Jayden at all. He doesn't come off as the kind of man who would cheat on a woman. And he knows exactly who you are and hasn't tried to change you." She narrows her eyes. "He hasn't tried to change you, right?"

"As a friend, he hasn't." I chew on my lip for a moment, wondering how much to divulge. "He admitted to being in love with me—"

"*Ohmigod*, I was right about you two." Her voice is almost a shriek.

At the sound of it, Cassie stops playing and glances up, her eyes wide with surprise and curiosity.

"Sorry, sweetheart," Ava says. "Mommy got a little excited for a moment. You'll understand when you're older." She returns her attention to me. "Are you in love with him?"

"I am." No point denying it. "But I can't be with a man who doesn't want me to do my job because he's too afraid that I'll be killed. It's different for you and Liam. He doesn't freak out when you go to your job as an elementary school teacher. He doesn't want to bubble-wrap you so you'll stay safe."

Ava chuckles. "We are talking about the same man, right? I think for most men, it wouldn't be a problem. But our men have seen too much to escape their fear for our safety. You just have to be patient and give Jayden the chance to adjust to your new career. And most of all, you have to be understanding of his fears. They're there for a reason."

"I get that. I go through the same thing every time he goes on a mission. But I'd never ask—and would never expect—him to give up his job because I can't handle the idea of something bad happening to him."

"Ah, but that's because you're a woman. You're innately much stronger than him. Men are wimps that way."

I snort a laugh, and my gaze drops to my finger where

Jayden's grandmother's engagement ring had been. My finger feels oddly naked without it.

Sad, even.

But as much as I trust Jayden with my heart—because I know he would never do anything to hurt me in that way—I can't be with a man who's afraid of letting me be *me*, because he's positive I'll die at some point on the job like his best friend did when they were on a mission together.

Unless Jayden changes his mind, I can't see us being anything more than friends and colleagues.

My heart slumps in my chest at the thought...and wonders if any solutions—beyond me being understanding—exist to help Jayden overcome his fears.

Ones that I could possibly google.

Preferably sooner rather than later.

33

JAYDEN

"**O**kay, boy." Mojo's leash dangles from my hand. He's got that happy expression he always gets when he figures we're going for a walk. "I need to go for a run." *Badly*.

And just like that, the happy expression flees, Mojo whimpers, and his ass crashes to the floor.

"Ah c'mon, Mojo. You know you love running."

He gives me those big brown eyes that Isabelle melts over, but which are currently calling me on my bullshit.

"Please." I'm not beneath pleading my case when it comes to my best friend.

My furry best friend.

Pleading my case when it comes to Isabelle isn't getting me too far.

The doorbell rings, and Mojo's happy expression returns. His ass lifts from the floor, tail wagging, and he eagerly waits for the door to open, ever hopeful the unexpected guest is of the dog-fussing variety.

I open the door. Liam's gaze travels down my body, taking in my T-shirt, running shorts, Nike running shoes, and the lack of my sling. It's currently taking a break on the kitchen table. "I don't suppose you've seen a physician in the last hour and a half, and he's okayed you for a run."

I inwardly cringe. "I haven't had a chance yet, but I'm sure he'd be okay with it."

My biceps twinges, disagreeing with my assessment. And the ache that has been behaving for the past few hours returns with full vengeance.

Liam doesn't miss the grimace on my face and grunts a disbelieving sound.

"I'm not going far. I just need to run."

I open the door wider so he can enter. Liam pets Mojo's head. "Look, I get why you need to go for a run."

I assume he's talking to me and not my dog, who prefers napping over running.

He straightens. "But I honestly believe you're wrong about Isabelle. She's smart and knows how to take care of herself. And it's not like I'm sending her into the same situations I send you and the rest of the team. Just like with the rest of you, her skills and experience will dictate her assignments."

"But she'll still be at risk of getting badly injured or killed." The words leave a sour taste in my mouth.

"Everything we do every day puts us at risk. You can't avoid it, regardless of what you do for a living. That's just life."

"Yes, but our job puts us at a greater risk."

Liam doesn't answer right away, knowing that what I'm saying is true. "I know it's tough when you love someone, and you're afraid something terrible will happen and take them from you. We're ex-military. We know that more than anyone. We've all lost someone in battle whom we loved. Deep down that messes with us.

"But you can't let that keep you from loving someone. Because let's face it, that's what this is really about, isn't it? If you weren't in love with Isabelle, you wouldn't have a problem with her new role."

I open my mouth to tell him that's not true, but he's got the don't-even-think-about-bullshitting-me expression on his face. Mojo is giving me the same look, only his is cuter—easier to roll my eyes at.

But not any easier to ignore.

Liam slaps my good shoulder. "Welcome to the club. And as acting president—and up until now the only member—let me give you some advice. The worst thing you can do is let what *you* think is the right thing dictate your relationship. I once made that mistake with Ava, and it cost me ten years with the woman I love. Those are ten years I'll never get back."

I nod because I know the story of what happened when he and Ava were engaged. He'd broken things off with her, believing it was for her own good.

He eyes me in the way my grandfather did, right before he sat me on his lap and shared his pearls of wisdom. Although in that case, it had nothing to do with women.

"Don't let your fears keep you from the woman who loves you," Liam says. "The one woman who understands how important your job is to you and accepts it as part of who you are. And don't make the same mistake all those women in your past made by repeating it with Isabelle."

He crosses his arms, daring me to argue otherwise.

"Are you done lecturing me?"

"Depends."

"On what?"

"If you listened to a single word I said and are planning to make things right."

Apparently, that's not all he has to say on the subject. "You and Isabelle work great together. But I can't partner you up if you're too preoccupied with her safety and it takes your head out of the game. So the next step is up to you. What's it going to be?"

"Can I get back to you on that?"

"Take all the time you need. Because like I said before, you aren't taking a step in the field until your arm is fully healed. And I'm expecting a signed doctor's note before I reinstate you." He looks down at Mojo. "Make sure he doesn't go running."

Mojo barks in reply.

"Good." To me, he says, "Figure out what you want to do about you and Isabelle, and let me know. I need to go coordinate things with our FBI contacts when it comes to Orlov."

He strokes Mojo's head one last time and turns to leave. "As soon as I find out what's going on with the mission, I'll let you know. And in the meantime, let that goddamn arm heal."

I shut the door behind him. "So what do you think, Mojo? Do I ignore that I'm in love with her, or do I accept that she's going to put her life at risk and just suck it up because I can't live without her?"

Mojo barks, telling me not to be a stupid idiot. There's only one option.

"Yep, that's what I thought, too."

34

ISABELLE

After the last few days I've been having, there's only one thing left to do...

I remove my hot air popcorn popper from the lower cupboard and pour the kernels into the chamber. Some girls eat ice cream when they're having a bad day or dealing with a bad breakup. For me, I prefer popcorn and a movie.

Preferably something with some major kickass action. Humor is always an added bonus.

I turn on the popper. Less than a minute later, the doorbell chimes—which I barely hear over the noise of the hot air circulating in the machine. Since I've got a few minutes before the kernels start popping, I leave it running and go to the front door.

I peer through the peephole and gasp at the tall hotness standing on the front stoop. My heart swoons—much to my annoyance—and I open the door.

"Hi, what are you doing here?" This isn't the first time Jayden has shown up unannounced, but given that we're at an impasse when it comes to his feelings about my job promotion, he's the last person I was expecting to see.

His gaze does a quick sweep of my body, lingering on my breasts for a beat longer than considered gentlemanly. His eyes darken—and I'm instantly reminded that I'm wearing my Hello Kitty pajamas, with the thin, faded T-shirt and sleep shorts.

And no bra.

My face heats up, even though he has already seen me naked. And then it fires up even more as the memory wiggles in of what we were doing the last time he saw me that way.

His gaze flicks to my face. "Movie night?"

"How did you know?" That's when I notice the sound of popping kernels behind me.

I open the door wider and let him in. Without waiting for a reply, I head for the kitchen. The front door clicks shut, and I sense him following me.

"What movie?"

"*Die Hard.*" Like I said, I'm in the mood for a movie with lots of ass-kicking, and you can't do better than *Die Hard* for that.

There's a smile in Jayden's voice when he says, "I don't suppose you're making enough popcorn for me, too?"

"Is that your way of saying you want to watch the movie?"

"It's my way of saying we need to talk, and I'm hoping you'll let me watch the movie with you afterward." He attempts to steal a handful of popcorn from the bowl.

I bat his hand away. "It depends on what you want to talk about."

"I want to talk about us. You and me."

The popcorn continues popping merrily away, oblivious to the tension between us. I don't mean the sexual tension that has sizzled at the edges for as long as I can remember. It's the tension of the unknown, not knowing what he wants to talk about, not knowing if I'm going to be happy with what he has to say.

"What about you and me?"

The words echo in my head, accompanied by my pulse pounding loudly in my ears.

Jayden turns off the popper. "I'm in love with you, Isabelle."

"As you've already mentioned," I say, bracing for the worst.

"And the thought of not being with you, of us just being friends and colleagues, isn't working well for me."

I know what he means. The idea of never being in his arms again is about as appealing as eating a handful of slimy, squirmy bugs.

Maybe even less so.

But he knows my stance when it comes to working with the team, and that won't change. I trust Jayden—trust him with my life. Trust him not to turn his back on me like his ex-fiancée did to him. Like my father did to my mother. But it's not enough.

I don't say anything. There's no point.

I know where this is headed. We're on a Ferris wheel, traveling around and around and around, but never really going anywhere.

He strokes his thumb against my cheek as if to memorize my features. "I don't like the idea of you risking your life." I stiffen under his touch. "But I'm also not interested in dictating what you can or cannot do. I just want to be the man you come home to. The man who plans to spend every moment of his life loving you—if you'll let me."

For a moment, all I'm capable of is blinking as his words replay in my head, searching for a hidden meaning. "You won't stand in my way when it comes to the job?"

"No, I won't. I'll be the one watching your back—like I would for any of the guys. The only difference is at the end of the day, I'll get to make love to you."

The corners of my mouth twitch. "Not interested in making love to them, huh?"

"Definitely not. I'm not saying that watching you risk your life will be easy. I'll make mistakes. I'll probably say stupid things from time to time. And I give you permission to kick me in the ass for doing that. But give me a chance to prove I'm a man of my word."

This time my mouth does more than twitch at the corners. It breaks into a soft smile. "I know you're a man of your word." That sentence has so many meanings, but I leave it at that. "Which is why I'll give you a chance, a trial period."

"And if I fail, you'll return me for a full refund?"

I laugh at his smug tone—the tone that says he's not going to fail. "Yes, something like that."

As soon as the last word has fallen, his mouth is on mine. It's a hungry kiss, but it's also tender. His lips move with mine in a soulful dance. Giving as much as they take. Tasting. Worshiping.

His arm goes around me. Mine go around his neck. "Did you mean it when you said the part about making love?" I ask. It's only been a few days since he caressed me, stoked the fire in my veins.

But it feels like a lifetime ago.

"Absolutely."

"Can we skip the movie and popcorn for a bit so you can live up to your promise?"

He lightly presses his lips to mine. "That's definitely a possibility."

I thread my fingers with his and lead him to my bedroom.

Light from the setting sun glows softly in my room, peering through the narrow gap in the gauzy white fabric that covers the window.

Jayden kisses the length of my jaw, each touch of his lips burning a path along my skin.

I unfasten the top button of his jeans, brushing my pinkie finger against his hardening length. He sucks in a soft breath.

The last time we had sex, it was rough and urgent. A compilation of an adrenaline rush after Jayden and Blake took down the two men who had kidnapped Landon and me, along with the adrenaline coursing through me from the argument Jayden and I had.

This time it's not adrenaline that drives us. It's something deeper.

This time the hunger we feel is like nothing I've experienced before. And because of that, we're not in a rush to rip off each other's clothes.

This time it's about discovering and exploring. It's about giving the other person pleasure and taking the time to get there.

Jayden moves to unfasten his sling.

"Aren't you supposed to keep wearing that?" I ask, already knowing the answer, whether he tells it to me or not.

"I'll put it back on afterward. But I want to make love to you, Isabelle, and I can't do that with the sling on. Not the way I want to."

"You promise you'll put it on again?"

"I promise." He tosses it to the side.

He then places his hand on my hip. The other shifts to cover my breast. The heat of his palm soaks through the fabric of my T-shirt, and a small whimper escapes me.

His thumb skims over my nipple, applying just enough pressure to tease. His gaze isn't on his hand and what it's doing to me. His heated eyes are locked on mine, watching my reaction—pushing me closer to the edge on the intensity alone.

My lips part slightly; my heart beats loud in my chest. Jayden's pulse flutters wildly in his neck, the speed matching that of my own.

He continues teasing me, in no rush to take things further. Patience seeps away, and I lean into his palm. His fingers move, and he pinches my nipple, sending a shot of need and liquid heat between my legs. I moan.

"Christ, Isabelle, I want to taste you so bad. I want to see you naked." With that simple request, he has me out of my clothes in record time, aided by my eager hands.

A minute later, I'm not the only naked one. I make sure of that. My fingers trace along the ridges of his stomach, his shirt now on the floor.

He nods at the bed, indicating for me to get on it. I make myself comfortable in the middle and grin as he crawls over to me like a panther stalking his prey.

Every part of him is a study of perfection. His long, lean muscles, his light-brown skin glowing in the setting sun, the ridges and valleys of his sculptured chest and abs, his sinewed arms and legs.

The only flaws are the battle scars obtained while in the military and while working for Liam. But they just add to his perfection—symbols of what he stands for.

Protecting his country and the freedoms we hold dear.

Protecting his colleagues, his brothers in arms.

Protecting those he loves.

Protecting the innocent.

God, you're beautiful.

"Most men aren't into being called beautiful." Amusement dances in his eyes.

Oops. "Did I really say that out loud...or can you now read my mind?"

"I definitely can't read your mind."

"Ahh, so the first option. And you *are* beautiful. To me. In a very manly way, of course." I grin, and my gaze drops to his hard cock, proud and erect.

I reach out to touch it. Jayden stops me before I have a chance.

"Not yet, sweetheart. I believe you promised I'd get to taste you first."

"Oh, I did, did I?"

He nods, and the hungry smile he flashes me has my lady bits wet in record time.

I spread my legs, creating space for him to fit. He cups the backs of my knees and spreads me wider. His hungry gaze turns even hungrier.

Never in all the years we've been friends have I imagined seeing him this way. For me.

He reverently kisses a path along the length of my inner thigh. My heart squeezes at how, because he loves me, this erotic moment between us feels so different, so breathtaking.

So right.

He reaches my sex and gently parts my lips. His tongue runs along one side of my seam to my core, giving it extra attention, flicking and swirling against it...and I almost shoot off my bed. *Oh God, the wonderful Almighty.*

My eyes squeeze shut against the powerful sensation trembling through me. Jayden chuckles, the sound vibrating against my clit. Which doesn't help the situation. I writhe and moan, unable to stay still.

He settles his hand on my hip, keeping me in place, then gifts the other side of my sex to the same delightful treatment. This gets the same response out of me, my hips jerking, although not as much as before, due to his hand keeping me steady.

I could so get used to this.

His tongue keeps tormenting my clit in the best possible way. I peer down at him. His beautiful head—with his shaved-short black hair—between my legs is the most gorgeous sight I've ever seen.

Unable to resist, I stroke my fingers over his coarse hair.

He looks up at me and smiles, and that smile is what almost does me in. It's tender, but at the same time, it's dirty and naughty.

It's my new favorite smile when it comes to Jayden.

It's one I wouldn't mind seeing every day for the rest of my life.

Jayden continues guiding me further and further to the edge, accompanied by my moans, "*oh, God*"s, and "*yes, like that*"s.

His fingers don't miss out on the fun. They plunge inside me, stretch me, drive me closer to the edge. Between his talented fingers and his equally gifted tongue, I'm on a runaway train. Destination: Ecstasy Valley.

And I've zoomed past the point of no return.

With one final flick of Jayden's tongue, a white-hot light surges through me, flooding every cell in my body, temporarily wiping out reality.

My inner muscles clench around Jayden's fingers, and his name—a mix of a gasp and a cry—tumbles from my lips.

I'm positive I might have slipped into a coma or unconsciousness, the orgasm that intense, that powerful.

After a moment, reality slowly seeps back into my brain, and I award Jayden with a content smile.

He moves up my body, kissing a path as he travels, igniting the fire in my stomach, my breasts, my neck. Then he kisses me senseless again.

"Do you have any condoms?" he asks, voice husky and hopeful.

I nod and point at the bedside table. He opens the drawer and removes a box that hasn't been used in more than a year.

"You might want to check the expiry date first. I haven't used them in a while."

Looking pretty smug at the news, he does as I suggest, and tells me they're still good. He opens a foil package and quickly slips the condom over his rigid cock.

"How's your arm doing?" I ask.

"Don't worry, it can handle me making love to you multiple times tonight."

I grin. "Multiple?"

"You didn't really want to watch *Die Hard* tonight, did you?"

My grin widens. "Not at all. Compared to sex with you, the movie is highly overrated."

"That's what I thought." Jayden positions himself between my legs, and slowly pushes inside me.

The seven modern-day wonders of the world include the Great Wall of China, Machu Picchu, the Roman Colosseum, and the Taj Mahal.

None of them compare to Jayden buried deep inside me, thrusting and circling his hips, filling every part of me with his red-hot desire.

With his love.

By the time I cry out his name once again, and he grunts out his release, I'm silently praying to anyone who is listening that nothing will happen to this gorgeous man—gorgeous both inside and out.

And that nothing will destroy the thin bond between us, the promise Jayden made to me.

35

JAYDEN

I wake up with my injured arm wrapped around a sleeping Isabelle, her bare back against my naked chest.

And my morning wood pressed against her ass.

The perfect place for it to be.

Better still would be inside her.

And that's exactly where I hope it will be shortly.

Sunlight bleeds into the room through the window. I can't see the alarm clock from where I'm lying, but if I'm to estimate the time, I'd say it's after 9 a.m. I blink the sleep out my eyes, not willing to move just yet. After we made love twice last night, we ate some food.

While naked.

There's nothing more liberating than cooking nude. If Adam and Eve had realized this beforehand, I'm positive they would have tied the snake around the tree and shoved the apple in *its* goddamn mouth.

We also started watching *Die Hard*—again while naked. With Isabelle in my arms.

But that soon evolved into me fingering her while Bruce

Willis began taking down the bad guys. We didn't see much more beyond that.

I'm sure Bruce will understand. The sex was phenomenal.

By the time we finally fell asleep—after another round of lovemaking—it was late.

I lightly kissed Isabelle's shoulder, with no intention of waking her. But if she should stir, I won't be complaining.

"Hi," a sleepy voice says. The owner proceeds to wiggle her ass against my very hard cock. Making it even harder.

Painfully hard.

The best kind of pain...unless it's not dealt with soon.

I lower my hand that's resting against her stomach and slip it between her legs. "You're already hot and wet for me," I say, my breath brushing against her shoulder.

"That might be because I was dreaming."

I circle her clit with my fingers. They slide effortlessly through her slick folds. "What were you dreaming about?"

"You. Doing this."

That response is rewarded with slightly more pressure on her clit. She creates a sound that's a cross between a gasp and a moan, then moves her ass, gently rubbing up and down the length of my cock.

I groan against her shoulder and nip the soft skin there.

From behind me, the opening theme music from *Star Wars* begins playing.

Shit.

My fingers freeze and stop what they were doing. Isabelle's ass does the same.

"Aren't you going to answer that?" she asks, recognizing the meaning behind the music.

"Maybe if we ignore it, they'll go away."

But alas, that's not the case.

The music stops—because the person has been forwarded

to voice mail. A second later, the music starts again, accompa-nied by Elton John's "Rocket Man" from Isabelle's phone.

"That's the song you picked for when work calls you?" I ask, reluctantly rolling away from her and grabbing my phone from the nightstand.

"I happen to love that song."

A fact I already know about her.

I answer my phone the same moment Isabelle does.

"Our informant confirmed that Vadik Orlov plans to escape the US today," Liam tells me without so much as a *Hi, how's it going? Hope I'm not interrupting the hot sex you and Isabelle would be having if it weren't for me calling you right now.*

Fuck. If Orlov leaves, it's highly likely he'll disappear from both the FBI's and CIA's radars. And then he'll sneak back into the country and create more havoc than he's already caused.

"Not only that," Liam adds, "but Bernard Bradshaw jumped bail and has gone missing. So it's possible he could be joining Orlov."

The doorbell rings from down the hall. Isabelle makes no move to get out of bed to see who it is.

"I need you both at The Warehouse within thirty minutes."

Because we can't exactly keep our weapons and ammo lying around the office, the stash is under high security in a building on the outskirts of town.

The doorbell rings again. This time for longer, as if someone has their finger held against it.

Isabelle scoots off the bed and hastily grabs her clothes from the floor.

"We'll be there," I say, before remembering that Liam has no idea I'm here with her.

But from the muffled noise on his end, it's clear none of the guys are surprised by my comment.

The doorbell continues its frantic ringing. Isabelle, now in her sleep shorts and T-shirt, races out the door before I can say anything.

The sensation of a million ants crawling over my body has me tossing my phone on the covers while scrambling out of bed. I quickly yank on my jeans, grab my phone, and chase after her.

"Wait," I tell her. At this point, even the doorbell seems exasperated by the person pushing on the button. "Let me answer it."

"I am capable of answering my own door." She peers through the peephole. "It's okay. It's Henri and Liza." She unlocks the door and pulls it open.

Different alarms blare in my head at the sight of the two slightly disheveled, visibly shaken individuals. They both look like they've seen a ghost, their faces as white as one.

"What's wrong?" I ask as they step inside the house.

"It's Josephine," Henri says. "Mr. Bradshaw—"

"The jerk doesn't deserve the title of mister," Liza declares with a grunt.

"What about him?" Isabelle presses.

"He came to talk to your grandmother, something about apologizing for the mix-up that happened with you at the resort."

Now it's my turn to grunt. Not mix-up. Try cover-up.

"She took him to her office to talk to him in private," Liza says. "Because whatever he had to tell her he didn't want to say in front of Henri and me."

"But when she didn't come back outside after thirty minutes, we went to see what was keeping her. That's when we discovered she was gone."

Isabelle stiffens next to me. "She didn't tell you she was going anywhere?"

Henri shakes his head. "We asked Juanita if she knew where

your grandmother had vanished to. She had no idea your grandmother had left. Josephine never said anything to her."

"That's when we realized something was wrong. Your grandmother always tells Juanita if she goes anywhere. It's kind of their unspoken rule."

"And there's no way in heaven she would leave without telling us. She wouldn't leave us on the balcony, waiting for her to return."

"Did you call her cell phone?" Isabelle asks them.

"It went straight to voice mail," Liza says. "I even tried calling her while Henri's driver drove us here. Still no answer."

No sooner has Liza finished telling us this than Isabelle is darting toward her room. She returns a moment later, her phone to her ear. Her gaze lands on me, and she shakes her head. "She's still not answering."

I speed-dial Liam. "We've got a problem."

36

ISABELLE

There have been several occasions in my life when I've been scared.

I'm not talking about seeing an enormous spider on the bathroom ceiling or a venomous snake (neither which is pleasant, if you ask me).

The first time I was scared was when I heard that my parents were divorcing. The second was when my mother was dying.

And the third time was when Orlov's henchmen kidnapped me.

But none of those combined equals the fear that surged through my veins after Henri and Liza told me what happened to my grandmother.

"Do we have any idea where they've taken her?" I ask the team, as Jayden and I enter the office at The Warehouse. On the drive over, I shoved the fear aside. There's no time for it now. I need to focus on the mission and not on how I'll hug my grandmother to death once we've rescued her.

Right—maybe death isn't the best word under the circumstances.

Liam turns to the huge board behind him, which is covered with several large maps and numerous pictures of guys I wouldn't want to meet in a dark alley at any time of day.

"We've pinpointed their center of operation to be here." He points to a black pushpin on the map of Berkley. "But we don't know if Bernard is there or at this location." He gestures to a green pin on the map of Sacramento. "So far neither Orlov, Bernard, nor your grandmother has been spotted at either locale.

"Which means there could be another hideout we don't know about. Somewhere that has allowed the Orlov family to operate under the nose of the Feds while they've focused their time and resources on the two known sites."

"Is there a chance he might have taken her somewhere else?" Landon asks me.

I study the maps of the three cities—including San Francisco—and the map that encompasses all three cities and the surrounding area. "If all those photos in his office are anything to go by, Bernard is sentimental." That, or he's just a show-off when it comes to the celebrities he knows. I'm hoping it's the former when it comes to locating my grandmother. "Which means there's a good chance he took her someplace that means something to them both."

"Because he's hoping to lure you and me back," Jayden finishes for me. I nod.

"So where did he take her?" Adam asks.

"I have no idea." I think for a second, mentally visualizing the photos of the two of them that are in his office. "The picture in his office," I say to Jayden, urgency racing in my voice and in my blood. "The one where they had their first date together."

"The winery?"

I nod. "That's the one. It was in Napa Valley." *Shit*, what was it called again? "Enchanted something." Like the Disney movie.

Jayden thinks for a moment before blurting, "It was in

Oakville," at the same time as I say, "Springs."

The other men watch us expectantly, waiting for us to puzzle it out.

"Enchanted Spring Winery in Oakville. That's where Bernard took my grandmother for their date," I tell them.

"But wouldn't the owners wonder why he's holding Josephine at gunpoint?" Adam throws me an apologetic look.

I shrug—more for the apology than the question.

"*Christ.*" Connor rushes over to his laptop on the conference table behind us and taps away at the keyboard. "I missed it the first time I did a background search on him because I didn't know exactly what I was looking for. And he was trying to keep the IRS from discovering the truth, too. He co-owns the winery. And I bet you can't guess who his partner is?"

"Vadik Orlov?" Landon ventures.

"Yes and no. The title is under the name of Chloe Reinhart. Reinhart is her mother's name after she remarried Bernard's stepson. Chloe is Vadik's granddaughter. The stepson went missing twenty years ago, and no one knows what happened to him."

Liam looks at the map again. "That has to be it. Okay, Connor and Jayden, you go in the van. And remember, Jayden, you're sitting this one out. You're backup for Connor if he needs it and that's it."

"Which means I'm babysitting you," Connor says on a chuckle. "Keep your hands to yourself. No touching the technology."

"Adam and Landon, you'll come with me." Liam turns toward the office door.

"What about me?" I ask.

Walking to the door, he pivots toward me. "This is your grandmother..." he says as if that's an excuse for what he's going to say next.

"I know—which is why I need to be there with you guys.

Look, before you tell me that I'm too emotionally involved and won't be of any use, let me say that's a load of horse poop. And you know it. Yes, he's got my grandmother, but that doesn't change anything. I need to do my job. This isn't just about my grandmother. It's about something bigger. It's about bringing these guys down before they can hurt anyone else."

"All right, you're with Landon, Adam, and me. Okay, let's load up."

PUSHING A FEW SPEED LIMITS, WE ARRIVE AN HOUR LATER, NOT far from our destination. Liam and Connor park where we can't be easily spotted, and where video cameras are less likely to be set up. Liam's government contacts have been appraised of the situation.

I grab my body armor and my gun from the back of Adam's SUV.

Jayden watches helplessly from the sidelines. I can't tell if he's frustrated at not being part of the action, or because he's not as okay as he said he would be with my involvement in the operation.

The man looks ready to go for a hard run—his go-to coping mechanism, along with riding his bike.

"Let me help," he says as I get ready to hook myself up to the radio. He picks up the earpiece and slips it into position. His fingers then sweep along the shell of my ear and down my neck, sending delicious shivers through me.

Concern and fear reside in his eyes, but they're only a shadow of the emotions in his gaze. Pride and love shine back at me...along with a spark of fire.

The fire I recognize from when he's turned-on.

I laugh softly. "Just keep thinking those horny thoughts, and before you know it, you and I'll be making good on them tonight."

"I'm counting on it."

I give him a quick kiss, nothing more than the brief press of our lips.

"Landon and Isabelle, you go that way." Liam points down the dirt road we're parked on. A grove of trees lines one side of the stretch of empty road. On the other, barbwire separates us from the vineyards. "Isabelle, listen to whatever Landon tells you. You're not to take any risks. And that has nothing to do with Jayden wanting to castrate me if anything should happen to you."

"I'm sure Ava will have something to say about that if he tries," Adam deadpans.

I nod, fully understanding what's at stake here—and I don't mean Liam's man parts.

"Adam and I will take the other direction," Liam says.

And with that, the four of us set off, doing our best to be inconspicuous.

"Is there any word yet if Vadik or Nikolai Orlov have been located?" Liam's question comes through the earpiece and is directed to Connor and Jayden.

"Nothing yet," Jayden says. "As far as the FBI can tell, neither man has slipped out of the country yet."

"Which probably means they have," Adam says. "There's always the chance the mobilization of his men is to distract the FBI from noticing either bastard has already left the country."

"Or to distract them from realizing Vadik never intends to leave the country. He's moved to another part of it instead."

I scan the area for signs that Bernard is on to us. The trees are too narrow to hide behind, the branches too thin to hold a grown man, which, fortunately, makes it more challenging for anyone to be stalking Landon and me.

"I don't think this place was designed to be the fortress that Orlov's businesses are," Landon says. "It really does look like nothing more than a winery, which means high-tech security won't be an issue for us. Our only concern is the bodyguards that might have tagged along."

"I don't suppose we have any idea how many that might be?" I ask.

"There's no way for us to know for sure until we come face-to-face with them, and that's never the ideal situation."

We walk for fifteen or so minutes before coming across a metal gate that's wide enough for trucks to access the property.

Landon checks that the gate isn't electrified. "They don't even have security cameras set up."

Which is great news for us.

Once he's happy we can proceed without being turned into tonight's barbecue, Landon unlatches the gate, and we squeeze past it.

With guns still drawn, we keep to the fence, a mess of barb-wire and vines. It would be better if we were doing this under the cover of night, but we can't wait that long.

For a second, I let in the thought of what Bernard or Orlov could currently be doing to my grandmother. Imagination is a dangerous thing. Just ask any kid who is positive the boogieman lives under their bed.

You become so focused on that, it steals your attention from where it should be—which in this situation isn't a brilliant idea.

As we move past a row of vines, two buildings come into view ahead of us: One is large and long like a barn, but Mediterranean in design. The other building also captures the Mediterranean feel but is smaller. Even though I can't see the front of the building, I'm positive the fountain from Bernard's photo is still there.

Both buildings were created to be seen, not to remain

hidden from the world. People come here for wine-tasting events.

The buildings aren't where you bring people you've abducted.

To the side of the smaller building, a portion of the parking lot is visible, the rest obscured due to our angle. It's unclear how many vehicles are in it, and how many belong to customers merely enjoying an afternoon at the winery.

"There's a black truck parked in front of the larger building." Landon pulls a pair of small binoculars from his pocket and reads the license plate number for Connor to look up.

A moment later he comes back with a name: Gabrielle Mendez.

Jayden's string of curse words shoulders its way through my earpiece.

"It's a common name," I say, quickly recovering from the shock. "It might not even be her."

There's a momentary pause. "No, it's definitely her. Connor pulled up her driver's license photo."

"Damn, she takes a hot photo," Connor says under his breath. His voice isn't as clear as Jayden's was.

"I'm no expert on wineries," I say, ignoring him, "but my guess is that the larger building is where they make the wine. Do you think my grandmother is in there?"

None of the men answer because this isn't the time for speculation.

"We're approaching from the other side." A moment later, Liam reads out the other license plate numbers.

Two are registered with men who have links to Vadik Orlov. One is listed to Tyler Mathews. I guess that answers which mobster he's connected to. The other three cars are registered to individuals who have no known links to Orlov.

"Regina and Dennis are listed as employees of the winery," Connor says. "The owner of the fifth vehicle isn't associated with either the Orlov family or the winery. Whoever was in the car might simply be customers."

"The question is, has Regina or Dennis seen Isabelle's grandmother?" Adam asks. "And do they even know why she's here?"

"I would like to know where Olov's men are currently located." The tension in Jayden's voice is tighter than a glued-on jam jar lid.

"I'd like to know that, too," Liam says. "Scorpio and Lady-bird, do you any visuals?"

"Nothing from where we are," I say. "But we can easily approach the larger building without being seen and check inside."

"Ten-four. Firecracker and I will hold our position in the meantime."

Landon and I make our way to the target. The side door is locked, as is the barn door in the front.

We continue our perimeter search and locate several windows about five feet from the ground, overlooking the low mountain range in the distance. Any other time, I would've stopped to enjoy it. Any other time, I would've considered the view breathtaking.

The window nearest us is opened partway. Landon and I inch closer to it, barely breathing.

"I'm going to check on what's keeping Vadik," a male voice, which I recognize as Bernard's, says.

"And I'm really sorry now that I dated you." Granny's voice is stiff. Uppity.

"That deeply wounded me." Except the last thing the old man sounds is wounded. More like amused. Which makes me wonder just how much of the soulmate gibberish he talked about the day Jayden and I first met him he actually believes in.

"I somehow doubt it. And since when did you associate with mobster trash?"

I guess he doesn't feel like dignifying that with a response. A moment later, the door clicks open and shut.

"Well, as nice as this tour is," Granny says in a tone I recognize. It's her I'm-getting-a-little-peeved-here-but-I'll-still-be-a-lady-about-it tone.

I wince—not because she's in trouble.

But because whoever's in the room with her is about to meet their reckoning.

"What the fuck?" Gabrielle's voice is a shriek that I'm surprised doesn't shatter the glass on this side of the building.

"Language, young lady." My grandmother's tone has switched to that of a schoolmistress from a century ago. I almost expect her to assign Gabrielle detention, or whatever it is they did in those days.

Landon and I exchange looks; then I cautiously peer through the window.

My grandmother and Gabrielle are in an office with a bar on the wall opposite the grand oak desk. And from the looks of it, red wine is dripping down Gabrielle's face and has stained her white sundress. My grandmother is holding an empty wineglass in her hand.

No one else is in the room.

Why the heck is Granny drinking wine?

Gabrielle wipes the wine out of her eyes. "What the fuck did you do that for?"

"You honestly didn't believe I would ask for a glass of wine to celebrate you kidnapping me, did you?"

Gabrielle appears taken aback by the question—like that's exactly what she thought.

"I didn't kidnap you. You came willingly with Bernard."

"When your ex-boyfriend tells you that he's going to kill your granddaughter unless you go with him, I'd hardly call that 'willingly.' Would you, Miss Mendes?"

Gabrielle appears not to have an answer for that.

"So what do you get out of all this?" Granny asks her.

"That's none of your business."

"Sure, it is. When it comes to my life, it's very much my business. Besides, what else will we talk about until those not-so-charming men return?"

I want to update the rest of the team on what's going on, but we can't risk Gabrielle overhearing us. And given Liam's team's radio silence, they might be in the same position we're in—unable to communicate without the risk of being discovered.

Even Jayden and Connor are silent, awaiting our reports.

"Are you doing this for love or for money?" Granny asks.

Gabrielle doesn't answer, but whatever is on her face is the only answer Granny needs.

"Please don't tell me you're in love with Bernard. Because, darling, you can do so much better than that old man."

Gabrielle snorts a laugh. "*That* old man is the same age as you."

"I never claimed to be a spring chickadee," my grandmother says with an indignant huff I know to be faked. She's a brilliant actress, but I know her too well. "But you are in love, no?"

Again, Gabrielle doesn't answer.

"It's not that boorish lawyer, is it? Tyler whatshisname?"

Gabrielle makes an *as-if* sound.

"Is he at least young and handsome?" Granny presses. "Oh, you simply have to tell me. I'm not getting out of this alive, so you might as well entertain me before I die."

"You won't die...not unless you don't cooperate."

Granny raises her chin slightly. "Maybe I don't want to cooperate. Maybe I'm happy to go down in history after dying in this great adventure. People are more likely to remember my name if I die at the hands of the mafia than if I die from a stroke. One will make me legendary, the other will leave me no different than any other star who died of old age."

She provides a dramatic pause before adding, "So tell me all about this love of your life. We have no idea how long we're going to be waiting, and I'm an old lady who has to live vicariously through others. Especially since it's been a long time since my dear sweet Philip died."

Philip? Grandad's name was Patrick.

She knows, a voice in the back of my head tells me. *She knows I'm here.*

"I mean if you're not going to tell me about your great love, then leave me be. Perhaps I could work on my knitting or cross-stitch." An impish expression crosses her face, which Gabrielle doesn't see because she's not looking in her direction. "Is the man you're in love with married or committed to someone else? That always makes for a juicy scandal."

Gabrielle swivels in her direction.

Granny flashes her a sympathetic, pitying look. "Don't worry. It's not you. Men are silly creatures. They tend to miss what's right in front of them. I'm sure the other woman in his life doesn't measure up to you."

I almost laugh out loud at the sincerity in her voice and on her face. The woman deserves an Academy Award for her performance.

Granny seems to have nailed it when it comes to whatever's going on with the man in Gabrielle's life. Gabrielle's shoulders shift slightly, in a move of resignation.

And *this* is who was teaching the sessions on how to have a happy and sexually fulfilling marriage?

Was she always hovering around Jayden and me during them because she knew we weren't married and was putting us on the spot on purpose?

I mean, sure, the outcome worked out great for Jayden and me, but she wouldn't have known that at the time.

"So who is this mystery man?" Granny asks softly.

"No one you know."

"Which means there's no harm in telling me. Is he here at the winery?"

Gabrielle shakes her head.

"Did you know he wasn't coming here? Or were you hoping for a brief interlude with him? A stolen kiss?"

That final line of questioning does the trick. "He's the grandson of the man responsible for bringing you here." *Nikolai Orlov? Is that the grandson she's referring to?* "And yes, I thought he was going to be here. But instead, his grandfather showed up."

"Is he married or committed to someone else?" The words are spoken gently, without judgment.

"Not that I know of. The committed part. I know he's not married." Gabrielle lets out a heavy sigh. "Maybe he really hasn't noticed I'm alive."

"Or perhaps he has, but he plays infield for the other team."

Despite the situation and her heartbroken revelation, Gabrielle chuckles. "I believe that's bats for the other team."

"That's so clichéd, and if there's one thing I'm not, it's a cliché."

She's right about that...in so many different ways.

I study the window, but there's no way for Landon and me to enter this way without Gabrielle noticing. A slight edge of helplessness leaks in. I hastily plug up the hole, barricading myself against all defeating emotions.

Apparently Granny has her own plans. While Gabrielle pours her heart out about the love of her life, who doesn't seem to notice she exists, Granny inches her way to the bar.

Gabrielle turns her back on her, long enough for Granny to grab a bottle of wine from the bar and swing it high above her head...

37

JAYDEN

"Are you getting anything?" I ask Connor. We've been sitting in the van for the past ten minutes without a single peep from the team.

It's not unusual for the guys to go radio silent when they're unable to communicate without giving away their positions. The last thing you want is for the bad guys to stumble across you because you're yapping like a bunch of old geese.

But even when that happens, Connor can still hear something, even if it's only sounds coming from the team's surroundings or the heavy breathing in reply to a question they can't respond to.

Except in this case, none of that has been true. He's been asking them for some sort of signal that everyone is okay, but all we've received in return is dead air.

And that's not good.

Somehow, our radio signals have been blocked. If that's the case, it means the two teams might not be able to communicate with each other, either.

Neither knows what the other team is doing or where they are located.

And that's not helpful.

At times, it can be damn dangerous.

"Still nothing," Connor says.

My phone rings. I check the screen and answer it.

"We're nearing your location," Blake informs me. "ETA is five minutes."

I called Blake and Virginia forty minutes ago, to inform them about what's going on. They're now part of the task force to take Orlov and his crime family down.

We end the call.

Helplessness slithers through me. I climb out of the van and begin pacing. The radio silence is like being in a dark building—without even a snatch of moonlight to guide the way. You're forced to navigate through the maze, unable to see or hear.

I don't like not knowing what's going on.

I don't like not knowing if Isabelle is in danger.

She's with Landon, I remind myself. *He won't let anything happen to her.* Just like he won't let anything bad happen to any of the team.

The voice doesn't say anything about how Isabelle shouldn't be in there. It stays silent, aware that she can take care of herself.

That's why I love her.

That's why I respect her choice to be an operative like the rest of the team.

But it doesn't mean I'm not going to worry about her.

I am human, after all. I'm not a robot.

A black SUV pulls up the dirt road where we're parked. Blake and Virginia climb out, and I get them up to speed on the radio communication issue.

Connor and I show them the map of the property and identify the locations from where the two teams last communicated with us.

"Have you identified yet if the other car belongs to a customer?" Virginia asks.

"As far as we are aware, that's all she is. We haven't had any communications with our team for the past fifteen minutes, so we don't know who is still on the property and if they're okay."

"Has Josephine Berkshire been located yet?"

"That's a negative with the last communications we received," I tell them, "but we have no idea if she's been found since then and by whom. All we know is that Gabrielle's truck was parked in front of what could possibly be the winery itself. The last I heard from any member of the team, it hadn't been ascertained at that point if she or Josephine were in the building."

"All right," Blake says. "This is your game. How do you want to play it?"

38

ISABELLE

"**S**hit," Landon says as Gabrielle slumps to the ground after Granny hit her with the wine bottle. "I want a grandmother like yours."

I grin at him. "She is pretty kickass, isn't she?"

Gabrielle will have quite the headache when she wakes up. On the bright side, she'll get to skip the hangover.

"But I'll admit," I say to him, "having an entire bottle of wine would knock me out, too."

We get to work on rescuing my grandmother. Landon tries to tell the guys that we've located her, but his voice goes out to dead air. He frowns. "What the hell?"

"Has that happened before?"

He shakes his head. "No, this is a first."

Granny opens the window farther and removes the bug screen. Landon gives me a boost up.

I pull myself all the way in, with Granny's help, and tumble to the floor. Then I check on Gabrielle. She's still unconscious, but who knows how long that will last?

While Landon hoists himself through the window—thanks

to his thick muscles and years of training with the SEALs—I search for something to tie Gabrielle up with.

Luckily for us—not so fortunate for Gabrielle—the person who uses this office has handcuffs in the desk drawer.

"Do I want to know what those are for?" Landon asks.

"Well, considering there's also a red silk tie in the drawer where I found them..." I leave the rest of the sentence hanging, letting him fill in the blanks for himself.

Gabrielle isn't visibly bleeding from the head, and her pulse and breathing aren't erratic, but she'll definitely need medical attention as soon as possible.

Between the two of us, Landon and I manage to gag her and handcuff her to the desk. I check her pupils. They're evenly dilated, and both constrict when exposed to my penlight.

"Is she going to be okay?" Granny whispers.

"Probably. But better her being out cold than getting us killed." I hug my grandmother. "You did great."

"Now you know where you inherited your super-spy skills," she says with a wink.

"Do you know if there's anyone outside your door?" Landon asks her.

"I have no idea. I only saw one man who looked like some sort of security guard. I doubt the lawyer who was with Vadik Orlov would stand around and watch the door. He didn't seem the type."

"What about Orlov? Any idea where he is?" I ask.

"I overheard him say something about talking to some customers, but I have no idea what they were talking about. I got the idea during the drive here that this winery is really a front for something else."

"You're lucky Bernard is a sentimental fool, and we figured out where he brought you," I tell her. "Otherwise, we wouldn't have known where to find you."

"It wasn't luck. He knew you'd figure it out. Or at least he hoped you were smart enough to figure it out."

I glance at the door, expecting someone to come bursting through it now that she's revealed that tidbit.

"You mean this is a trap?" Landon asks.

"I think so. Which means you've got to get out of here before they return. Where's Jayden?"

"In the hidden surveillance van."

Granny releases a long breath, her shoulders sagging slightly. "That's good. Now we just need to get you out of here." Her gaze is directed at me when she says it.

"We're not going anywhere without you."

"You have to, Isabelle. You're the bait. Without you, they can't get to Jayden."

"What are you talking about?" Landon asks.

"That's all I know. I don't know the details, but Jayden did something in the past that bit Vadik in the mobster-butt. And he's not happy about it. It was just dumb luck for him that Bernard knew me well enough to call in a favor. It's been Jayden all along that Vadik's wanted."

"It's going to be okay," I tell her. "Nothing's going to happen to him. He's safe in the van." Thank God for that.

My heart beats fast, a bird fluttering its wings inside my chest, rattling the cage bars.

He's going to be okay. He's going to be okay....

As long as no one goes looking for Connor's van, Jayden will be safe.

Us on the other hand...

Landon presses his ear to the door and listens for a minute. He draws his gun and points at the wall, indicating for us to stay close to it. Then he twists the doorknob and cautiously opens the door.

He checks to see if the coast is clear and gestures for us to follow him. Granny is behind him. I bring up the rear, keeping an eye on our surroundings. Whoever was guarding Granny's room didn't bother to stick around. They must have wrongly assumed that Granny was no match for Gabrielle.

Which is good news for us.

The entire corridor contains nothing but giant wooden barrels lined up on either side of the space. Anyone could be hiding between them, and we wouldn't realize it until it's too late.

The wooden ceiling above us is steepled. At the far end is what looks like an exit. At the other end are low voices: two males and a female. Something about the female's voice sounds familiar, but all the voices are too low to hear what they're saying.

Well, I'd say it's a no-brainer where we need to go.

Except, Landon doesn't seem interested in heading for the exit. He's listening—and for a fleeting second, fear causes his eyes to flare slightly.

But it's gone just as quickly.

He points at me, and my grandmother, after which, he points at the exit. He wants me to take Granny to safety, but why isn't he planning to come with us?

A third male voice adds to the mix. Jayden's voice. Whatever's going down isn't looking too rosy. And now Landon's decision to stay behind makes sense.

My heart rate kicks up again, my breath follows suit, and the sensation of a giant spider crawling along my skin ambles up my spine.

I look behind me at my grandmother. I need to get her out of here, but if Jayden is in trouble, I can't abandon him. I need to save him...and then ream him out for disobeying Liam's order to stay *in* the van with Connor.

From the expression on Granny's face, it's clear that she also has heard Jayden. And she realizes that not only is Jayden in trouble, Landon wants me to turn my back on the man I love to get her out of here.

She points to herself...and then to the space between the two giant upright barrels standing next to us.

I nod in understanding.

It's not safe for her to go to the exit herself, and we have no idea what's on the other side of the door. So as long as Landon and I don't get ourselves killed, she'll be okay if she stays hidden for now.

She squeezes her body between the two barrels. Once she's hidden, Landon and I creep forward, listening to the conversation around the corner.

"You won't be walking out of here a free man," Jayden says, "so you might as well put down your gun and let her go. Killing a federal agent won't score you any points. The criminal system's funny that way."

So the cavalry is here...so to speak.

Except it doesn't sound like the FBI is doing too hot right now, if what Jayden is saying is any indication.

"Says you," a male voice I don't recognize says. It's an older voice with a strong Russian accent. It's also rough and unperturbed at how things are unfolding.

Mainly because from the sound of things, they're moving more in his favor than they are for the good guys.

For now, anyway.

Landon peers around the massive wine barrel, careful not to be spotted. He straightens. "Vadik has Virginia hostage and is holding a gun to her head." He keeps his voice to slightly above a whisper.

"How many of our guys are with them?" I ask.

"Just Jayden, Virginia, and Blake."

Thanks to the issue we're having with the earpieces, we have no idea what's going on with everyone else. We have no idea if the rest of the team is okay.

"What about the bad guys? How many of those are there?"

"Four. Vadik, Bernard, someone with an extremely thick neck and muscles to match, and a man who looks like he could be Tyler."

"Could be?"

"Let's just say his photo on his firm's website hasn't been updated in a few years."

"What is it you want in exchange for the agent?" Jayden asks, his voice calm and soothing, as if he's trying to lull Vadik to sleep like a baby.

"You," is Vadik's simple answer.

"Me? Is there any particular reason?"

"Because you broke my granddaughter's heart and you will pay for what you did."

"Who's your granddaughter?"

"Suzanna Neumann."

A stunned silence fills the space for a heartbeat. "Wait, you kidnapped Josephine Berkshire because my ex-girlfriend—your granddaughter—cheated on me and broke *my* heart?"

More silence. "My sweet Suzanna would never harm a soul." Unlike her grandfather, apparently.

"Well, she did, while I was serving in the military. I was away and she was screwing a close friend of mine at home....So let me get this straight. All this, Bernard luring Isabelle and me to his resort, kidnapping Isabelle, and then kidnapping Josephine is all because you believed I had cheated on Suzanna?"

"No—not entirely. I vas angry that you and your little band of warriors put a wrench in our scheme to escape the country a few weeks ago. When I learned from Bernard Bradshaw about your connection to Isabelle, I decided to shoot for a two-for-one when it comes to revenge."

"Taking the bad guys down is our job. Just like your job

seems to be doing illegal activities so law enforcement is kept busy. You're the Ying to our Yang."

Vadik laughs, the sound so deep, I could almost imagine him as Santa at Christmas.

An evil Santa, mind you.

"Did you know I was going to be at the resort or was that a convenient fluke?"

"Maybe a little of both. I discovered that Isabelle's grand-mother once knew Bernard. So I had already made arrangements for him to manipulate things to bring you two to his resort. It vas the least he could do since our family trees are connected in one way or another. But as it turns out, you and the rest of your team were attempting to make my life a nightmare. Unfortunately, the bullet that had your name on it missed its target, and so we continued with the original plan once you showed up at the resort."

What feels like a gun barrel nudges me from behind, and my heart picks up speed, scrambling into my throat.

Oh. Shit.

"Drop your gun," a gruff male voice commands. Don't know what he has to be grumpy about. He's not the one with a gun poking him.

I do what I'm told and lower it to the floor. He nudges me forward, his gun pressed in my back again.

Landon slowly turns around. I mouth, *He's got a gun.* Henchman gives him the same command to drop his weapon. Landon reluctantly places his gun on the ground.

With further prompting from the henchman, Landon and I walk around the barrels to where Jayden and the others are standing. Like where we were a moment ago, giant wooden barrels line the walls of the hallway.

I cringe when Jayden spots me. His worst nightmare is coming true. But given that his situation isn't much better, he can't really complain. The only difference is the gun isn't pointing at his head—it's aimed at Virginia's.

A scary jack-o'-lantern grin breaks out on Vadik's face. "I shouldn't be too surprised you're here, Isabelle, given your grandmother is a guest here."

"Where is she?"

His henchman doesn't say anything, so I assume he hasn't found Gabrielle yet—and has no idea Granny has escaped.

"Don't worry. You'll have your happy little family reunion soon enough." He waves us forward.

Jayden takes a step toward me.

"Don't even think about it, Mr. Price." Vadik redirects the gun at him. My heart, not having succeeded in escaping just yet, jams in my throat, making it difficult to breathe.

I try to swallow it back down.

A movement on top of a barrel near him catches my attention. But whatever it was disappears the moment my gaze darts to it.

There's no time to dwell on it. A loud bang—like a gun firing—comes from the direction Landon, the henchman, and I were a few minutes ago.

I startled. I'm not the only one. Whatever was on the barrel didn't appreciate the loud noise. It comes sailing through the air like a large flying squirrel with the shriek of a banshee.

And lands on Vadik's head.

Vadik does his own shrieking, not expecting the creature's assault.

That's the only distraction we need. Jayden and Blake lurch forward, toward Vadik and Virginia.

I swivel around to confront the henchman, who's no longer paying attention to either Landon or me. He's turning toward the wooden barrel that has seen better days. Wine sprays from a newly formed hole in it, painting the floor in a sea of red.

My gun lies abandoned on the ground, no longer where I'd left it, the wine ocean spilling under it.

A pained moan breaks from the henchman's lips, and he stumbles toward the barrel and the gun.

Landon dives for the weapon. I hurl myself at the man, wrapping my arm around his thick neck.

He's taller and all-around bigger than me, but my unexpected attack throws him off enough that Landon gets to the gun before the henchman can even move a few feet.

I wrap my legs around him, pinning his arms to his side, including the one holding the gun.

He tries to shake me off. He doesn't have much success.

Landon snatches up the gun and levels it at him. "I suggest you put the gun carefully down, and then I'll get Isabelle to release you."

For a second, I fear he's going to ignore Landon and back up, slamming me into a nearby barrel to dislodge me.

Instead, he lets out a defeated sigh and awkwardly places the gun on the floor.

Landon kicks it away.

Behind me, there's a crash of activity and voices. I peer over my shoulder to discover Liam and Adam, along with men in swat gear, streaming into the building.

On the floor near the door is a tabby cat, busy cleaning itself.

I release my hold on the henchman and drop the short distance to my feet. I quickly step away before he has a chance to grab me—if he's stupid enough to try—and find myself engulfed in the familiar arms of Jayden.

Before I can say anything, he spins me around, and his mouth captures mine.

And...I melt into him. Maybe it's partly because of the adrenaline coursing through me, but I can't kiss him enough.

The sentiment seems to be echoed by him. Our kisses are

hungry, tender, consuming, sweet. I'm vaguely aware that we have an audience, but for now, I don't care.

And neither does Jayden.

A wave of applause and hoots and wolf whistles breaks into our moment. It's only then that we reluctantly untangle our tongues and separate enough to look around us.

We're not the only ones who're locked in an embrace. Virginia and Blake appear a little dazed by the onlookers they too had forgotten about until a moment ago.

Jayden releases me. "We should get back to doing our job." He nods toward Granny, who's beaming at me like she did the day I graduated from college.

I hug her hard. "Were you the one responsible for putting the hole in the barrel?" I nod at the one in question. The escaping wine has reduced to a trickle. Most of the barrel's contents are on the floor.

She giggles. "Not intentionally. I kind of pulled the trigger and almost dropped the gun. The poor barrel got in the way of the bullet. May it rest in peace."

I hug her again. "Do me a favor?"

"What's that, darling?"

"Unless you know how to use a gun, how about we leave them to the professionals?"

"Sounds like a good plan." She grins at me again. "Sooo... about Jayden..."

"What about him?"

"I hope this means you two have worked things out between you...and you've both stopped being oblivious fools when it comes to how much you love each other."

Before I can respond, Jayden's healthy arm is around me again, from behind. "Most definitely. You've got your wish, Josephine."

She narrows her gaze at him. "My wish is to be a great-grandmother. I don't suppose your sperm will give me what I want."

He laughs, and I gasp with a horrified "Granny!"

She doesn't appear to care. Her smile widens.

"I'm all for that," Jayden says. "But it's also up to your granddaughter."

"We haven't even discussed getting married one day," I say to no one in particular.

"I'm all for that, too," he murmurs huskily in my ear, much to the delight of my grandmother. She rubs her hands together, mentally planning the wedding and everything else.

I glance over my shoulder at him. "Is that your way of proposing?"

"Don't worry, when I propose, you won't have to ask me if I just proposed, and there won't be FBI agents running around the crime scene."

I chuckle. "Hopefully when you propose, there won't be a crime scene."

"That too."

The next hour is spent with the FBI questioning us about what went down. Bernard and Gabrielle are arrested. By the time the agents found her, she was conscious and a little peeved at finding herself handcuffed to the desk.

Eventually, we're free to go, after the paramedics check Granny over.

"Now, how about I get my two favorite girls home," Jayden says to us both.

As Granny walks away on Landon's arm, Jayden says to me, voice husky again, "I'm especially looking forward to soaking in your bathtub, preferably with you in it. My arm feels like it could use some TLC."

I slap him playfully on his other shoulder, pretending to give him the stink eye. "It wouldn't be if you had done what you were told. Weren't you supposed to stay in the van with Connor?"

"We lost communications with the entire team, and I didn't know what was going on. But if it makes you feel better, I did wait until Blake and Virginia showed up."

"So you didn't really trust that I'd be okay?"

Everything about him positively glows at my question. "Are you kidding? I was dying to watch you take down the bad guys. And I'm happy to do that on a regular basis." He kisses the end of my nose. "*Partner.*"

And then his lips find mine again in a very unprofessional kiss.

EPILOGUE

ISABELLE

Five Months Later

The best thing about Sunday mornings in November?

Staying in bed with my best friend turned boyfriend, Jayden.

Especially after an extra hot and sweaty lovemaking session with him. I'm not sure how much of that can be attributed to the resort, but those sessions with Gabrielle certainly didn't hurt—even if the person conducting them ended up being somewhat of a fraud. The FBI learned that she had a psychology degree, but most of her "educational background" in the area of having a fulfilling marriage and sex life came from magazines—like *Cosmo*—and online articles.

Fun articles like "Ten Sexual Positions Guaranteed to Leave Him Begging for More," "How to Know If Your Spouse Is Cheating," and "Twenty Ways to Spice Up Your Marriage and Your Bedroom."

Apparently, her computer history provided hours of entertainment for the FBI agents investigating her.

But at the end of the day, her stupidity was my gain when it came to Jayden. So other than when she held my grandmother hostage, I really can't complain.

Jayden gives me another long and languid kiss that leaves every cell in my body drunk on satisfaction and need. I moan softly, signaling I'm ready to make love to him again.

But instead of getting my hint, he rolls away from me, tugging at the bedding.

"Hey, where're you going?" I grab at the covers to keep from getting cold now that my personal furnace is vacating the bed. Outside my window, San Francisco is bathed in a dim morning light—made dimmer due to the rain and the clouds blanketing the sun.

"To feed Mojo and take him for a short walk."

Even though Jayden and I still live in two separate houses, we alternate each week whose home we stay in. But even when he spends the night at my house, Mojo comes with him.

I wouldn't have it any other way.

I make a move to get out of bed but don't get very far. Jayden leans over, still in his naked glory, and tenderly kisses me. "Stay where you are. Once I've finished dealing with Mojo, I have every intention of coming back to bed."

"I can make breakfast while you're gone."

He removes his jeans from the floor. "Nope. I've already got that covered."

"Are you sure?"

"Positive."

While he's gone, I check my messages on my phone and read a chapter from the thriller I've been reading. Not that I've had much time to read since Jayden and I became a couple.

I don't mean we've been too busy having sex for me to find the time. I mean, we *have* been busy in that department, but now that we're a couple, we're doing more things together than we were as best friends. And not just the typical couple-related activities like watching movies and going out for dinner.

We've been practicing together at the shooting range, training at Paradise. Hiking. Biking. Running.

Practicing martial arts.

All the fun stuff.

But we've also been cooking together and snuggling on the couch, watching TV, and working on jigsaw puzzles. Only now, to make things more challenging, we do them without the pictures.

By the time I've finished the chapter, the front door clicks open, and I can hear the sounds of my two favorite guys returning home.

This is followed soon after by noises coming from the kitchen. They then stroll into the bedroom. Jayden is carrying a tray with coffee cups, steam rising from them. Mojo has a white paper bag dangling from his mouth, which I recognize. It comes from the bakery in my neighborhood.

"You bought breakfast from Home Sweets Bakery?"

Just add this to the long list of why Jayden is the best boyfriend, ever.

"Possibly." He tells Mojo to give me the bag.

The big goofy dog eyes his tall, handsome owner, and with his tail wagging, presents the bag to me.

Practically drooling, I remove the bag from his mouth. Fortunately, it's free of dog drool. "So what did Jayden get me?" I ask Mojo. "Blueberry or cherry cheesecake muffin?"

Both would be excellent choices.

I open the bag, but instead of a muffin, a small white cardboard box—the kind you put desserts in—is inside.

My smart and sexy and witty boyfriend has brought me something even yummier for breakfast than the typical standard delights.

"What's the special occasion?" I ask, lifting the box out of the bag.

"You'll see."

Without being told, Mojo sits and watches me expectantly, as if waiting for me to share my treat with him.

I open the box and peer inside.

Then gasp.

It's not the slice of my favorite chocolate cake that causes the reaction.

All right, that might have something to do with it...because it is chocolate cake after all.

Jayden's grandmother's vintage engagement ring—the one I wore on the mission—is sitting on the icing. The large teardrop diamond and the tiny embedded diamonds glitter happily at me.

Jayden gets down on one knee, and my darn eyesight becomes blurry.

"Isabelle, you're my best friend and my partner in crime at work, but I'm—"

Mojo—no longer sitting—licks Jayden's face.

Jayden turns to his goofball of a dog. "Do you mind? We're having a moment here?"

I giggle and attempt to blink away the tears while Jayden's distracted.

Mojo whimpers what I'm guessing is an apology and goes back to sitting.

"That's better." Jayden turns to me. "I'm hoping you'll also be my partner in life. Isabelle, will you be my wife?" His hopeful expression is almost my undoing. There's no way I could ever say no to that.

And why would I?

Jayden is everything I could possibly want. He *is* my everything.

Besides, the guy proposed to me with my favorite chocolate cake. This moment couldn't be more perfect.

"I would love to be your wife. More than you can possibly imagine."

Jayden removes the ring from the icing, wipes it with a cloth napkin from the tray, and holds it out to me. I present him my hand, and he slides the ring onto my finger.

It was breathtaking the first time I put it on as part of our cover. But now that I know Jayden loves me—and what the ring symbolizes—my prior feelings toward it pale in comparison to this moment.

It's the most gorgeous thing I've ever seen.

Jayden pushes himself to his feet and joins me on the bed. He tenderly kisses me and brushes my hair from my face. "Christ, I love you."

This time when he kisses me, it's more possessive, but no less tender than before. Our tongues swirl against each other, taking their time to explore. Every part of my body hums with need and love.

The familiar tune from Jayden's phone steals us from our moment—more so when Elton John's "Rocket Man" accompanies it.

Wow. Our boss really knows how to kill a moment.

[TOP SECRET]

AN HOUR LATER, JAYDEN AND I ENTER THE CONFERENCE ROOM. Liam, Connor, Adam, and Landon are waiting for us, all seated around the table.

They watch us expectantly as we walk in together, holding hands.

"She said yes," are the first words out of Jayden's mouth. His excited grin makes my insides go all warm and squishy.

"We told you she would," Liam says, unfolding himself from his chair.

The four men congratulate us. Hugs are exchanged.

"You called us down to see if Jayden went through with the proposal?" I ask. They could've waited until tomorrow if that's the case.

"No, I called everyone in for another reason." Liam gestures for us to take our seats. Coffees from The Coffee Nut are waiting at our usual places. "We've been asked to help, once again, with the Orlov case. Even though Vadik and his men at the winery were arrested—and are currently facing life in prison—the Feds have yet to locate his grandson, Nikolai Orlov. As long as he's still free, the Orlov family will continue to commit crimes. He was marked to take over the family business once his grandfather stepped down, and it's suspected he's doing just that. Only now he's deep underground."

"And the Feds want us to flush him out?" Landon asks.

"That's exactly what they want us to do. But we're doing it through his cousin, Chloe Reinhart."

"Chloe? Isn't she the owner of the winery?"

"Yes, the winery that the Feds suspect she has no idea that she owns. Her name is on the legal documents, but the Feds have nothing beyond that to indicate she's ever been on the property. They interviewed the employees, and none of them have actually met her. Or at least, none of them have met the woman in the photo they were shown.

"They're hoping that she knows where her cousin is hiding, or at the very least, that he'll attempt to contact her."

"Would he really take that risk if he believes the Feds are looking for him?" I ask.

"It's possible. As kids, the two were very close. Back then, Nikolai would do anything for Chloe and was super protective of her. The Feds don't know why, but it's clear there was a special bond between them. They're hoping it's still there, even though he has yet to reach out to her—as far as they're aware."

Landon picks up his coffee. "So they want us to do surveillance on her?"

"It's more than that. They want someone to get close to her. Get to know her and gain her trust. But they're also concerned for her safety. They have reason to believe that one of Orlov's enemies has issued a hit on her.

"The Feds obviously can't put her under witness protection because then Nikolai won't be able to contact her, and they won't be able to nail him."

"What do we know about her?" Jayden asks.

"She's an elementary school teacher. Single." Liam pushes the manila folder in front of him toward Landon. "And she's about to become your girlfriend..."

EXCERPT FROM SPYING UNDER THE MISTLETOE

Landon

Life is sometimes nothing but a series of mistakes.

Mistakes that leave you wondering a few hours later what the hell you were thinking.

Mistakes that seem like a brilliant idea at the time.

"Ooh, coffee," my latest mistake says, walking into the kitchen, wearing nothing but a hockey jersey. *My* hockey jersey, which was hanging in my closet until a few minutes ago.

"I'm going to need that soon." I nod at the item of clothing.

The blonde, whose name I can't quite remember, sidles up to me. I met her at the bar Adam, Connor, and I went to last night. I hadn't gone there to get laid, but here I am, with a strange woman in my town house.

"I didn't know you play hockey," she says with a seductive purr. It was a turn-on last night. Now, not so much. "I loooove hockey."

Something about the way she says this hints that it's not entirely true. I recognize the look in her eyes from my days in junior hockey.

She's not a real fan of the game. Hooking up with hockey players is her sport of choice.

I'd dealt with a few of those in my past, back before I realized I'd never be good enough to play in the NHL.

I give her a single nod—because there isn't anything more to say on the subject. She's just reminding me why I don't typically bring one-night stands to my place.

Not that one-night stands are a habit of mine these days.

Blondie is one of those rare occasions.

She doesn't get the hint and leans against the granite kitchen counter. "Can I have some, please?" Her gaze drops to the mug in my hand, and I stiffen.

But while I'm not exactly happy she's still here, I'm not going to be an asshole and kick her out of my home.

Yet.

If she decides to overstay her welcome, I'll politely ask her to leave.

I remove a mug from the kitchen cabinet, fill it partway, and hand it to her.

"Thanks." She takes a sip and pouts at me. "You've already showered?" she says, stating the obvious. My hair's still damp.

My goal had been for her to wake up while I was in the shower and be the kind of woman who bails while the guy's preoccupied.

Instead, she slept the entire time and only woke up when the coffee had finished brewing.

"I was hoping we could shower...together." She flashes me a look that reminds me of Mojo—my colleague's Bernese mountain dog—whenever he sees his favorite treat.

Then she winks at me...which lasts an incredibly long time. Like her eye has frozen shut. "Oh, darn it. My false eyelashes are stuck together. Can you help me, Landon?"

Sorry, sweetheart, you're on your own.

Before I can voice that out loud, "Hit Me with Your Best Shot" plays from my phone on the kitchen table.

Saved by Pat Benatar.

"Sorry, I have to take this." *I don't suppose you'll be gone by the time I return....*

I pick up my phone and head upstairs to my office.

Inside, I close the door behind me. "What's up?" I ask Liam. My boss.

The owner of Quade Security and Investigations.

My former brother in arms.

Liam doesn't call the team on a Sunday unless it's super important. He's a family man through and through—especially since his daughter was born over a year ago.

Cassie and his wife, Ava, are his world.

"I need you to come into the office this morning. I'm calling the entire team in."

"I'd ask what this is about, but now's not a good time for me to talk." I have no idea if Blondie's the curious type—if snooping gets her off. "As soon as I get some baggage out of my house, I'll be there."

Liam has been my friend for too long to miss the hidden meaning between the words. "You know, if you found a nice woman to settle down with, the overstaying-their-welcome baggage wouldn't be a problem."

"You sound like my mother."

"Your mom is a wise woman."

We end the call, and I head downstairs. Blondie is still in the kitchen, in my hockey jersey, coffee mug in hand, in no particular rush to leave. Her eyelashes are no longer stuck together.

"I have to go to work now," I tell her, hoping she gets the hint this time.

She frowns, her pout resembling that of a toddler denied a

cookie more than it resembles the pout of a supermodel selling sexy lingerie. "Work? But it's Sunday."

I shrug because it is what it is.

"You never did tell me what you do for a living." She sips on her coffee.

"I'm a janitor. The usual weekend guy called in sick."

Rule #1 when it comes to hookups: Never tell them my real job.

Even if I don't mention the off-the-website part of the job—the part involving secret government contracts—telling women I work for a security and investigation company leaves them with all kinds of alpha-hero fantasies.

It makes me, in their eyes, more desirable, more exciting, than someone who cleans an office building for a living.

The frown between Blondie's eyebrows returns. "This is a really nice place for a janitor."

I don't dignify her comment with a reply.

Fortunately, she finally gets the hint, puts the mug on the counter, and heads upstairs to hopefully get changed. She returns a few minutes later in the dress she was wearing last night. Her hair is no longer messy.

"I had fun last night," she says, batting her eyelashes at me. They miraculously don't stick together this time. "I would love to see you again. Maybe we could catch a movie and dinner later this week?"

Her tone is not of someone hoping to be a booty call. It's more along the lines of wanting something I can't give—my heart.

Or what's left of it.

No, a woman didn't cheat on me or do me wrong. Just the opposite. My post-college girlfriend was the love of my life. I was positive she was it—the woman I would one day marry.

At least that had been my plan until she went out with

friends. The next time I saw her, she was in a coma and on life support.

Her parents removed her from it a month later.

After that, I joined the military. And on more than one occasion witnessed a brother die—and each time, like with my girlfriend, I was unable to do anything about it.

"Sorry," I tell Blondie, "but I told you last night it was a one-time-only deal. That hasn't changed."

She shrugs, the disappointment on her face nothing more than a flicker. A minute later, the front door clicks shut behind her.

I grab my jeep keys and head out the front door. The crisp November air is heavy with the promise of rain.

A faint whimper, almost a squeak, draws my attention to a bush on my property. I walk over to the sound and crouch next to the bush, where a small tangle of reddish-brown fur with large floppy ears lies.

"Hey, little guy, what are you doing here?"

The puppy lifts its head slightly and gives another whimper. It doesn't have a collar, doesn't look familiar.

I hold my hand out to him, letting him sniff it, and stroke his soft head. "Are you injured?"

ACKNOWLEDGMENTS

The idea for the Love Undercover series came about in an unusual way. Two years ago, I took a Romance Writers of America (RWA) workshop about the CIA. I mentioned it to a friend, and she told me I should write a spy rom-com series. At the time, I was busy writing the By the Bay and Copper Creek books, so a new series wasn't in the works. But one of the topics covered during the workshop focused on female agents during the Second World War. I became fascinated by their stories, so much so that I started doing research for a historical novel.

It was Brenda St. John Brown, a fellow romantic comedy author, who suggested that maybe I *should* write a spy rom-com series. She knew about my research. Because I was writing *Decidedly by Chance* at the time, it was easy to introduce Jayden and Isabelle (and the other operatives) in that story. It made sense to write *While You Were Spying* as a spin novel from the By the Bay series.

When I hinted to my Facebook group (Stina's Sweethearts) about the potential new series, their enthusiasm confirmed that this was the direction I needed to go next. So thank you to the RWA chapter (Kiss of Death) that had the CIA workshop, Brenda, and my Facebook group. All of you are the reason the Love Undercover series exists.

I would also like to thank the fans of the By the Bay series and especially those individuals who wanted more of Liam after he was introduced in *Decidedly Off Limits*. Even though I hadn't planned for him to have an additional role in the series,

I changed my mind after so many requests for his story (*Decidedly with Mistletoe*).

This book wouldn't be the same without my editor Bev, as well as Hope and Jessica from Flat Earth Editing for the copy-editing and proofreading. All three individuals helped make this book sparkle. The same is true of Brenda St. John Brown, who always shares her brilliant suggestions and wisdom when it comes to my romantic comedies.

And finally, hugs and kisses to my husband Ralph, my three kids, and my cat Callie for your love and support over the past several years.

ABOUT THE AUTHOR

Born in Brighton England, Stina Lindenblatt has lived in a number of countries, including England, the U.S., Finland, and Canada. This would explain her mixed up accent. She has a kinesiology degree and a MSc in sports biological sciences.

In addition to writing fiction, she loves photography, and currently lives in Calgary, Canada, with her husband and three kids.

For news about her books and to sign up for her newsletter, check out her website at:

stinalindenblattauthor.com